RETURN OF THE DEAD

Book Two in the Realm of the Dead Series

Jeremy Dyson

DARTMOOR
PUBLISHING

Dartmoor Books

CONTENTS

For my wife and my mother...

The two women that have always had my back.

CHAPTER ONE

When the vultures are circling, something bad is about to happen. I never used to see many of them, but ever since the dead started walking, I see them all the time. That's how I can always tell when we got trouble nearby. I lower the binoculars and wipe the sweat from my eyelids.

"Scout," Steven whispers. "What do you see?"

There isn't anyone around for miles, but he is accustomed to whispering now. We all are.

"Nothing good," I tell him. I lift the binoculars again and peer at the brittle brush on the hilltop and wonder what lies on the other side. The vultures continue to circle and wait. I heard that was only a myth. Supposedly, vultures don't actually circle. Maybe it was just something we imagined before, but it's real now.

Steven keeps pacing behind me, hovering like he is one of the damn vultures. He can be a pain in the ass, but he is good with a machete. He also doesn't try to get me to sleep with him. Thank God for that.

"We need to get closer," I say. I lower the binoculars and stand up.

"Come on," sighs Steven. "Why?"

"You know why," I grumble. I grab my pack off the ground and shoulder it.

Steven hesitates. He gazes at the birds over the horizon with his languid, blue eyes. With a sigh, he lifts the filthy royal blue baseball cap off his head and slicks back his sweaty ginger hair with his fingertips. He removes a canteen from his backpack, unscrews the top and chugs down half of his water. This is the part where he tries to say something that will change my mind.

"Well?" I prod. I wish he'd just get on with it.

"We're pretty low on water." Steven shakes his canteen so I can hear the small amount of liquid slosh inside.

"I got two bottles in my pack. We're fine."

Steven looks down at his boot, nudges a rock with it and sighs.

"Okay then," he resigns. "Let's go."

We struggle down the rocky slope beneath an awning of leafy trees. The creek between the hills is emerald green and glistens beneath the morning sun. A cacophony of bird calls and the crisp scent of sappy pine trees fills the air. A scene like this is almost enough to make you forget how bad everything is if you let it.

We stopped last night at a clothing store just west of what used to be Eminence, Missouri. Another day or two on the road and we will finally reach Fort Leonard Wood. A couple of weeks ago, we overheard a radio transmission. The broadcaster claimed the military base was operational and free of the undead. It still sounds too good to be true. We have been on the road since this whole thing started nearly two months ago and it was the only good news we had heard so far.

About halfway down the slope, I lose my footing on the craggy soil. A rock shifts beneath my boot and sends me sprawling on the ground.

"Damn it," I curse. If there is anyone nearby, I just gave away our position. I can't afford to let my mind wander like that. Not anymore.

"You okay?" Steven asks. He rushes to my side and offers me his hand. I grab onto his wrist, and he pulls me up.

"Fine," I groan. "Fucking Ozarks." I wipe my dirty palms off on my jeans and readjust the straps of my pack as we continue toward the shore.

"Ain't so bad," Steven says. "Kind of quiet and peaceful out here."

"If you like that sort of thing."

My husband, Kevin, used to drag me along when he would go hunting and fishing all the time, so I know how to deal with the outdoors. That doesn't mean I enjoy it.

I step into the creek. The cool water seeps into my boots and sends a chill through my body. I wade deeper into the water before I pause and look back over my shoulder. Steven still lingers on the shore.

"Come on, you big baby," I urge him.

Steven looks up and down the creek as if I hadn't already checked for the easiest spot to cross. He sighs and follows me into the water.

"This sucks," Steven complains. "Did I mention that already?"

"Don't make me tell little Stevie that his dad was being a big pussy again."

The water reaches my waist and I lift my pack over my head to keep it from getting wet. My eyes scan the trees along the shore for any signs of the dead. The leaves are still and quiet. The morning calls of songbirds are the only sound. We reach the shore and I shoulder my pack again. I look up at the steep incline and the dark shade beneath the trees.

"You sure about this, Scout?" Steven asks.

"What kind of question is that?"

"Just a question," he shrugs.

"No, it's a stupid question," I snap. I can be a little harsh sometimes. Sue me.

"You think it's them?" Steven wonders. He means Bishop and his thugs. The first time we saw them they had a yellow flag with a black rattlesnake coiled in the middle of it. Maybe it's just my fear of snakes, but it made me nervous about them right from the get-go. We had several run-ins with some of his guys since then. None ended well.

"Might be," I whisper. "But if it is them, we need to find out what they're up to out here."

"No," Steven disagrees. "We don't, Scout."

I turn and start to climb the hill with water sloshing around in the bottom of my boot. The incline is steep, and I have to grab onto tree trunks to pull myself up to the crest of the hill. The vultures circle in the air. I take out my binoculars and scan the area. Nothing moves.

I lower the binoculars and retrieve the Glock from the holster strapped to my thigh. I raise a finger to my lips and look at Steven. We creep forward through the woods. Steven starts his mouth-breathing behind me, and I resist the urge to turn around and tell him to shut the hell up. You'd think he'd know better by now.

Sticks crackle beneath Steven's boot and I freeze. I turn to throw an irritated glance his way, but my eyes widen when I hear a guttural moan off to the left. I crouch down and scurry for cover behind a nearby bush. Steven leans against the bole of a tree. He peers around one side and then the other.

I peek through the leaves of the bush, but I don't see the son of a bitch. The distant moan reverberates through the woods again. My eyes scan the trees until I spot a long, thin piece of black metal sticking up out of a ravine to the right. There is no telling what lies at the bottom of the ditch.

"Let's get the hell out of here," whispers Steven.

I shake my head.

"You got a death wish or something?"

"Quit being such a chickenshit," I snap.

We crouch as we make our way along the ridge toward the ravine. As we get closer, I realize what I spotted was the blade of a helicopter. The battered chassis comes into view as we approach the edge of the ditch. The bird sits belly up in the dirt. The windows are shattered, and sunlight glints off the bits of glass on the ground.

I spot the corpse of a soldier on the ground next to the crash. The thing is pinned to the ground by a blade from the tail rotor. The long piece of alloy impaled his sternum then sunk deep in the dirt. It pushes itself up when it catches sight of us. The rotor blade stirs his intestines as they spill out onto the ground.

I look around to see if there are any more of the dead in sight, but the woods are still and quiet. I take out the Glock and point it at the face of the soldier and pull the trigger. The shot echoes through the trees.

"Search the helicopter," I tell Steven. "I'll keep an eye out."

Steven drops his backpack and approaches the bay door of the chopper. After several seconds at the door, he pokes his head inside. He steps in and disappears into the darkened cabin. A moment later, I hear him howl, followed by several thwacks of the machete.

"You all right in there?" I call out to him.

"Yeah," he says. "Just dandy."

I circle around the helicopter and scan the debris on the ground for anything useful. When I come across a two-way radio, I pick it up and try to turn it on. No luck. Maybe it is broken, or the battery could be dead. I unzip my pack and shove the radio inside anyway. Perhaps James will be able to get it working again.

I resume my search of the wreckage and stop when I come across a book on the ground. It's a copy of The Stand. After I glance around to make sure we are still alone, I bend down and retrieve the paperback. The paper is damp from the morning dew. From the faded cover, I can tell it has been sitting out here for a while.

"Ready," Steven informs me.

"Find anything?" I ask.

"The pilot," he says. "Nothing else. Had a feeling this was a waste of time."

He puts his hands on his waist and glares at me. I can't help but smirk. He lowers his eyes and shakes his head. It's not like Steven could ever stay mad at me. That's just not who he is. I tilt my head back and watch the vultures circle.

"Let's get going," I say.

The noise from the round I fired off will have carried for miles. If there is anyone around, alive or dead, they will probably come looking for us. We climb back down the hill to the creek bed. We cross the lazy water and stop to wring out our clothes on the shore.

I squeeze the water from my filthy green army jacket. It still had some blood on it from the dead soldier, so I don't mind it getting wet. I turn away from Steven, pull off my tank top, and twist the fabric until the water stops dripping. Then I slip it back over my head. I turn back around and catch Steven staring. I can't blame the guy. The world is a lonely place for everyone.

"Quit looking at me like that," I bark at him.

"I wasn't," he insists. He looks down at his boot that is pushing a rock around on the ground. His reaction makes me smile for a second. I don't understand how someone can shy away from their feelings after everything that has happened. I slip my arms through the sleeves of my jacket and grab my pack.

We struggle up the steep hillside and make our way back through the forest until we reach the truck in the clearing. I look back at the sky and notice the vultures are gone. The birds are probably feasting on that rotten corpse by now. Since there isn't much in the way of roadkill anymore, the vultures mostly feed on dead humans now. They either had to adapt or die.

I slip off my pack and climb into the passenger seat of the truck. Sunlight glints off the windshield and irritates my eyes. I flip open the mirror on the visor. One look at the dark circles around my eyes is enough to make me regret looking. Not that being pretty even matters anymore. I used to care about how I looked. Now, looking good would only bring more trouble. That's the last thing I need. From my pack, I retrieve a pair of cheap aviator sunglasses and a hair tie. I collect the split ends of my damp brown hair in a ponytail and cover my eyes with the shades.

Steven opens the door and slides in behind the steering wheel. He lowers the visor to grab the keys he tucked away there and cranks the truck to life. His head turns slightly, and he stares at me for a moment.

"You sure you're okay?" Steven asks.

"Can we not do this?" I sigh.

He shifts the engine into gear and pulls the truck around to face the narrow road. Then he presses the brake. He puts the truck in park and swivels in the seat to face me.

"I can't just pretend I didn't see it," he huffs.

"I wasn't going to do it," I relent. "It was just a moment of weakness."

"Scout," he sighs. He drops his gaze and shakes his head.

"Don't lecture me, Steven. Please, just forget it ever happened."

"You had a gun in your mouth, and I'm just supposed to ignore that?" Steven grips the wheel with one hand tightly and leans toward me. Anger flushes his face.

I notice a corpse wandering out of the trees across the road. The clothes it has been wearing for weeks hang in filthy tatters. Watching the miserable thing makes me realize how a sane person would decide to call it quits. The fact is, I don't know why I keep going except that I'm still afraid to die.

"Steven." I gesture at the corpse in the road. "We need to get moving."

"I'm not letting this go," he whispers.

He grabs the stick, shifts the truck into drive, and accelerates toward the road. We drive past the corpse and the smell of death drifts in through the window of the truck.

CHAPTER TWO

S teven pulls off the road into the empty parking lot of a rundown lodge about a mile or so outside of town.

"We can walk the rest of the way," he suggests.

I nod and open my door and shoulder my backpack. It's always a good idea to keep a low profile when we reach a new area. I'm pretty good at hiding myself, so I usually recon everything first to make sure it is safe for the others. They don't call me Scout for nothing. Well, they also don't know me by anything else. I generally prefer to do this sort of thing alone, but Steven insisted on coming along this morning. Probably because he was itching to talk to me about last night.

A pair of bodies shrouded in a layer of chert rest in the dusty gravel. Shattered ground floor windows underscore the dark and weathered exterior of the lodge. A gentle breeze blows the open front door and squeaks the hinges.

"Let's have a look inside," I tell Steven.

"I was afraid you'd say that," he sulks.

"Baby," I scoff.

Glass fragments snap beneath my boots as I step onto the wood floor of the lobby. The room is dim, quiet, and destroyed. Overturned tables and chairs are piled near the front and rear doors. Several reeking corpses house swarming flies and maggots. I reach into my pocket and pull out a bandana. I keep it tucked in there along with a sheet of fabric softener for times like this when I can't handle the smell. It's something you never get used to. I tie the fabric around my face like a surgical mask.

"This place is trashed," whispers Steven.

"Thought maybe there would be a kitchen or something like that," I say.

"No room service in a dump like this," Steven says. He glances around the lobby and reaches into the chest pocket of his flannel shirt to fish out a pack of cigarettes. His rough hands remove one from the pack and he lights it. He draws in a long drag and then exhales and watches the smoke drifting around the stagnant air. I hate the smell of cigarettes, but even that is better than smell of the corpses.

The silence in the room is broken by the sound of floorboards creaking on the second floor. I look up at the ceiling and wait to hear the sound again.

"Sounds like somebody is home after all," Steven says.

Steven parks his smoke between his lips, and rights a toppled chair. He sits and smokes and watches me.

"Just one of them by sound of it," I whisper.

"Don't look at me," Steven says as he exhales a cloud of smoke. "I got the last one."

I guess he is right. Sure, we could just leave without dealing with the thing upstairs. We could leave it for someone else to find, but there's always the chance that it will find the next person that comes along first. I already have enough on my conscience without thinking about that.

I slip the knife out of my pocket and ascend the staircase. The steps groan beneath my feet no matter where I put them. At the top of the stairs, I find a dark hallway with half a dozen doors marked by silver numbers. Instead of checking all of them, I wait and listen. Everything seems quiet behind the first pair of doors. As I approach the next rooms, I hear feet dragging across the floor inside of room number three.

I clutch the doorknob in my hand and ready the knife. The handle turns quietly, and I ease the door open to see the corpse of an old woman in a nightgown. She faces the window where the rising sun pours into the room. For a moment, I wonder if she might be alive, but the thing lets out a hoarse moan. She is dead all right.

With a few quick steps I cross the room before the corpse has time to turn around. I grab a handful of the long grey hair and plunge the knife upwards at the base of the skull. The body goes limp, and I lower it to the floor, and then I pull my knife free. I grab the sheet off the bed and clean the congealed blood off the blade. After I take a look around the room for anything of use, I start to walk out in the door. In the doorway, I pause and look back at the body on the floor. I take a second to go back to the bed and use the sheet to cover it up.

None of the cheap motel rooms even have a minibar so this was just a total waste of time. One of the toilets in another room still has a tank full of water, so I fill a couple bottles. When I open the door to the last room, I discover a disturbing scene. A wooden chair sits in the middle of the room. Handcuffs dangle from the backrest. Behind it I see the badly mutilated body of a man in the corner. He looks to be a soldier by the pile of army green clothing soaking in a puddle of blood beside him. I have no idea what might have happened here, and I don't want to either. All I know for certain is the corpses had nothing to do with that. I quickly close the door and retreat back downstairs.

"Find anything?" Steven asks.

I decide not to mention the gruesome scene I discovered upstairs to Steven. Sometimes it is better not to know. I toss him one of the water bottles and it slips through his fingers and hits him in the chest before it falls to the floor. Steven reaches down and picks it up, twists off the cap, and fills his canteen.

"Try not to gulp it all down right away this time," I tell him.

Steven studies my expression closely for a moment as he pours the water.

I'm afraid he'll try to engage me in another heart-to-heart, so I wander towards the back door. I step outside onto a wide deck that overlooks an empty wooden dock. The water trickling downstream and the breeze moving through the trees calms my nerves. I pull the bandana down around my neck and breathe the country air. The moment almost makes me feel alive again.

"You ready to get moving?" Steven calls.

"Sure," I call back. "Just give me a minute." I take a deep breath and close my eyes, but when I listen, I hear a vehicle approaching from town. I spin around and hustle back inside.

"Someone's coming," I hiss at Steven.

The chair topples over as he scrambles to his feet. Steven hurries to the front entrance and presses his body against the wall. He peers out at the road, watches, and waits. I crouch down behind a couch near the back door and stare at Steven as I listen to the vehicle slowing down. Through the open front door, I watch as a blue pickup comes to a stop in the middle of the road. A yellow flag waves from pole mounted in the truck bed. I count two people in the cab and four more in the back. They carry a couple of heavy guns, too.

Steven looks back at me and shakes his head. He thinks we are out-gunned, and I know he is right. I know we can only hope they decide to keep driving.

One of the men standing in the bed points to the fresh tire tracks and the driver pulls off the road toward the lodge.

We just lost our ride. Damn.

Steven scurries across the room and follows me out the back door. As we run toward the dock, I hear the truck tires crunch over the gravel as the vehicle crosses the parking lot. I sprint to the end of the dock and leap into the water. Steven splashes into the stream beside me and we wade across the river to the opposite shore. When we reach the tree line, we stop to look back at the lodge. Several figures enter the building and begin searching inside. I can hear their voices but can't make out the words.

"Please tell me you have the keys," I say.

"They're in the truck," Steven admits. "Old habit."

"Jesus," I sigh.

"Think they saw us?" Steven whispers.

"No," I say. "I'm sure they can smell your cigarette, though. They will know we're close."

"Let's get the fuck out of here then." Steven slinks away into the woods, snapping every little twig on the ground along the way.

I don't want to give up the truck. It's getting harder and harder to find a working vehicle. We might have some luck finding a new ride in town, but there is a good chance we might only run into even more trouble there instead.

"Damn it," I curse and follow Steven through the dense curtain of trees. "Wait up."

Steven pauses and leans against a tree as he scans the surrounding woods.

"You're going the wrong way," I tell him.

"No, I'm not," Steven insists.

"The town is that way." I jab a finger in the opposite direction for emphasis.

"You can't be serious," Steven snorts. He folds his arms across his chest. "We need to go back and warn the others."

"It's over four miles. We need to keep going and hope we find another car in town." I turn and walk away before he can argue with me.

For several minutes, I ignore the sound of his clumsy footsteps behind me. I usually don't mind being around Steven, but it's turning out to be a bad day. The way things are going, it might get a lot worse. If those guys were with Bishop, then we're going to be in for some trouble. I was too far away to get a good look at their faces, but it probably was them. Just my luck.

We follow along the river until we come to a road. A red, wood-covered bridge that leads to town spans the rocky riverbed. I crouch behind a boulder and look for any signs of movement in the street. The only sound comes from the nearby water trickling over the rocks. I nod to Steven, and he follows me out to the bridge. The old boards creak beneath our boots as we cross. We pause again before exiting the cover of the bridge.

Several shamblers lurk in the distance on the main road through town. A few vultures feed on a corpse rotting in the middle of the street. Their beaks tear the putrid flesh from the bones. I reach into my pack and locate my binoculars. I scan the abandoned cars up the block. One bullet-riddled truck has a flat tire. Two sedans have crashed into each other. A minivan holds half a dozen shamblers that smack their heads against the windows. There are more cars further down the road, but I can't tell if they are in any better shape from this distance. I notice a restaurant called Horstmann's on the corner of the nearest intersection. The greasy spoon seems like the only place to eat in town. The tinted windows don't allow me to see inside, but at least the glass is intact. Maybe we can check inside for more food or water since this trip is taking longer than expected.

"Looks clear," I inform Steven. "Let's check out that diner."

"Nah." Steven brushes the idea away with a wave of his hand.

I stop and turn to look at him. "Why not?"

"I don't know," he muses. "Seems like an unnecessary risk."

"You were the one that was all concerned about how low on water we are," I tell him.

"And you told me we had enough," he smiles. Bastard just loves to give me a hard time.

"Shut up." I ball my fingers into a fist and slug his shoulder. Steven winces and grabs his shoulder in mock pain.

"You're such an idiot," I remind him.

He starts to say something but the sound of a vehicle approaching town intervenes. I watch the road as we race toward the diner. Steven whips open the door, and we duck inside. I quickly glance around the dimly lit dining area. Nothing moves. Through the windows, I see a pickup truck emerge from the covered bridge. It has to be the same group from the lodge. Just behind it, our truck exits the covered bridge. The caravan glides down Main Street.

Metal clangs against the tile floor behind me. The corpse of a waitress behind the counter flails her arms at us and knocks napkin dispensers and saltshakers across the floor. Out of the corner of my eye, I spot another waitress crawling out from beneath a booth in the corner. The doors to the kitchen swings open and the wiry body of the busboy lurches into the room. From a hallway in the back of the cafe comes the sound of someone banging on a door. The staff shambles towards us. Their clumsy bodies knock into tables and chairs.

I glance over my shoulder and see the truck inching down the road. The racket caused by the corpses in the diner did not give away our presence yet, but we can't shoot the things while the trucks are so close.

Steven slides his machete from the sheath. I slip out a hatchet from a loop on my pack. The corpses close in on us. I can even read the name tags on their uniforms.

"You get Marci," I tell Steven. "I'll get Valaen."

He nods as he brings back the machete and slashes the waitress across the face. I raise the hatchet and drop the blade on Valaen's head with all my strength. My first strike glances off her skull and knocks her to the ground. I bring the weapon down again and it fractures the back of her skull. After the third blow, the body goes still.

I look up to see the busboy. Alfredo is stitched into his grimy black polo shirt. The corpse lunges at me and knocks me back. The hatchet falls from my fingers as I stumble over a chair and topple to the floor.

"Steven!" I yell, probably louder than I should have. Me and my big mouth. I kick at Alfredo with my boot. The move knocks the busboy to the side as he falls on me. I struggle to get to my feet, but grease and the slimy blood from the waitress covers the floor. Alfredo gets to his knees and moans and opens his mouth. I reach for the hatchet. Then Steven puts a bullet through his skull. The head of the corpse tilts to the side and his brains splatter onto the windowpane.

"Damn it," I grunt.

Steven shrugs his shoulders and lowers the gun. He had no choice but to shoot the thing. There wasn't time to do anything else. I grab the edge of a table and pull myself to my feet. Through the window blinds, I see the truck down the street. I stare at the illuminated brake lights and wait for the truck to move.

The passengers on the bed of the truck ready their rifles and scan the street. One of the men gestures back toward the cafe, then white lights on the rear of the truck light up.

"They're backing up," I say.

The corpse in the back of the restaurant continues to pound on the door. I run down the hallway to check for a back door, but it just leads to the bathrooms.

"The kitchen," Steven pleads. He grabs my pack and turns me around. I follow him through the swinging gray door into a kitchen that reeks of grease and decay. Abandoned plates of food rot on the countertop. A large refrigerator barricades the rear entrance. Each of us grabs an end and we slide the large unit over the tiles. The legs grind over the surface. We clear the exit and push through the door into the bright midday sun. I squint my eyes to try and see but before my eyes adjust a man's voice urges me to get down.

"Show me your hands," another deep voice chimes.

I raise my hands and shield my eyes. As my vision returns, I make out three figures with assault rifles leveled on us.

"Whoa, there," says Steven. "We're not looking for any trouble, guys."

"Get on the ground," orders one of the men. His mouth bulges on one side from a wad of snuff tucked in his gums.

I hesitate while I blink my eyes and the faces of the men emerge from the glare. Steven falls to his knees beside me and raises his hands.

"On your knees, princess," the man repeats.

"For fuck's sake," I sigh. "Just shoot me and get it over with already."

The tobacco guy lowers the rifle. He cocks his head to the side and chuckles.

"Sorry," he tells me. "Guess this ain't your lucky day."

He whirls the weapon around. The stock of the rifle advances towards my face then everything goes black.

CHAPTER THREE

I hear distant murmuring as I open my eyes to see the grimy tile floor of the diner. When I try to move, I discover my hands are cuffed to the back of a chair I am sitting on. I can't recall where I am or how I got here. Several blurry figures move around the room, having some conversation that I can't understand for some reason.

"Wake up!"

A hand slaps me across the face and startles me. Everything snaps into focus. My eyes dart around the room. A blonde woman by the bar lights a cigarette. A trio of men holding rifles and shotguns stand guard at the front entrance. In a booth along the wall, a man with a grey crew cut seated between an anxious pair of dark-haired women smirks at me. Steven struggles in a chair beside me. He cranes his neck around to look at me and wrestles with the cuffs around his own wrists.

"Morning, princess." Rough fingers grasp my jaw and lift my chin up until I'm looking at a middle-aged man wearing a faded jean jacket. His bearded face smiles down at me. I shake my head away from his grip and bite at his fingers as he tries to grab me again. Even though I am not quick enough to sink my teeth into him, he pulls his hand back. His deep-set brown eyes stare down at me as he laughs softly.

"I heard you were feisty," the man grins.

He turns and paces slowly across the room. His gaze shifts between me and Steven.

"Do you know who I am?" the man asks me.

I catch myself thinking up smart-ass responses but decide I better keep my mouth shut and stare at the floor. I'll let things play out and see where this goes.

The man takes a seat on a tabletop a few feet away and rests his leather boots on the chair below. He picks up a knife off the table, which looks an awful lot like my knife. The guy stares at me as he runs the tip of his finger along the blade.

"I'm waiting," he reminds me.

"I've never seen you before in my life," I finally tell him.

"You've never seen me before. That is true," the man agrees. He waves a man with a mullet over from the counter. "But I believe you have seen my pal Owen before. Didn't you, Scout?"

I recognize the man from our encounter at the grocery store a couple of weeks earlier, but I just lower my gaze and stare at the floor.

"Owen tells me that you're the one who used this big ass knife to stab him and then left him for dead," the man informs me.

"I don't know what you're talking about," I mumble. My mind feels foggy, and the words are difficult to form. The room spins and I struggle to keep my eyes open. "You must have us confused with someone else," I insist.

"Isn't this her, Owen?" the man asks. He drapes an arm over Owen's shoulder and raises the knife with the tip pointed at my face. "Take a good look at her."

"Sure is, Bishop," Owen grins. "That's her all right." It's easy to see he has been waiting for this moment.

"Damn," Bishop grins at me. "I got to admit I am a little impressed. That is some cold-blooded shit, princess."

"Maybe Owen should learn to keep his goddamn hands to himself," I growl.

"I'll kill you, bitch," Owen seethes as he takes a step in my direction.

"Easy," Bishop laughs. He clasps Owen by the shoulder to keep him from attacking me. "Everybody just relax."

Owen steps back and crosses his arms over his chest and resumes scowling at me.

"Now, you seem like a bright gal, Scout. You can probably understand that there is another reason that I've had my guys out looking for you for the last couple of weeks," Bishop says. He reaches up and scratches his temple with his index finger. "It's getting harder and harder to find the right kind of people."

I glance around at the diner full of questionable characters. I wouldn't trust any of them either.

"Take Owen for example," Bishop says. "He's a tough guy. Never asks for too much. Never gets out of line. And he's about as loyal as they come."

Owen straightens up his stance and smiles at Bishop. He doesn't seem to notice when Bishop stops smiling and fixes a cold stare on him.

"The thing is you just can't count on Owen for shit," says Bishop. He turns and plunges my knife into Owen's abdomen.

Owen gazes down at the knife in his stomach with his mouth gaping. Bishop pulls the blade out and stabs the man in the sternum over and over again. I turn my head to avoid seeing what happens next but can't help hearing Bishop grunting every time he drives the knife into the groaning man. Finally, Bishop lets the limp body fall. He lets out a deep breath as he stares down at Owen. Fresh blood drips off the blade of my knife onto the diner floor.

Bishop turns around and stares at me while he wipes the blood splatter off his jaw with the forearm of his jacket sleeve.

"You should see the look on your face, princess," Bishop grins.

"You're insane," I say. The words come out before I think about what I'm saying.

"Insane?" Bishop says. He lifts the knife, stabs the tabletop with the blade, and leaves the knife sticking up there. With a tired sigh he collapses into the chair right next to the body on the floor.

"Maybe the whole damn world is insane, and I'm just doing my best to fit in," he smiles at the thought for several seconds. Then he lifts his hand up and smacks the table. "I need a smoke, Dom," he says.

The blonde woman at the bar fishes in her purse and pulls out a pack of cigarettes.

"It better not be one of those skinny pussy straws that you like to smoke," Bishop warns her.

The woman steps across the room and hands him a red pack of cigarettes and he looks up and studies her expression as she steps over the body beside him. Before she returns to the bar, she pauses and narrows her eyes at me.

Bishop grins as he lights the cigarette and gestures for Dom to keep walking. He takes a long drag and blows the smoke into the air. Then he just stares at the space above my head for a long minute and he lets his head sway slightly from side to side as though a song is playing that only he can hear. Finally, he blinks and his gaze locks on me again. Then he glances down at the cigarette between his fingers and flicks the dangling ash onto the corpse on the floor.

"Really is a shame about Owen," Bishop sighs. "You see, I didn't want to kill him. Hell, I even kind of liked the dumb bastard. But he let you and your merry band of fairy assholes steal our shit, and that kind of incompetence does not help the cause."

"Cause?" I scoff. "What cause?"

"Saving the damn human race," Bishop says. "Can't you see that?"

"Seems like you're just helping destroy it," I say. "You're a psychopath."

"Bullshit," Bishop says. "Hell, didn't we offer to take you people in? We told you we would protect you. But instead, you killed two of my guys, stole one of my trucks, not to mention a shitload of my guns."

"We never killed anyone," I tell him. "They started shooting. The dead did the rest. Those assholes had it coming."

"Maybe they did," Bishop concedes. "But that doesn't change a damn thing. Someone still has to pay. My people need to see that only I can protect them. They need to understand what happens when someone gets out of line. There has to be justice."

I lower my eyes and shake my head.

"Maybe you think my methods are a little... extreme. But you need to wake up, princess. The world is an evil place."

"Mostly because of people like you," I say.

The fingers of the corpse on the ground beside Bishop begin to twitch as Owen returns from the dead. I fix my gaze on Bishop and try not to look at the body again. He stares back at me and smiles. Maybe he won't notice until it's too late.

"It's a real shame how things turned out, Scout," Bishop says. "See, I got a real good eye for talent. We could have really used someone like you. You and me could have been very, very good friends, princess."

"If you even think about touching her—" Steven warns him.

"You ain't gonna do shit," Bishop says. "Goddamn pussy."

"Fuck you," Steven spits.

The corpse lets out a moan as it starts to sit up. Bishop lounges in the chair beside it and watches me with a smug smile. Even though he is aware of the threat beside him, he continues to watch me and wait. It's like he wants me to see how fearless and insane he can be.

"You know what I love best about all this?" Bishop asks me.

The corpse climbs to its knees and gazes around the room.

"You used to only get to kill someone once before. But now..." He pauses to grab the knife off the table and drives the blade under the chin of the dead man until it skewers his head. The corpse continues to move his jaws and gurgle as Bishop stares into his vacant eyes. Finally, Bishop drives the knife up further until the thing falls limp again. He pulls the knife out and the body hits the floor with a thud.

"Let's cut the shit," Bishop sighs as he collapses back into the chair. "I don't suppose if I ask nicely, one of you is going to tell me where the rest of them are hiding," Bishop says.

"We don't know where they are," I tell him. "We got separated over a week ago. For all we know they might be dead by now."

"She's lying," Dom says. I turn my head and glare at the woman with the blonde pixie hair as she puts out a cigarette on the lunch counter.

Bishop studies her face out of the corner of his eye and then he turns his cold stare at me.

"I'm telling you the truth," I say.

"Deny it all you want," Dom scoffs. "You're still lying. I used to be a lawyer. I know a liar when I see one."

"So, who'd you have to blow to get this cushy job?" I sneer.

Dom lights another long cigarette and gives me the finger.

"Come on now, Scout," Bishop sighs. "No reason to make this harder on yourself. Where is James?"

"I'm not telling you sh—," I begin to say, but Steven talks over me.

"She already said she doesn't know," Steven sighs.

"I'm sorry, I don't remember asking you a damn thing," Bishop turns his head and snarls at Steven. Then he suddenly gets to his feet and slugs Steven in the face.

"Don't interrupt the lady when she is talking," Bishop warns him as he settles back into the chair across from me. He clenches his jaw as he stares at me and waits.

"Even if I knew where they are, I would rather die than tell you anything," I say. "So, you might as well save us all some time and just shoot me right now. You'd be doing me a favor anyway."

Bishop leans back in his seat and crosses his arms over his chest as he considers my words.

"I actually believe you," Bishop tells me. "You're a real piece of work, princess."

"Just get it over with," I urge him.

Bishop swivels in his seat to look at the grey-haired man in the booth and signals him to come over with a slight nod of his head. The man leaves the women at the booth and smirks at me as he crosses the diner. He leans down toward Bishop and whispers something into his ear. Bishop peeks at Steven out of the corner of his eye and nods a few times when the man is finished. He resumes giving me his disturbing stare while he puckers his lips and contemplates the situation.

"I was really hoping you would be more reasonable, Scout," Bishop frowns. "You're really forcing my hand here. You see, one way or another, I'm going to get what I want."

CHAPTER FOUR

The man with the grey hair pushes the table closer to me and Steven, and then he positions the chair across from us and takes a seat. He glances down and straightens the silverware on the napkin before him.

"My name is Arkady," he says with a hint of a Slavic accent. Maybe it's Russian, I can't be sure. He gives me and Steven a friendly smile that puts me on edge. Nobody should smile like that a mere five minutes after witnessing a murder.

"Don't worry," he says. "All I want is to have a talk and see if I can help you both."

"We've got nothing to say to you," I tell him.

"That is unfortunate," Arkady sighs. He notices Steven eyeing the pack of cigarettes that Bishop left on the table and picks them up. Arkady opens the pack, retrieves a cigarette, and parks it between his own lips and lights it. "I would prefer to end this quickly and spare you both some pain and anguish. Maybe even see if we can resolve this unfortunate situation without further violence."

"Sure," Steven says. "That's all we want. We never wanted any trouble."

"Shut up, Steven," I warn him. Steven looks at me and I shake my head.

We watch Arkady smoke the entire cigarette in silence as he stares intensely at me. Something about the lack of talking makes me want to say something, but I resist the urge.

"In the end everyone talks," Arkady finally says, "I want you to keep that in mind. Do not feel bad about it when it happens, because that is the only way this ends. Most people only end up regretting they did not talk sooner and avoid much unnecessary suffering." He picks up the fork off the table and slowly turns it in his fingers as he subjects us to another painfully long pause.

"Where are the others?" Arkady asks.

Steven almost says something but then he catches himself. He drops his gaze and stares at the pack of cigarettes on the table.

"Would you like a cigarette?" Arkady asks him.

Steven doesn't respond, but Arkady removes another cigarette from the pack and holds it out for Steven to lean in and take it between his lips.

"You see," Arkady says as leans across the table and lights the cigarette. "I'm just here to help. Let us sort everything out like reasonable men."

Arkady scoots his chair back and steps around the table. He removes the handcuffs from Steven's wrists but leaves me cuffed to the chair.

"Is that better?" Arkady asks.

Steven nods as he leans forward and rubs at the pink marks on his skin left by the cuffs. I realize it is just going to be a matter of time before Arkady is able to get Steven talking and he gives up everything.

"You have to make them understand," Steven says. "We didn't do anything wrong."

"I can tell you are a good man," Arkady says. "You just got caught in an unfortunate situation."

"Right," Steven says. "If James never brought us to that damn store none of this would have ever happened."

"Shut up, Steven," I hiss again.

"A man like that will only put your friends in jeopardy again," Arkady says. "It is just a matter of time."

Steven turns his head to look at me, beads of sweat forming on his brow.

"If you cooperate perhaps your son will still be spared," Arkady says.

Steven stops rubbing his wrists and locks eyes with the grey-haired man.

"Yes," Arkady smirks. "I know about the boy. It would be a shame if something were to happen to him."

"Stop," I say before Steven has a chance to respond. Maybe I can make up some other story to keep him from talking to Steven.

Arkady smirks. "I am listening," he says.

"They're at the church." I didn't even see a church in town, but it's safe to guess there is at least one.

"The church?" Arkady considers this a moment. He picks up the fork off his napkin and examines it as he turns it around in his fingers. "Are you sure?"

"Yes," I stammer. I can't tell if he is trying to trap me or not.

He turns to look at Steven.

"Put your hand on the table," Arkady orders him.

Steven hesitantly lays his hand on the table.

"Is the rest of your group at the church?" he asks Steven.

Steven turns to give me a questioning look. He has no idea how to answer.

"Yes," he finally nods. "That's where they are."

"I see," Arkady sighs.

Steven lowers his eyes. I watch in horror as Arkady lifts the fork and drives the tines into the back of Steven's hand. Steven howls in pain and tries to get out of the chair but Arkady quickly steps around the table and grabs Steven by the wrist. He twists Steven's arm behind his back and clamps a hand around the back of his neck and slams his face down onto the table.

"We were already at the church this morning," Arkady hisses. "There are a couple hundred corpses barricaded inside." He fixes his eyes on me as he yanks Steven's arm up and pops his shoulder free from the socket.

Steven grimaces and wails in agony. I feel the tears in my eyes as I sit there and watch him in pain and can do nothing to stop it. This was all my fault.

As Steven stops screaming, I hear laughter across the room. Bishop leans against the lunch counter sipping out of a bottle of cola. He smiles when he notices me looking at him.

"You see what you have made me do, Scout?" Arkady asks me as he presses Steven's face against the tabletop. "I tried to help you and you deceive me. This is happening because of you."

Arkady releases his hold on Steven and pauses to smooth the fabric of his oxford shirt before he returns to his seat. Steven manages to sit up in the chair again and stares at the pool of blood around his hand that is impaled with the fork. His breath is strained and rapid as he turns to look at me. I notice he begins to shake.

"I know you are feeling a lot of pain right now, Steven," Arkady says. He reaches behind his back and his hand returns with a revolver. "Just tell me where they are, and I can make it go away."

Steven stares at the gun as Arkady flips open the cylinder. Sweat trickles down his ashen face.

"Go to hell," Steven growls.

Arkady smirks at him and silently begins removing the bullets from the cylinders one at a time.

"It feels like the mood has become rather unpleasant," Arkady says. He sets five bullets down on the table, then spins the cylinder and flips it closed with a flick of his wrist. "How about a little game to liven things up?"

Steven and I both stare at the revolver in silence. We both know exactly where this is going.

"By the look on your faces, I don't think you need me to explain the way this game works, but I will do so just in case," Arkady says. "I'm going to ask you each some questions. Every time you do not answer or take too long, you will have to try your luck. The game ends when one of you decides to talk or is dead."

Bishop leans his back against the counter and watches with interest as he runs his fingers across the dark stubble of his beard. The son of a bitch is really enjoying the show.

Arkady cocks the hammer back and then he centers the tip of the barrel against Steven's forehead. Steven begins to tremble. The pain from his dislocated shoulder and the fork lodged in his hand and the terror of a gun pressed to his head is too much for him to handle any longer.

"Where is the rest of your group?" Arkady asks Steven.

"Please, God," Steven begs the man. Spittle trickles over his quivering lips as he speaks. He shakes his head as he looks down and begins to sob. "Please. Don't do this, man."

This is it, I think. He can't possibly take anymore.

"Time is up," Arkady says. He pulls the trigger.

I flinch at the sound of the hammer clicking, but the gun doesn't fire. I let out a breath that I'd been holding hostage in my lungs. Even though I am relieved that Steven is alive, and his brains aren't covering the wall, I know this is far from over. Now it's my turn. I hear the hammer of the revolver being pulled back again and turn my head to see Arkady pointing the pistol at my face. He raises his arm and presses the gun against my forehead.

"Your turn, Scout," Arkady smiles. "Same question."

I close my eyes and try to think of something nice instead of the nauseous feeling in my stomach and how bad my hands are shaking. The only memories that come back at the moment are all the horrible things I've been trying to forget.

"Too long," Arkady says but Steven breaks before he pulls the trigger.

"Hold on, man. Hold on!" Steven screams. "I'll tell you where they are. Just please, stop this."

Damn it, Steven. I open my eyes to see the anguish on Steven's face. I can tell he isn't going to hold anything back now. He wasn't willing to watch me die in front of him.

Arkady watches my expression and smirks but keeps the gun pressed against my skull.

"They're still alive," Steven says.

"Where are they?" Arkady demands.

Steven hesitates for a moment. He looks into my eyes that plead with him to keep his mouth shut.

"I'm sorry," he says.

A gunshot rings out and one of the guards at the door drops to the ground. Then an assault rifle opens fire and peppers the restaurant windows with bullets. Arkady moves the gun from my head and fires a round toward the front of the diner as he moves away. If Steven had not said something that bullet would have killed me. It was my turn.

I lean over and topple my chair. The wooden seat splinters and breaks as I drop to the ground to take cover behind an overturned table. It's better than nothing. Rotten food, shards of glass and bits of furniture rain down on me as I curl up in a ball. I call out to Steven but can't hear anything over the sound of gunfire. Feet run past me toward the back of the restaurant. I try to crawl across the floor to get to the kitchen but it's difficult to move with my hands cuffed behind my back. Soon the firefight moves outside. I hear a truck peel out on the pavement followed by a few rounds of bullets piercing metal. The restaurant falls silent once again. I check myself to see if I'm hit, but somehow, I came out unscathed.

"Steven!" I call out into the restaurant.

"Yeah," he coughs. "Over here."

I manage to push myself up to a sitting position and look around the restaurant. The girls that were with Arkady cower beneath a table against the wall. I get to my knees and peer over the table toward the front of the diner. There is no sign of Bishop anywhere. I locate Steven between two other bodies sprawled face down on the floor near the entrance and crawl through the broken glass to get to him.

"Hang in there," I tell him. I begin to search the body of the guy beside him hoping to find a key to the handcuffs. Before I can locate it, the door to the diner flings open. I look up to find a woman with a blonde ponytail

wearing a tank top and camo pants, and she is pointing a gun at me.

CHAPTER FIVE

"Who are you?" the blonde woman demands. She glances around the restaurant. Her eyes find the women crawling out from beneath a table. She looks down at Steven and then she locks her eyes on me again.

"Scout," I stammer. "You mind getting these cuffs off me?"

"Not until you tell me just what the hell was going on in here," the woman says. She looks over her shoulder and nods at a soldier just outside the door. Four soldiers enter the diner and begin sweeping the room and checking the bodies.

"You showed up just in time," I say to the woman. "Those people took us hostage and tortured us."

"Why?" the woman demands.

"They've been after us for a couple weeks," I say. "The guy in charge, Bishop, is forming some kind of army in this massive underground facility."

"You know where it is?" the woman asks.

Even though I would be dead if they didn't show up, I'm still not sure how much information I should give this woman. Besides, it's kind of a long story and Steven is still bleeding on the floor.

"Please, I'll explain everything, but my friend needs help," I say and tilt my head toward Steven. "Is there like a medic here or something?"

Her eyes glance down at Steven as he groans on the floor.

"Please," I beg.

"Check him out, Hernacki," the woman orders one of the soldiers. The youngest member of the squad, a dark-haired kid with a sparse beard, hustles over and crouches beside Steven.

"Thank you," I say to the woman.

"The cuffs are staying on you for now," the woman informs me. "Nothing personal. I just don't know if I can trust you yet, Scout."

"Can't say I blame you," I admit. I still don't know if I should trust them either. They saved our asses, but they must have some other reason for being here. I doubt they were just being good Samaritans.

"Hey, Jess, this guy is pretty fucked up," Hernacki says.

"Do what you can for him," she shrugs.

Hernacki looks back at Steven uncertainly.

"Isn't he a medic?" I ask.

"We don't have a medic anymore," Jess answers.

I struggle up to my feet. Jess watches me closely but doesn't make a move to stop me. I glance through the window at a pair of military Humvees parked outside. Our truck is still parked on the street as well. At least we got that back. Even if it is riddled with bullet holes now.

"Listen," I say. "The rest of our group is a few miles outside of town. One of them is a paramedic. If you'll just let us go, I can get help for my friend."

The woman seems to think about this. She cranes her neck to look at the girls in the back of the restaurant.

"What's their deal?" she asks. "They with you?"

"I don't know who they are," I snap. "Look, I don't have a lot of time here."

"You said it's a few miles away," she says. "You going to carry him all that way?"

"That's our truck outside," I tell her.

"That thing?" She jerks a thumb towards the truck. "Good luck with that."

"I'll figure something out," I say.

"Fine," she says. She turns to glance at the soldier beside her. "Give her the key for cuffs, Hernacki," she orders.

"What key?" he asks.

"Christ," she sighs. "Open your survival kit."

Hernacki sets his pack down on the table and digs out a soft-cover kit. He retrieves a handcuff key and steps behind me to unlock the cuffs. Jess crosses her arms and watches me from behind her sunglasses. I rub at the indents in my wrists left by the cuffs.

"We're normally not in the business of picking up strays, Scout," says Jess. "But given the circumstances, we can escort you and your friend back to your group on one condition."

"Okay," I agree. "Anything."

"I want you to fill me in on all the details of what happened here and tell me everything you know about Bishop."

"Fine," I say. "Thank you, Jess."

"My friends call me Jess," she says. The woman gives me a hint of a smile. "You can call me Agent Lorento."

I nod. There are a million questions going through my mind, but I decide it isn't the time to press her for information.

"Load him up, too, Hernacki," Lorento tells the young soldier.

"Hey, Piper," hollers Hernacki. "Give me a hand getting this guy in the GMV."

A lanky soldier outside moves to the back of a Humvee and retrieves a stretcher. He hurries inside, slipping past me with a warm smile.

Another pair of soldiers remain outside. I start to wonder just how big this unit is. A burly soldier with hair the color of straw pauses to speak to a black soldier with a heavily bandaged arm.

"Keep your eyes peeled, Morris," orders the burly soldier before he follows Piper inside. He rests his rifle on his shoulder as he surveys the room. His blue eyes pause on the two women.

"What are we doing with those two?" the soldier asks Lorento.

"We have other priorities, Hoff," Agent Lorento states. "Just question them and turn them loose unless they have any viable intel."

"You're just going to leave them here?" I interrupt.

"Scout," sighs Agent Lorento. "If you think you can trust them and want to take them in, that's your business. I've got enough problems to deal with already, though."

"Then they can come with us," I tell her.

"Suit yourself," Lorento shrugs. She steps aside to let soldiers carry Steven through the door.

I look around the diner to locate my pack. The majority of my supplies have been dumped on the floor next to the lunch counter. I spot my pack hanging off a chair and grab it and begin stuffing my clothes, binoculars, ammunition, and food inside.

"We got incoming," Hernacki announces as he returns from the truck.

"Bishop?" Lorento asks.

Hernacki shakes his head.

"Couple hundred corpses coming up the road," Hernacki says.

"Let's move out," Lorento orders the soldiers.

Lorento and the soldiers head out the front entrance. I shove the last of my belongings into my pack and spot the bloody knife next to the body on the floor and I grab it. I'm about to get up when I notice something shiny clutched in Owen's hand. It's the keys to the truck. Maybe this awful day

I'm having is going to turn around after all. I pry open his cool fingers and remove the keys.

I get up to leave and notice the two women still standing next to the table. There is no reason to think that I can trust them, but I can't bring myself to leave them here to fend for themselves. That's just not who I am.

"You can die in here or you can come with us," I tell them as the gunfire erupts outside. "It's your choice."

"We're coming," says the younger girl as she steps over a body on the ground and hurries toward the entrance.

I follow the two women out the front door as the massive crowd of the undead files into the street from around the next block. The town was nearly deserted a few hours ago, but I recall Arkady mentioning the church was full of the dead. They must have opened the doors and released them all into town to cover their retreat. Crazy bastards.

"Let's go, Scout," Lorento yells over the rumble of the truck engine.

I escort the two women to the military vehicle, and they climb into the back seats.

"I'm going for the other truck," I tell Lorento as I toss my pack in the back of the Humvee so it doesn't slow me down.

"They're right on top of us," she yells as I turn and sprint for the truck. "You'll never make it."

To hell with that. I've been through too much today and it was partly because of that goddamn truck. I'm taking the damn thing with me.

Gunshots ring out behind me and bullets zip by my head as the soldiers provide some cover fire. I don't know if I am more scared of getting shot or the corpses, but I run like hell. The first corpse reaches the truck before me, and I skid to a halt as the dead man in the black suit shambles in between me and the door. A bullet punches the thing in the chest and staggers it for a moment, so I rush at it with the knife in my hand and shove the blade as hard as I can into the eye socket of the corpse. The stiff slides off my knife and onto the ground.

I fling open the truck door and move to get inside but another corpse grabs my wrist as I try to shut the door. A dead woman in a yoga outfit pulls my arm towards its face and opens its jaws. Instead of trying to fight it off, I just yank the door closed on it as hard as I can. The thing lets out a moan as the door shoves its head into the frame of the truck. I still can't get the door closed, so I open it slightly and pull it hard again as I fumble to get the key into the ignition. The door crushes the head of the dead woman against the frame again, fracturing her skull and spraying flecks of congealed blood around the inside of the cab.

More corpses begin to surround the front of the truck. The engine sputters alive and I open the driver side door to let yoga pants tumble onto the street. Corpses climb onto the hood of the truck as I grab the shifter and throw the truck in reverse. I slam on the gas and crank the wheel to spin the truck around. The bodies of the dead topple off onto the street. The tires squeal as I shift the truck in drive and punch the gas again.

Once I catch up to the convoy, I look back at the swarm of bodies in the rear-view mirror. They still pursue the vehicles even though it would be impossible to ever keep pace. The dead just don't know when to give up. As we cross the covered bridge and follow the road away from town, I realize I still never really learned how to give up, too.

CHAPTER SIX

The military vehicles pull to a stop in the gravel parking lot outside the clothing store. I bring the pickup skidding to a stop and head for the door, but when I try the handle, the door doesn't budge. My knuckles tap the glass a few times.

"It's Scout," I say.

Silence.

"James," I call out and bang a fist on the glass. Something isn't right. There is no way Bishop got to them before us. He would have gone back to get reinforcements first. There is no sign that anything happened, so I don't understand why they would just disappear.

"Fawn?" I cup my hand to the window and peer into the darkened store. "Stevie?"

A silhouette shifts inside the building. The figure pauses behind a rack of clothes and studies me. After several seconds, the person approaches the door. The deadbolt retracts, and James pushes open the door and greets me with a smile.

"Saw these big ass trucks coming and we nearly took off running," he laughs. He steps outside and cocks his head when he notices the bruise on my cheekbone. His eyes flick towards the truck and back at me. "What happened?" he whispers.

"Bishop," I explain. "Steven is pretty banged up."

Hernacki and Piper help Steven out of the back of the Humvee.

"God almighty," James sighs. He grabs the handle and holds the door open for the soldiers. "Come on, get him inside," he urges.

Once the men pass inside, James follows them through the door and calls Fawn to come help. The soldiers shove papers and bags off the front counter to set Steven down.

"Hurry it up, Fawn," James hollers as takes another look at Steven.

"I'm coming," she sighs. Fawn shuffles over from the back of the store, carrying her medical bag and rubbing anti-bacterial lotion on her hands. Her auburn hair is pulled back into a messy bun, which is how she always wears it when she needs to help someone. She takes a look at Steven and starts to tend to his hand first.

"Dad?" calls a soft voice from behind me.

I spin around and spot Stevie peering around the corner of the dressing room. I hurry across the store and squat down in front of him and grab his shoulders.

"Hey kiddo," I smile.

"What happened to my dad?" he says. He tries to look over my shoulder to see what is going on in the front of the store.

"He's okay," I tell him. I place my hands on his cheeks and pull his face closer to mine to get him to focus on me. "Your dad is going to be just fine."

When this all began, Stevie watched his dad take a wrench to the things that used to be his mom and sister. The pain of what he experienced is still evident in his eyes every day. Looking at him is almost enough to convince me that it's better my own boys never have to witness the end of the world.

Stevie fights back the tears welling up in his eyes. He throws his arms around me and buries his face in my shoulder. The kid is just seven years old, and his dad is all he has left of the life he had.

I detect the scent of whiskey and look up to see Nick leaning against the dressing room door. He takes a swig from a bottle and wipes his haggard face with the sleeve of his blazer.

"Is everything fine?" he slurs.

"Yeah," I say, even though everything is far from fine. I've learned to just avoid talking to Nick once he has the bottle in his hands, which is usually about ten minutes after he wakes up. Everyone has their way of dealing with things, or not. The stubborn man still refuses to take off the damn clothes we found him wearing when he was passed out in a puddle of his own piss in a bowling alley bathroom. Even though he begged us to leave him alone, it didn't seem right. I'm still convinced there is still a decent person inside of him somewhere.

"Kid must have slipped past me," Nick groans. He combs his fingers through his graying hair. "Little shit."

"I got him," I say. "Can you start packing? We're going to have to get moving soon."

Nick shrugs, and then he turns and takes another swig from the bottle as he returns to the back of the store. I take Stevie by the hand and lead him outside to a bench next to the front door.

"Want a candy bar?" I ask.

Stevie smiles and nods his head.

"Wait here," I tell him. "I'm just going to grab it out of my pack."

I turn and head back to the GMV. Agent Lorento leans against the front of the vehicle. With her arms crossed, she watches me from behind a pair of sunglasses as she listens to the two women from the diner. I open the back door and unzip my pack and dig through the contents. The candy bar I had in there earlier was gone. I could have left it on the floor of the diner. More likely one of those bastards with Bishop stole it when they went through my stuff.

"Damn it," I sigh.

"Something wrong, honey?" asks Hoff.

I lift my eyes and notice him sitting behind the wheel, watching me in the rear-view mirror. He tosses a handful of sunflower seeds in mouth. I zip up my pack and drop it on the ground beside me.

"My friend that we brought back has a son," I say.

Hoff furrows his brow. Then he turns and spits a seed shell out the window.

"I was going to give him a candy bar I'd been saving, but now it's gone."

"I didn't take it," says Hoff.

"I know," I laugh. "I didn't mean that. I must have lost it at the diner, or those guys took it. I know it's just a candy bar, but I thought it might help distract him."

Hoff reaches into the cargo pocket on his pants and pulls out a protein bar.

"Take it," he says and hands it to me over the seat.

I smile. My heart races for joy at the sight of the protein bar. It's likely close enough to a candy bar to still bring a smile to Stevie's face. I close my fingers around the wrapper of the bar, but then I hesitate. I lock eyes with Hoff. These days even a gift this small usually comes with an expectation of repayment. The big guy notices my expression and gives me a small nod of encouragement to take the food.

"Compliments of the Navy Seals," he says.

"Thank you." I smile and head back to where I left Stevie sitting on the bench. He swings his legs that aren't long enough to reach the ground and stares at his sneakers. The shaggy mop of dark hair hanging over his eyes makes me feel guilty for not taking the time to trim it when we weren't running for our lives. I know something so small might not be very important considering the state of everything, but a mother always notices these things, I guess. I sit down beside him and open the wrapper. He hears the crinkle of the plastic and lifts his head. The sight of the chocolate bar brings a smile to his face. I hand him the candy bar and watch as he takes a bite.

"Thanks, Scout." Crumbs sprinkle from his mouth as he talks. "My mom never used to let me have candy."

"Well," I say. "I'm sure this time it would be okay."

"How do you know?" he asks as he takes another bite.

"Because if I were your mom, I'd want you to have it," I smile.

Stevie stops chewing and looks up at me.

"You know you could be my mom if you wanted to," he says. "I don't have one anymore."

I try to smile but looking at the kid beside me just makes me want to cry. He has been hurting so much these past weeks. Maybe I should just tell him what he wants to hear, but I can't handle the thought of hearing him call me mom. I just want to hear my own kids say it one more time.

"I know it's hard to understand, kiddo," I tell him. "But I can't be your mom."

"Why not?" he asks.

"That's just not how it works," I sigh. "Your mom is always going to be your mom. I could never take her place no matter how much I might want to."

"Even if she dies?" Stevie asks.

"Yes," I tell him. "Besides, I'm already your best buddy, and I like that a lot."

"Me too," Stevie agrees. "You want some?" He holds out the candy bar to share it with me.

"It's okay. Your dad got it just for you," I say.

Steven lets out a scream of pain inside the store. Fawn must be relocating his shoulder now. His son stops chewing for a moment.

"He's going to be fine," I assure the kid. "Just be sure you remember to thank him when you see him, okay?"

Stevie nods and takes another bite. He holds up a fist in my direction as he chews. I make my hand into a fist and touch it with his then pull my hand back and open the fist and make an exploding noise. Stevie does the same. Exploding fist bumps always make him smile.

I rub his shaggy hair and lean back on the bench, so the kid doesn't notice the anxious expression on my face. Most likely his dad will be okay. His injuries are painful but not that severe. My main concern is that we get out of here before Bishop arrives. He knows we're close. It's just a matter of time before he finds us again.

Agent Lorento leaves the women standing near the military vehicles and strides over to the entrance. Her casual pace is that of a person that feels confident and in control of the situation. I'm usually pretty good at reading people, but I am not sure about her motives, so her presence gives me an uneasy feeling. She leans a shoulder against a support beam for the storefront porch and smiles at Stevie when he looks up at her.

"He's a cutie," she says to me. "Yours?"

"No," I shake my head. "His dad is the man you picked up with me."

Agent Lorento nods. She tilts her head and peers over the top of her sunglasses and squints at Stevie.

"Now I see the similarity," she says, as if she didn't believe me without seeing it for herself. "Keeping a kid safe in this kind of environment must be tough. But you seemed to handle yourself pretty good back there."

"Look," I sigh. "I know you've got some questions you want to ask me so can we just get on with it. It's just a matter of time before Bishop and his guys come back around looking for us."

"Piper says he is sure he tagged Bishop as they were getting in the truck. That will slow them down a bit. Plus, they let those corpses loose to make their getaway, so they can't just drive back through town."

I sigh and my shoulders relax a bit.

"I was hoping those two girls from the diner would have some good intel," Lorento continues. "They weren't as helpful as I hoped. Both confirmed what you told me about the underground facility, but they aren't sure of the location. That's their story at least," Lorento smiles. "You mind telling me why Bishop is after you?"

"It's a long story," I say.

"Give me the short version," she insists.

"Well, a couple of weeks ago we stopped to check out this grocery store and ran into a few of their guys on their own supply run. They seemed all right at first, real friendly. Offered to take us in with them as long as the men would fight, and the women would put out. When James told them no, they got violent. They were well-armed and outnumbered us, but we managed to escape. The dead got a couple of them. Bishop has had his guys out looking for us ever since. We had no idea what we were getting into then."

"What do you mean?" Lorento asks.

"I mean, we thought it was just a dozen guys we were dealing with. We had no idea who Bishop was. If we had any idea those guys were part of an army, I don't know, maybe we wouldn't have fought back then."

"Do you have any idea how big this army is, Scout?"

"Big," I sigh. "I trailed the group back to the underground compound, but I never got inside. I just staked the place out for a day, watched trucks coming and going. Security was tight. I'd guess he has to have at least two or three hundred people in there. Could even be a lot more than that."

"Where?" Lorento asks.

"Near Springfield. It's one of those massive storage and manufacturing facilities built into the rock."

Lorento turns her head, stares at the trees, and considers the information. After several moments she lowers her gaze.

"Anything else?" she adds.

"Sorry, that's everything I know," I say.

"You've been a big help, Scout," Lorento smiles.

"Wish I could help more," I sigh.

"Maybe you can. Do you remember how you got to the compound?"

"Sort of. I'm sure I could find my way back there, but I don't remember the names of any of the roads to give you directions."

Lorento crosses her arms and stares down at her boots and considers my response.

"You mind if I ask you something?" I say.

"Depends on the question," she says. "But you can try to ask me anyway."

"What do you guys want with Bishop?"

"It's kind of a long story," Lorento smiles. She clearly finds humor in throwing my own excuse back at me.

"Give me the short version," I insist.

"Let's just say he has something of mine," she says. "And I want it back."

The door of the clothing store swings open and James steps out onto the porch. I get up from the bench when I see Fawn pushing through the door behind him. She peels a pair of bloody latex gloves off her hands and tosses them on the ground.

"He's going to be okay," Fawn sighs and wipes the sweat from her brow with her forearm.

I spread my arms and wrap them around her and pull her close.

"Thank you," I say. "You're amazing, Fawn."

"I bet you say that to all the paramedics," Fawn laughs. "Now, he's pretty banged up and lost a bit of blood, so it'll be a few days before he fully recovers."

"Can I go see him?" asks Stevie.

"Sure," smiles Fawn. "Just stay quiet and let him take it easy so he gets better."

Stevie nods, and then he runs inside the store.

"You must be James," Agent Lorento says. She moves past me and extends a hand toward James.

"I am," James smiles. He slowly reaches out to shake her hand gently.

"Agent Jessica Lorento," she announces. "Scout tells me you're the man in charge."

James glances at me. He smirks and crosses his arms.

"I guess you could say that," says James. "But I like to think we're all equals here."

Lorento nods.

"I just want to say I really appreciate what you did for Scout and Steven. There aren't too many people willing to stick their neck out to help someone else anymore."

"That's very true," agrees Lorento.

"So, if there is anything we can do to repay you, just ask. We don't have much of anything to offer in the way of supplies."

"Actually," begins Lorento, "I was hoping you might be willing to come along with us. The fact is we have a common enemy, so the smartest thing we can do is work together."

James shoves his hands in the pockets of his jeans and sighs. His brown eyes stare down at his cowboy boots for a long moment as he considers the request.

"I see," James says. "We'll need a minute to talk it over." He looks at me and jerks his head then moves toward the doorway of the store.

"Of course," Lorento agrees. She turns and heads back toward the soldiers gathered near the military vehicles.

"I'm not sure about all this, Scout," James says.

"We don't really have a choice. Bishop knows we're in this area," I explain. "He's going to come looking for us soon. We can't keep running forever. At least with these guys we stand a fighting chance."

James settles his gaze on me. His weary brown eyes plead with me to say something that will convince him of the right decision.

"Bishop isn't a guy we can reason with. Steven and I would be dead if these soldiers didn't show up," I say. "We can trust them."

"All right then," James agrees. "Let's load up."

CHAPTER SEVEN

There is hardly room for all of us after we load the pickup and the military vehicles with our supplies. I help Stevie climb into the front seat of the bullet-riddled truck and hand Fawn the keys.

"I'm going to ride in one of the Humvees," I tell her. "See if I can find out some more information."

"I'm still not sure about this," Fawn sighs. "These guys want us to fight with them. We're not soldiers. We are doing just fine on our own."

"No," I tell Fawn as I close the truck door. "I know how you're feeling, but we were not fine. We need all the help we can get."

I give her a hug and as I look over her shoulder, I notice Hoff and the two women from the diner getting into the other truck.

"It's going to be fine," I assure Fawn, then I let go of her and walk toward the Humvee.

I still haven't had a chance to talk to the women from the diner either. Lorento seemed to think they are probably harmless, but I have to find out what their deal is, and whether or not we can actually trust them.

"You riding with us?" Hoff asks me as I approach him.

"You got room?" I ask him back.

"Sure," Hoff says. He turns to Morris in the passenger seat and jerks his thumb and the soldier gets out and heads for the other Humvee with Lorento and the rest of the squad.

I climb into the truck and glance back at the two women from the diner in the backseat. Now that I actually take a closer look, I notice the bruises all over both of them. It makes me curious what kind of nightmare they went through, but also a little afraid to ask.

"I never caught your names," I say.

"I'm Val," says the young girl with a long brown ponytail. She looks up from her hands that are tucked between her thighs and looks at me. "Valerie. That's Nicole."

"I'm Scout," I smile. "Are you doing okay?"

"These seats are brutal," Nicole complains from the backseat. "But other than that."

"We're fine," Val says. "Now that we got away from those assholes."

"Lorento tells me you were inside their compound?" I ask.

Valerie nods. Hoff starts the truck and I wait for the loud engine to turn over and begin idling to speak again.

"What was it like in there?" I wonder.

"Horrible," Val shudders. "It's the worst place imaginable."

"Quit being so dramatic," Nicole snaps. "The worst thing about that place was having to listen to her whining the whole fucking time."

"Shut up, Nicole." Val brings a hand up and wipes a tear from under her eye.

"Listen," Nicole says to me. Her gritty voice grates my ears like sandpaper. "There aren't exactly any four-star hotels around anymore. It's safe there. As long as you keep your mouth shut and do what you're told, you get to live."

It almost sounds like Nicole would consider going back if she could. Maybe they didn't have it good there, but at least she was alive. For some people surviving is all that matters. It was less frightening than facing the uncertainty of the world outside.

"Do you have an idea how many people are there?"

"A lot," Val says. "A couple hundred men are in the militia. The rest are just regular people."

"Why don't they do something about Bishop and his thugs?" I ask.

"The militia keeps them safe," Val says. "The only reason they are there is because they aren't the kind of people that can survive on their own. We all know Bishop is a monster, but he was also our only hope to stay alive."

"At least they had cigarettes there," Nicole adds. "Don't suppose you got any of those? I get real cranky if I don't have some."

That explains a lot.

"Sorry, I don't smoke," I tell her. "But I'll see what I can do."

Nicole murmurs and sighs and turns her head to stare out the window again.

"They have a lot of supplies there?" I ask Val.

"Sure," says Val. "They've got everything. Clothes. Food. Anything you want as long as you have something to offer them."

"Like what?" I say, but Val doesn't need to answer. She looks down at the floor and presses her lips together.

"The things I would do for a pack of smokes right now," Nicole sighs.

Hoff folds up the map in his hands and glances at the side mirror to see if the rest of the trucks are ready to go. I can't tell for certain if he was paying attention to the conversation at all. He clears his throat before he reminds us to buckle up.

"You think they'd at least put a little cushion in these things," Nicole complains as she shifts in her seat.

"Get comfortable being uncomfortable," Hoff says as he shifts the truck in drive.

We drive a few miles in silence down the open country road. I glance over at Hoff and notice the name stitched on his uniform. It is different from the name Lorento called him by. His eyes stare at the road before him without moving or blinking for some time.

"Why do they call you Hoff?" I finally ask him.

"Huh?" he says. The soldier takes his eyes off the road quickly to glance in my direction.

"The name on your uniform says Lewis," I say over the noise of the engine. "So why does everyone call you Hoff."

Hoff grins. The question seems to lighten his mood a bit.

"You ever seen Knight Rider?" Hoff laughs. He turns the wheel and accelerates onto the highway.

I shake my head.

"You know David Hasselhoff?" He turns his head to spit a sunflower seed shell out the window.

"I think so," I nod.

"Well, David Hasselhoff plays this guy with a talking car. When I first joined up with the squad the guys always made fun of me for talking to Lucille. That's what I called her. Lucille was a real beauty, a 69' Camaro SS, all black," he grins.

I return his smile and shrug. I don't know shit about cars.

"So anyway, they started calling me Hasselhoff, but eventually that got shortened down to Hoff."

"I see. Does everyone have a nickname?"

"Sure," Hoff nods. "Like Morris. We call him Motown on account of his singing."

"He can sing?" I say.

"No," Hoff grins. "He most definitely cannot sing."

We both laugh.

"Everybody gets a nickname. We still got to pick one for Hernacki. He just joined up before the shit hit the fan, so we haven't figured out what to call his dumb ass yet."

"What about Piper?" I ask. "How'd he get that nickname?"

"You don't want to know." Hoff laughs and shakes his head.

"You're probably right," I blush. "I don't think I want to know."

"What the hell kind of name is Scout for a girl anyway?" he asks. "Is that your real name?"

"Real enough," I say.

Hoff grunts. He steers the car into the opposite lane to avoid a corpse in the road.

"I'm still kind of surprised," I change the subject. "We didn't think there was any government left."

"What makes you think there is?" Hoff asks me.

"You guys seem like you're following orders of some kind," I explain. "That means there must be someone calling the shots, right?"

"Hardly," Hoff shakes his head. "We haven't had contact with any military or government personnel since we left Chicago. Personally, I don't think there is any one left to give orders."

"So, what are you guys doing out here?" I ask.

"That's classified."

"Who cares? You just said there is nothing left of the government."

"Classified is still classified until someone says it isn't," Hoff explains.

"Forget I asked." I roll my eyes. This conversation is getting me nowhere. The truth is I don't really care about what Lorento and her soldiers want to accomplish. It doesn't matter anymore. No one can fix this deep shit we're in. It's too late for that. The only thing that matters now is that we might stand a better chance of surviving tomorrow.

Hoff steers the truck to the right onto a country road heading north and keeps his eyes on the road to avoid my stare.

"You planning on staring at me the rest of the way?" Hoff finally asks.

"Maybe," I tell him.

The soldier grins and shakes his head.

"Can you at least tell me where we're going?" I press him. "I don't like being left in the dark."

Hoff glances over at me and considers my expression for a moment. Then he turns and spits a sunflower seed out the window.

"Iowa," he says. "We're headed to Iowa."

"Iowa?" I ask. "I thought we'd be headed to the military base. What the hell are we going to Iowa for?"

Hoff takes his gaze off the road and raises an eyebrow at me.

"Right," I grunt, and roll my eyes. "Let me guess. It's classified."

"You catch on quick," he laughs. "Sorry Scout. If you want more info, you'll have to grill Lorento. She's running the show."

"Something tells me that won't go too well," I mutter.

"She's a real piece of work, ain't she?" Hoff laughs.

"I thought she was just having a bad day," I say. "Please don't tell me she is like this all the time."

"No," he says. "She is usually way worse than this."

"Good to know," I laugh.

"Just be sure to stay on her good side," Hoff grins.

CHAPTER EIGHT

We ride along the empty road through the Mark Twain National Forest without any signs of trouble. I know the rest of the trip is probably not going to be this easy. The drive to Iowa might have only taken six hours or so before, but now it might take several days if we're lucky. The dead swarm the streets of every small town. We could try to stick to the back roads, but even that isn't exactly safe. There is no telling what we might run into along the way.

As nightfall approaches, Hoff pulls the Humvee to a stop in front of a small tire shop that sits about a quarter mile down the road from a small town. The population, according to a sign on the side of the road, used to be nearly seven hundred people. It doesn't seem like a lot until you see their bodies all prowling the street in search of food.

"Looks pretty good," Hoff says as he shifts the truck in park.

I get out of the truck and scan the area. The windows and front door of the building still appear secure. June bugs buzz in the surrounding trees. The pink clouds in the west shroud the setting sun. I gaze at the sky for a few moments. Fireflies flicker in the dusky light. It looks like I will make it through another day.

Barely.

"Check it out, Hernacki," Lorento says. She slides out of the passenger seat of the other Humvee and glances at the surrounding trees on each side of the road.

Hernacki straps on his helmet and readies his rifle with precision as he hops off the rear of the truck.

"Move it, kid," Lorento urges him. "We don't have much daylight left."

The rest of the soldiers remain stationed with the vehicles as Hernacki approaches the store. Lorento folds her arms across her chest and leans back against the passenger door of the truck.

"You a meteorologist or something?" Lorento asks me.

"What?" I ask.

"You keep looking up at the sky," she says. "I noticed you doing it several times already. At first, I thought maybe you were praying, but you don't strike me as the religious type."

"No, I wasn't praying," I shake my head. "I watch for vultures."

"Vultures?" Lorento cocks an eyebrow at me. "I never pegged you for a birdwatcher."

"Not like that. It seems like the birds have started to follow the dead around," I say. "They stalk the large crowds. A few will also hang around if one of the stiffs gets stuck or can't move. They feed off it for days until there is nothing left but bones."

Lorento glances around the treetops as she listens.

"If you see vultures," I continue. "There's trouble nearby. The more you see, the more trouble you got."

"And when you don't see any birds around you know it's clear?" Lorento asks.

"Well, no," I concede. "It might just mean you have a different kind of trouble to worry about."

"You're pretty resourceful," admits Lorento. "I hadn't noticed that about you."

"You seem to be paying pretty close attention," I say.

Lorento flashes a smile, and then she turns her head to watch Hernacki as he emerges from the shop.

"We're in luck," Hernacki says. I turn to see the soldier holding the front door of the building open. He grins and waves us over. "The door wasn't even locked."

"Keep it down, Hernacki," Hoff scolds. He closes the door of the Humvee and drapes the strap of his rifle over his shoulder.

"All right, clear the entire building and get the trucks in the garage," Lorento tells the men. "Don't screw around. It's almost dark."

The soldiers ready their rifles and line up on each side of the entrance. One by one the men vanish into the darkness of storefront. Lorento retrieves a satchel from the back of the Humvee and pulls out some kind of electronic device. She stands at the back of the vehicle looking at the screen with her brow furrowed. At first glance it looks like a cell phone, but when I look more closely, I notice it's something else. My curiosity gets the better of me and I decide to approach her. Lorento notices me out of the corner of her eye as I get close, and she quickly shoves the device back in the satchel and pulls the strap over her shoulder.

"Yes, Scout?" she asks.

"Is everything okay?" I say. "You look worried."

"It's been quite a while since everything was okay," she smirks.

Suddenly she decides to crack jokes. It's clear she will do whatever it takes to avoid giving me any information.

"That's not what I meant," I sigh.

"I know," she says. "The truth is we are not nearly as close to our objective as we need to be. We lost a lot of time today, and every minute we lose puts our mission at risk."

I turn my gaze toward the road, not wanting to hear any more of her empty explanations. I keep hoping for an answer that isn't coming.

"I can't stress that enough, Scout," Lorento continues. "The fate of the world is at stake."

I roll my eyes. Lorento scowls at my reaction. Her speech seems absurd. I can't see what a condescending intelligence agent and a handful of soldiers can possibly accomplish to prevent the end of humanity.

"I'm sorry," I explain. "It's just a little hard for me to believe there is anything that can be done to stop this based on what I've seen."

The garage door slides open, and the soldiers emerge from the building.

"All clear," Hoff reports.

"Let's get these trucks inside," Lorento orders.

The soldier nods as he opens the door to the truck. He turns the key and steers the truck into the garage. Lorento waits beside me silently as everyone moves inside. I take a step toward the garage, but the agent reaches out a hand and grabs the sleeve of my jacket.

"I can tell you want answers, Scout" Lorento whispers. "But I need to be sure that any information will stay between us."

I look away from her again and turn my eyes to the small sliver of moon above the treetops on the horizon. I can't stand to look at anyone when I get angry at them. I've heard about as many of her excuses as I can stand. She sighs and removes her sunglasses and hangs them over the collar of her shirt.

"We're going to Iowa to locate a helicopter pilot," Lorento says.

"A pilot?" I ask.

Lorento nods.

"He will fly us somewhere safe?"

"Well, it's a little more complicated than that," she sighs.

I cross my arms over my chest and wait for her to continue.

"In the early days of this crisis, the government assigned this unit to help me locate a scientist and escort him safely to a secure military facility in New Mexico. When we stopped to refuel the helicopter at FLW we encountered a hostile force of significant size. We tried to negotiate with them at first, but the situation quickly escalated, and the scientist fell into their hands during the ensuing firefight. We had no choice but to retreat to the helicopter, but we took some heavy ground fire, and the aircraft went down. Our medic and the helicopter crew were all killed in the crash. The rest of us managed to escape with mostly minor injuries."

"How long ago did all this happen?" I ask her.

"Several weeks ago," Lorento says. "It took some time before this squad was recovered enough to begin our efforts to track Bishop down. By then his men had already cleared out of Fort Leonard Wood and took most of the supplies along with them. We didn't manage to locate them again until this morning."

"So how do you know this scientist is even still alive?"

Lorento reaches into her satchel and removes the device I'd noticed earlier.

"This tracks a GPS transmitter that I planted in the pocket of our scientist's pants shortly after we met. We found his bloody clothes in a lodge along with this..." Lorento returns the GPS to her satchel and removes a tape recorder. She clicks a button, and the tape begins to play.

"Hello there, blondie," Bishop growls. "As you probably guessed, I found the chip your friend, Dr. Schoenheim, had in his pants. Don't worry, he's doing just fine. We're all having a real good time here. Ain't that right, Doc?"

Bishop pauses as a man wails incoherently in the background.

"With a little encouragement, the doc told me all about you and your friends and your mission to save the world," Bishop laughs. "Now see that's where we don't agree. It seems to me this whole situation is fixing everything that was wrong with the world. The corrupt, greedy politicians are gone. All the lowlifes in the ghettos and the prisons are eating each other alive. No more terrorism. No more war. No more illegals coming here to—"

Lorento clicks off the recording.

"He goes on for quite a while, but you get the idea," she says. "Needless to say, his message wasn't very convincing, and his actions against the government and military make him a traitor and an enemy of the state."

"Why wouldn't he just kill this Dr. Schoenheim?" I wonder.

"Bishop envisions himself as the last hope to save humanity," Lorento says. "Not just from this outbreak, but from going back to the way things were. In his mind, this whole outbreak is an opportunity to set everything right. While he doesn't want to return any means to resolve the crisis to the government, he would certainly use the research to his own benefit. If he holds the power to stop the dead, we'll all have no choice but to play by his rules."

The thought gives me a chill.

"So, we get the pilot, get the doctor back from Bishop somehow, and then we all fly off to New Mexico?" I ask.

"That's the objective," Lorento says.

Something still doesn't make sense. I gaze at the open garage for a long moment as I consider the details of our conversation.

"Why don't we go after Bishop now?" I ask Lorento. "Then we can drive to New Mexico."

"No offense, Scout," Lorento says. "This is my job. I call the shots. You have to trust me when I say we will have a better chance of pulling this off and transporting the doctor if we have air support. We need the pilot."

"If you're in contact with him, why doesn't he just fly down here or whatever. Seems like that would be a whole lot easier for everyone."

"It would be," she agrees. "Except he doesn't know he's coming here yet."

"What do you mean?" I wonder.

Lorento retrieves the GPS device from her satchel again. She presses a couple of buttons and shows me a red beacon on the map display.

"I told you I know where he is. I never said we were in contact," she says. "That's the reason we're running out of time, Scout. With no computers online to update these satellites the accuracy of this receiver degrades more and more each day. It may be twenty miles off today, but tomorrow could be eighty. Within a couple of weeks, we might not know what state he is in."

"So, we might be looking for a needle in a haystack," I say. "For all we know, we might get up there and find out he's dead and wandering out in the woods somewhere."

"Well, potentially," Lorento says. "There's also one other minor potential problem. Our pilot might take some convincing to go along with all this. Well, a lot of convincing. He can be quite... difficult."

"What man isn't?" I scoff.

Lorento lets out laugh and then slaps a hand over her mouth. She ducks her head and giggles quietly into her fingertips for a couple seconds. It's the first genuine reaction I've seen from her all day. She might actually be human after all.

CHAPTER NINE

T he soldiers surround a workbench with a travel map spread open before them. They have some ration boxes open and look to be preparing some meals in plastic bags as they discuss the possible routes that could take us to Iowa. Other than the small battery powered lantern beside the map, the garage is shrouded in darkness. The cavernous room smells of rubber, fuel, and years of cigarette smoke. It takes a moment for my eyes to adjust to the darkness. I scan the room looking for James and the others. A hand suddenly seizes my arm and startles me.

"Don't think I forgot about you, Scout," Fawn says.

"Jesus, Fawn, don't do that to me."

"Sorry," she laughs. "Steven told me you took a pretty good shot to the head earlier today. Let me check you out."

I let Fawn pull me toward a glass doorway that leads to the sales floor of the tire store. There are stacks of rubber tires and a couple of display racks filled with air fresheners, floor mats and bumper stickers. Along the front windows is a waiting area with half a dozen chairs, a coffee table full of automotive magazines, and a small bin of toys in the corner.

Fawn nudges me, and I reluctantly take a seat in the chair next to Nicole.

"Do you remember what my name is?" Fawn asks.

"Of course, I do," I sigh.

"Please, just answer the questions."

"Fine," I say. "Your name is Fawn."

"Do you know what day of the week it is?"

"It's Thursday, I think, or Friday," I shrug. "Gosh, who is actually keeping track of that anymore? This is stupid, I'm fine." I move to get up but Fawn grips my arm and pulls me back down.

"Just another minute," she insists. "Do you have a headache?"

"Throbbing."

"Any feelings of nausea?"

"A little," I inform her. "Just the same feeling I get every day now."

"You sure you aren't just pregnant?" Nicole chimes in.

Somehow, I resist the urge to find out if she can take a punch.

Fawn removes a penlight from her pocket and clicks it on. She flashes the light in my eyes and studies their reaction to the light. She flicks the light back off and I'm left totally blind for several seconds until my eyes readjust to the darkness.

"You don't look so great, but you'll be fine," Fawn concludes. She grabs my hand and places a couple of tablets in my palm. "These should help with the headache."

"Thanks, Fawn," I say. I toss the pills into my mouth and reach out to grab a bottled water from the paramedic. She pats my knee and gives me a smile before she moves to the service counter and returns the penlight and pills to her medical bag. She grabs a different medication and some clean bandages and comes back to tend to Steven next.

For a long time, I just sit in the chair and watch Stevie play with a toy dump truck on the floor of the waiting room. The little boy makes rumbling and beeping noises as he steers the yellow vehicle around in circles. It makes me feel better just to watch him playing like a normal kid for once. When I look over at Steven again, he has fallen asleep in the chair. Fawn must have really given him some strong stuff for the pain.

The service door to the garage creaks open and Lorento and the soldiers file into the storefront. They pass out some rations to us and I get Stevie to leave the dump truck long enough to take a few bites of food. I grab a bag of corn chips and eavesdrop on Piper as he starts telling Nicole and Val some odd story about a guy named Jervis and a camel.

I stop listening when I notice Lorento slip out of the room. For several minutes, I listen to the sound of her voice in the garage. Even though I can't make out her words, something gives me an uneasy feeling. Then I finally realize what seems off about it. I don't hear anyone else talking out there except her.

I leave Stevie to play by himself and slip behind the counter to reach the service door. Before I push the handle to open the door, I pause and reconsider. I am probably just being paranoid. Still, my curiosity gets the better of me and I ease the glass door open. Lorento emerges from the darkness and meets me at the door.

"Did you need something?" Lorento asks me. She closes the cover of her satchel and gives me a smile.

I lean to the side and peer over her shoulder. The garage behind her appears to be empty.

"I just thought I heard you talking to someone," I explain.

"That's strange," Lorento says. She steps around me and returns to the storefront without meeting my eyes.

After she leaves, I take another look around the dark garage. Maybe I am just imagining things, but somehow, I doubt that is the case. There is still something she definitely doesn't want me to know about. After our talk outside, I started to feel like I could trust her. Now, I am not so sure again.

As soon as we have finished our meals, the soldiers bring out a crate of weapons and give us all a crash course on how to handle them. Hoff brings me an automatic rifle equipped with a scope and suppressor along with a .45 caliber handgun.

"Picked these out for you," Hoff winks at me. "Think you can handle them?"

"Sure," I say as I take the weapons. I check the safeties before I prop the rifle against the wall and slip the pistol into my thigh holster.

"It's the same shit that we carry," he explains. "I thought the suppressor might make it a little easier for you to handle."

"Now I'm not even going to miss the Glock I had before," I tell Hoff. "Thank you."

"What about sleepy over there?" Hoff jerks his head to Steven.

"It doesn't matter," I tell Hoff. "He's a terrible shot with any gun."

The soldier laughs and pulls out an old hunting rifle and leans it against the wall beside Steven.

"Do you happen to have a machete?" I ask Hoff. "Steven will probably miss the one he had."

"Might be one in the GMV," Hoff tells me. "I'll take a look."

The soldier turns around and settles his eyes on Fawn sitting behind the service counter.

"How about you, gorgeous?" Hoff asks Fawn.

"Oh, I don't use guns," Fawn blushes. "Thank you, though."

"Don't use guns?" Hoff asks.

"Fawn doesn't fight," I tell him. "She doesn't believe in it."

Hoff rolls his eyes. The big soldier waves Morris over and the two men carry the crate back out to the truck.

I can understand his reaction. It's hard to accept that someone could still be that opposed to using a weapon, but Fawn has never killed a living creature. Not even the dead. She has always relied on us to keep her safe.

James sits down in the open seat beside me and props his cowboy boots up on the coffee table and starts unwrapping a granola bar.

"Guess this all worked out pretty good so far," he says. He glances back at the door to the garage.

"Tell that to my face," I remind him.

"It doesn't look that bad, Scout," he laughs. He takes a bite of a granola bar and glances toward the garage again. "Did Lorento mention where we're going?"

I fight back the urge to tell him the truth.

"No," I lie. I know I can trust James with my life, but he is just too honest, even when that isn't the smartest thing to be. He will just feel obligated to tell the others, so it's better not to put that burden on him. I look up and see him eyeing me. I must have hesitated too long before I answered. He knows. Damn it. Honest people can always tell when someone is lying.

"I'm still not sure I trust them," James says. "But I might just be starting to lose my faith in people. Maybe I'm just a glass half-empty kind of guy, but it seems like there aren't many good people left these days. Sometimes I doubt I'm a good person anymore either."

"It's all right," I assure him. "You're a good man, James."

I know James still has had a hard time with the outcomes of some of the decisions he has made. He even feels guilty about Bishop's men that were killed by the dead in that grocery store. Even if he has done nothing wrong, he always does whatever he can to make things right. Sometimes that just isn't possible, though.

I notice Stevie has stopped pushing the truck around and rubs his tired eyes. Since his dad is still snoring away, I guess it will be up to me to get him to sleep tonight.

"What do you say we get you ready for bed, kiddo?" I ask Stevie.

"Please can I play for just five more minutes?" he asks me.

"You need to get your rest," I tell him.

Stevie sulks and lets out a frustrated sigh.

"I tell you what," I say as I pick up the truck off the floor. "We can take this with, and you can play with it tomorrow. Deal?"

"Okay, Scout," Stevie yawns. He watches as I unzip his Captain America backpack and pull out a blanket before putting the dump truck inside.

"Can you tell me a story?" Stevie asks.

"It's already pretty late, kiddo," I tell him. "And I am tired, too. Maybe tomorrow night."

"My mom used to always read me a book when she tucked me," Stevie says as I cover him with the blanket.

"Stevie, I'm not your mom," I remind him.

"I know," he says. The tears start to build up in his eyes and he rolls over so I can't see his face.

I feel awful for making him sad. He is such a sweet kid, but the pain from losing my own children still feels fresh every day. I know I am not able to care for him the same way a mother would. Maybe, for his sake, I can try to fake it.

"Once upon a time..." I begin...

CHAPTER TEN

A hand clamps over my mouth and startles me from sleep. My eyes dart around the room but all I see is darkness.

"Shhh," a man whispers into my ear. The warm breath on the side of my face gives me a chill. My heart races.

I try to pull myself free, but the rough hands grip me tighter.

"Easy," the voice assures me. "You're okay, Scout."

I recognize the sound of Hoff's voice and I stop resisting. He feels my muscles relax and then he uncovers my mouth.

"Jesus Christ, you scared the hell out of me," I hiss.

"Shh," Hoff whispers.

"What the hell is going on?" I whisper.

"We got company outside," Hoff says. "Wake everyone up. We need to move out now."

I nod my head, and then the soldier retreats silently to the garage. I turn to nudge James but before I can a hand smacks against the glass at the front of the store. The sound causes everyone to stir from their sleep except Nick.

Another hand thuds against the glass. The dark shadows fill the windows as the dead converge on the building.

"Everyone get your stuff and get to the trucks," I whisper. My hands locate the strap of my pack and the barrel of the rifle.

The hands of the dead begin to pound at the glass. I can't understand how they know we are inside. Something must have alerted them to our presence. Splinters begin to appear in the large storefront windows.

"Hurry up!" I urge. I shoulder my pack and ready the rifle as I back towards the door. Others rush past me as I hold my position. Nick is the last one remaining in the storefront.

"Son of a bitch," he curses and knocks over at stack of tires. I blink into the darkness to see what he is doing.

"C'mon, Nick," I hiss.

"Shut up," he yells back.

I'm about to turn and leave him when the windows shatter and glass rains down on the tile floors. I raise the rifle and open fire. The powerful rifle causes me to lose my balance and bullets spray wildly into the night. Corpses pour into the building. The dead knock tires and chairs aside as they push through the lobby. Nick stumbles into my back and knocks me toward the dead as he charges into the garage. Fingers brush against the sleeves of my jacket. A hand clamps around the barrel of the rifle and pushes it down toward the floor. I try to pull the rifle free as the dead close in around me. I kick blindly and manage to hit something, and the rifle is suddenly released sending me stumbling back into a stack of tires.

The engines of the vehicles turn over. Someone calls my name in the garage. I stay on my feet and fire off several more rounds to slow the dead long enough for me to back through the doorway. Once I am in the garage, I turn and sprint toward the taillights of the idling trucks. The soldiers open fire as the dead crowd the doorway. I reach the back of the Humvee and Lorento reaches out a hand to help pull me up into the back of the truck. I collapse onto the floor as the truck begins to accelerate. The first vehicle plows into the garage door and knocks the metal panels off the tracks and rumbles into the night.

I climb back to my feet as the second truck rumbles through the open garage. The air around us fills with the moans of the dead. The headlights of the vehicles illuminate hundreds of corpses surrounding the building. One of the soldiers tosses out a grenade that sends a thick cloud of smoke into the darkness. Muzzles flash as everyone begins to fire blindly into the growing crowd of corpses. The vehicles inch forward, churning bodies beneath the tires.

The corpses grab on to the vehicle and try to climb into the bed. I grab the rifle and point it at the face of a dead farmer in muddy overalls and pull the trigger. Chunks of his skull spray into the air. His body flops back onto the crowd that surges forward behind him. I fire again and again until the bullets are gone. I reach for my pack to reload but, before I can, the engine growls, and the truck accelerates through the smoke and into the road. The corpses pursue us but as the trucks speed down the highway they disappear into the darkness behind us.

It takes me a few moments to catch my breath. My hands shake and my heart pumps violently in my chest. I can't understand how so many of the dead happened to descend on the store at the same time. It is like they knew we were inside. Those things just aren't that smart. None of it makes any sense.

"You okay, Scout?" Lorento places a hand on my shoulder gently.

"What the hell happened back there?" I ask.

"I'm not sure. Hernacki said they all came down the road together. It's almost as though someone lead them right to us."

"It had to be Bishop."

"I think it's safe to assume that it was," Lorento agrees.

As the truck rolls into town, I scan the darkened buildings along the road. If this was Bishop, we may still be in a lot of danger. Now that we have been flushed out into the open, we are much more vulnerable. Maybe we are right where he wants us.

"Shit," I mutter.

The crack of a rifle interrupts my thoughts. The lead vehicle swerves in front of us. I'm thrown back down to the floor as the driver hits the brakes to avoid crashing into the back of the first truck. Bullets begin to pelt the

Humvee from every direction. I cover my head with my arms and curl into a ball on the bed of the vehicle.

"Go!" I hear Lorento scream as the truck accelerates again. The engine growls and the truck swerves and I hear the soldiers firing back at the darkened building. A moment later the gunfire stops. I slowly raise my head and see Steven covering his son next to me. Beside me Lorento changes a fresh magazine into her weapon. She studies the road behind us.

"They're coming," she says.

I look back and see several sets of headlights in the road. Then more headlights appear until I can't tell exactly how many vehicles are giving chase. I get to my feet and pick up the rifle.

Lorento grabs the radio from her belt and talks into the microphone. "We need to pick it up, fellas."

"Piper's hit," Hernacki says. His voice cracks in panic. "He can't drive like this."

"I'm good," Piper argues. His muffled voice in the background is barely audible.

"You got shot in the fucking neck, man," Hernacki says. "We need to pull over."

"No," orders Lorento. She pauses and lowers the radio for a moment as she thinks. "Damn it," she whispers. Lorento raises the radio to her lips. "Piper, hang in there for a few miles. We need to lose them. Hernacki, do what you can for him, then get in the turret."

"I thought these trucks were supposed to be bulletproof," I say.

"I wish," says Lorento.

"Can't this thing go any faster?"

Lorento ignores me and turns toward the front of the vehicle. She grabs a large grenade launcher on the hood and begins removing it from the rack. I watch as she loads the RPG and crouches down to hoist it onto her shoulder. This whole situation is getting insane. The headlights from the approaching trucks draw closer. It won't be more than a few minutes before the lighter vehicles catch up to us.

"When they get close, I need you to lay down some fire for me, Scout." Lorento says. Her voice remains steady and even. "Think you can do that?"

I nod and grip the rifle.

Fawn drives ahead in the pickup as the military vehicles pull side-by-side on the road. I spot Hernacki in the turret of the other Humvee, while James and Morris ready their rifles in the back.

"I can help." Steven appears beside me with the rifle in his hands. I glance back at his son, cowering against the wall of the front cab. His lip quivers as he cries.

"It's going to be okay," I tell Stevie. All I can do for now is tell him something that feels like a lie and hope that it isn't.

I look back to the road behind us and see the headlights advancing on us. They are close enough I can make out the silhouettes of the men in the trucks and the barrels of the rifles in their hands. There's got to be at least a dozen trucks.

"Here we go," says Lorento. "Give 'em hell."

I pull the trigger and fire wildly at the vehicles. The drivers swerve as the incoming bullets hit hoods and windshields. The passengers fire blindly back at us. When my magazine is empty, I reload I take out a full on from my bag and reload it. I glance over at the other truck and see James firing away. When he pauses to reload a bullet rips through his chest. The shot knocks him backwards and splatters the back of the Humvee with blood. For a few seconds, I can't even manage to move while my mind tries to make sense of what I just saw.

"Keep shooting, Scout," Lorento yells.

I rotate my body and squeeze the trigger again. Tears begin to blur my vision so I can't even see where I'm firing. Before my magazine is empty, Lorento stands up and steadies herself. She fires the RPG at the lead truck. It smashes into the grill and explodes, lifting the truck off the ground. The pickup crashes back down to the pavement sideways and rolls along the road as it bursts into a ball of flames. The vehicle to the left veers off the road and slams into a tree. The driver on the right slams the brake and collides with the other pursuing vehicles. I watch the destruction as we speed away and the remaining pickups give up the chase.

"That will give them something to think about," says Lorento. She lowers the rocket launcher and retrieves her radio. "We just bought ourselves a little time," she says. "Good job, boys."

"Shit, man, Piper's in bad shape," Hernacki responds.

"Take over behind the wheel for him, Hernacki," Lorento says. "Hoff, find us a place to regroup."

CHAPTER ELEVEN

Hoff pulls the truck off the road onto a long dirt driveway that winds into a dark forest of trees. I hadn't even noticed there was a driveway until we were turning off the road. That should make it tough for Bishop to track us down again. As soon as the truck pulls to a stop in front of dilapidated farmhouse, I hop out and run to check on James. His shirt is soaked with blood and his lifeless eyes stare at the sky.

"Jesus," I whisper.

Fawn rushes over to see what happened and gasps when she sees James in the back of the truck. She brings a cupped palm to cover her mouth as she lets out a sob. I put an arm around her shoulder as she turns toward me and buries her face in my neck.

"Fawn!" Hoff calls as he opens the front door of the Humvee. Hoff and Hernacki haul Piper out of the truck and carry him toward the house. Fawn wipes her eyes and leaves to grab her medical bag from the pickup and lugs it up the driveway.

I'm so sick of crying. Sick of losing people. And I'm tired of facing what comes next. I pull out his knife from his belt and turn his head to the side. Then, I bury the blade below the base of his skull. I remove the knife and wipe the blood on the sleeve of my jacket. I stare at the wet blood on the fabric. It looks black in the moonlight.

When I finally lift my eyes, I see Lorento standing behind the Humvee. I look down to avoid her gaze and realize I am still clutching the knife in my hand. I retrieve the sheath from James' belt, slide the knife inside, and tuck it away in the pocket of my jacket. I climb off the truck and return to the other vehicle to get my pack. Lorento trails behind me, studying my movements. I'm just hoping she will leave me alone right now. I'm not ready to deal with anyone at the moment, but especially not her.

"What are you doing?" she asks me.

"I have to bury, James," I say as I head back to the Humvee.

"Bury him?" Lorento sighs. "Now?" She checks her watch and then looks at the darkened windows of the farmhouse.

"Yes," I snap. "I'm going to bury him because he is my friend. That's what normal people do. I'm not going to dump him on the side of the road and let the wild dogs eat him just because you're in a hurry."

I brush past her and stalk back to the other truck. Lorento shakes her head and follows behind me.

"I just meant that we might not be safe here very long," Lorento says. "Bishop is not going to give up, especially after what just happened."

"I know that," I growl. I let out a long sigh as I stare at James in the back of the truck. I can't keep it together anymore. I lower my eyes and let out a sob.

"Come on," Lorento says as she puts a hand on my back. "I'll give you a hand."

Lorento helps me move James into the grass. She locates a shovel among the gear in the back of the Humvee and we take turns digging his grave in the moonlight.

"I'm sorry about your friend," she says. It almost sounds sincere, but not quite.

"I'm sorry for losing it," I tell her as she digs the spade into the earth. "I know you're just trying to help, even if you have a fucked up way of going about it."

"Thanks, I think," she smiles.

"I just don't know if I can handle any more of this," I admit.

"From what I've seen you don't know how to give up," Lorento says. "Probably never gave up on anything in your life."

I think about it for a few minutes. There were lots of times I wanted to give up on things. Hell, I swore a million times I was not going to stay in my crappy marriage or be a servant to my kids for the rest of my life, but no matter how miserable I felt at the time I could never do it. Given everything that happened, I wish for just one more minute of that miserable life every single day I wake up now.

"I quit writing," I finally say. "When I was younger, I used to think I'd write a novel someday."

"Really?" she says. "Why did you give up?"

"Well, when we had the kids, I never had time," I admit. "I still carry the notebook around with me, though. It's one of the few things I took with me from home. God knows why."

"Sounds like you still didn't give up to me," Lorento pants. "You're just still getting around to it. Your turn."

I take the shovel from her and resume moving the dirt. By the time we finish digging, the dawn of a new day begins to brighten the sky. We lower James into the ground and begin pushing the soil back into the grave. After the last shovel full of dirt, I take a minute to catch my breath. Maybe I should say something nice, but I just stare at the grave instead. Words don't really mean anything once you're dead.

I hear footsteps approaching and turn my head to see Hoff heading down the drive. In the dim light it takes a moment before I notice the dark bloodstains all over his uniform.

"How is he?" Lorento asks.

Hoff grimaces.

"Is he gonna make it?" Lorento presses.

"He is stabilized for now, but he lost a shit-ton of blood. I don't think we can move him. Not without killing him."

"Jesus," Lorento sighs. She props her hands on her hips and turns her head toward the sun climbing above the tree line to the east. "We'll have to go without him."

"Negative," says Hoff. "I'm not okay with that. That's not an option."

"We'll come back for him in a few days," Lorento continues. "He'll have a better chance if we leave him behind with Fawn."

"What?" I say. "No."

Hoff folds his arms across his chest.

"It's either that or I have to go inside and put a bullet in his head so we can proceed with our mission," Lorento warns.

"Jesus," gasps Hoff. He looks at me briefly and notices my incredulous expression.

"You heard me," Lorento snaps. "Don't make me do that, Hoff. Make the right call." She clearly isn't messing around.

The soldier scratches at his golden beard and sighs. He considers the situation for a long moment. Lorento takes a step toward the house and reaches for her weapon, but Hoff grabs her arm to stop her.

"Fine," he relents. "But we can't leave him here alone."

They both look at me and wait for me to speak.

"Fawn will stay with him," I tell them. "I don't like it, but she probably would refuse to leave someone that needed help anyway."

"All right," Lorento agrees before she turns and walks back toward the truck. She opens the door and sits down on the passenger seat and picks up a bottle of water. She takes a gulp and looks back at the two of us. "Just make it quick. The sun is up, and I want to be back on the road in twenty."

Hoff holds open the door and waits for me to step inside before trailing me into the derelict farmhouse. It reeks of mold, urine, and smoke. Every room is filthy and littered with trash. The only furniture is a busted lawn chair that tilts to one side. Squatters must have been living in this place for years before the outbreak. Still, it wouldn't be the worst place I've been since this started.

Piper rests on a stained mattress in the corner of what used to be a family room. Hernacki is hunched over on one knee beside him and clasps the injured soldier's limp hand in his own.

"I know everyone is tired," I say. "But we need to get back on the road."

"What about Piper?" Hernacki asks me. "We can't leave him here." He hops up, gesturing at his comrade on the floor. He sees my grim expression and turns his eyes toward the soldier beside me. "Hoff?"

"Orders," Hoff says.

"Bullshit," Hernacki gripes.

"I don't like it much either," Hoff agrees. "He'll have company here and we'll be back for him soon."

I notice Steven sitting beside his son on the moldy floorboards across the room. Stevie is passed out with his head on his filthy Captain America backpack. His dad brushes his teeth with his bandaged hand as he winces in pain. He looks even worse today than he did yesterday. I cross the room and collapse on the floor beside him. I know we need to get on the road, but I just need to rest a minute. Steven pulls the toothbrush out of his mouth and rinses it with a water bottle.

"How are you holding up?" I ask him.

"Not bad, all things considered," he says. He seals the toothbrush in a plastic bag and returns it to his pack.

"I'm sorry that had to happen to you back at the diner," I tell him. "I wish it would have been me instead."

"He could tell you would be tougher to break," Steven says. "So, he tried to get me to talk."

"Were you going to?" I ask.

"Yeah," he admits. "I was about to tell him everything to keep him from pulling the trigger."

I shake my head.

"I know it doesn't make sense. But Stevie needs you as much as he needs me now. And I need you," he sniffs. "I don't think I could wake up every day and tell him things would still be okay if you weren't around."

"Steven," I sigh. "He needs you, not me. You're his father. I'm just..." I search for the right words. I look down at the ground as if I might find them down there.

"The truth is I was never a great dad," Steven says. "I traveled a lot for work. His mom was always the one taking care of him. I'm just trying to do my best for him now, but I'm not always sure what he needs."

"You're a great dad," I assure him. I put a hand on his shoulder but quickly remove it as he winces in pain.

"Jesus, Scout," he groans.

"Sorry," I whisper. "I'm so tired. I forgot which shoulder it was."

Steven smiles and shakes his head. One of the truck engines turns over outside. It's time to get moving again.

"You ready?" Hoff asks.

I look up and see his hand held out to help me up. I take it and pull myself off the floor.

"Yeah, thanks," I tell him.

"I'm going to have one of my guys stay behind, too," Hoff informs me. "Lorento will have a fit, but she can go fuck herself."

I can't help but smile at his defiance.

"Morris is a good soldier. He'll keep them safe," Hoff assures me.

"Thanks, Hoff," I smile at the big soldier before he turns and heads out to the truck.

It's a relief to know one of the soldiers is staying behind, though I don't know that it will do any good if Bishop or his men show up here. We don't seem to have any other options though, especially if we don't have a lot of time.

I walk over and crouch down next to Fawn, who is still cleaning blood off her hands and arms. She looks up at me slowly with bloodshot eyes and a tired smile.

"Will you be okay keeping an eye on him here?" I ask.

"I'll do what I can for him," Fawn shrugs. "It's not much unless we can find more supplies."

"Make me a list and I'll do my best," I tell her and give her a pat on the shoulder. "We'll leave the pickup behind for you in case you need it."

Fawn gives me a nod and lets the bloody towel fall to the floor. I can tell she would rather come with me, but she could never leave an injured person that needs medical attention. It would haunt her forever.

"Be careful, Scout," she says. She stands up and gives me a hug.

"You know me," I say.

"That's exactly why I'm reminding you to be careful," she sniffs.

She lets go of me and I turn to find Steven hovering behind me.

"Better wake him up," Steven frowns as he glances back at his exhausted son.

"It's okay," I say. "I'll carry him so he can sleep."

"Thanks, Scout," Steven says. He collects his rifle and his pack and winces in pain as he lifts the bag off the ground.

I scoop up the sleeping boy in my arms.

"Where are we going, mom?" he mumbles.

"It's Scout," I whisper in his ear. "Go back to sleep."

CHAPTER TWELVE

We pass a sign marking the edge of Mark Twain National Forest and for the next several miles, the convoy cruises north at top speed. I keep an eye on the sky for scavenger birds and sniff the air for signs of rot. As we approach a town, a faint scent hits my nostrils. I grip my rifle tighter as a factory comes into view. The town streets are surprisingly clear, but that smell is coming from somewhere close. I scan the skies again and spot a cluster of black shapes over the center of town.

"Damn it," I mutter and raise the rifle to peer through the scope. The road ahead seems clear at first, but when I scan off to the right, I see a horde of the dead in the parking lot of a Walmart.

"It's always the fucking Walmart," I growl. It's true. When the shit hit the fan some idiot in every dinky town came up with the foolproof plan of barricading themselves in a big box store. Haven't met anyone that ever made it back out of one alive. They usually just managed to draw every walking stiff in town until the things smashed through the windows and killed anyone inside. It was always just a matter of time.

"Must be a blue light special going on," Steven smirks.

"That's K-Mart, you dipshit," I correct him. "Focus."

I peer through the scope again to gauge the numbers of the dead. The whole goddamn town must be there. I grab the radio and click on the mic.

"There's a big crowd coming up on the left. The road is clear, but we have to move fast before they hear us coming," I urge.

I hear Lorento's voice, but I drop the radio back in my pack and raise the rifle to check through the scope again. The crowd has already noticed the loud growl of the engines approaching and swarms toward the sound. The sight of all those lifeless faces coming at me is so horrifying that I pull my eye away from the scope.

"How many?" Steven asks.

"Too many," I tell him.

A minute later, the whole horde in the parking lot comes into view as we reach the last intersection before the store. Hernacki starts firing the big machine gun on top of the lead vehicle. Fifty-caliber bullets mow down the corpses closest to the street, but the crowd behind them surges toward the sound of gunfire. The dead trip over the fallen bodies as they stumble into the southbound lanes.

"We're not gonna make it," Steven panics.

I raise my rifle and open fire on the corpses as they close the distance. To get around them, Hoff swerves the truck to the right and jumps the curb. The sudden motion causes me to lose my balance and stop shooting.

Steven grabs hold of my shoulder to keep me from toppling out of the truck. The Humvees speed between several cars parked out front of an auto repair shop. The wide trucks scrape the other vehicles as they pass between them and knock the mirrors off the doors.

As the trucks roll back over the curb and into the road, I look back at the crowd of corpses trailing the vehicle. Hundreds and hundreds of emaciated dead bodies trudge along behind us on the only possible route through town. Good luck getting around that, Bishop.

We reach an overpass at the edge of town and our caravan slows down to navigate through a cluster of crashed vehicles on the road. I glance back to make sure the crowd behind us isn't getting too close. That's when I notice the horde of the dead has turned around and is heading in the other direction.

Over the loud engines of the Humvees, I notice the distant rattle of machine guns. I lift the rifle and peer through the scope. Beyond the swarm of corpses in the road, I spot the squad of pickup trucks stopped in the road. A yellow flag flutters in the breeze above the vehicles. I scan the faces and fire off a round when I spot Bishop in the passenger seat of a black truck. I doubt my bullet found any of them, but it makes me feel better to see the vehicle jerk to the side as their heads duck for cover. Once the pickups turn around and retreat from the corpses, I lower the rifle and reach for the radio once again.

"We got trouble," I inform Lorento over the radio. "Bishop."

"Where?" asks Lorento.

"Behind us," I tell her. "He hit some traffic back there, but it won't take him long to catch up unless we can make these trucks go any faster."

"Keep your eyes open, Scout," Lorento replies. "Let me know the second you catch sight of them again."

The trucks begin to pick up speed as the road infiltrates the thick Missouri forests once again. We sit silently in the back of the Humvee with our eyes glued to the road behind us and wait for the threat to come. I know for certain that we can't outrun them forever like this. It's just a matter of time now. We have to figure out some other way to slow them down, and we have to do it soon.

CHAPTER THIRTEEN

As the sun climbs higher in the sky, we approach a gas station on the edge of a small city. We roll through the center of town on Market Street and pass by a looted electronics store, a Mexican restaurant with a large sombrero on the sign, and a candy store called Sugar Momma's. The two-lane road widens to create a center turn lane through the shopping district. The extra room makes it easy to weave through the dead walking along the asphalt. I notice a few taverns, wineries, and a gift shop as we reach the north side of town. This place must have been a tourist spot, which around here can only mean we're near one of the major rivers.

After we pass a couple historic motels, the bridge comes into view. The trucks roll onto the overpass. We cross over a pair of train tracks before the rushing water begins to flow beneath the road. As we near the opposite shore I pick up the radio.

"Do we have any explosives?" I ask.

"You thinking we should blow the bridge?" Hoff responds.

"The thought crossed my mind," I say.

"I can probably do that," Hoff says. "I think I got enough C4 to do the job."

"How long would it take, Hoff?" Lorento asks.

"Maybe ten or fifteen minutes."

"Not worth it," Lorento says. "We might not have that kind of time."

The vehicles slow on the empty bridge and come to a stop just at the edge of the shore.

"What are you doing, Hoff?"

"Hang on," Hoff grunts. "Closest other town that crosses the river is close to thirty miles away. If they're still behind us, taking down the bridge could buy us at least an hour, maybe more."

There is a long pause before Lorento responds.

"Make it quick," Lorento says. "But try not to screw it up."

Hoff and Hernacki get out of the trucks and begin rigging the bridge with explosives.

"I'm going to check on Stevie," Steven says.

I nod and watch as Steven struggles to get down off the rear of the truck and hobbles around to visit his son in the backseat. After taking a glance back at the other end of the bridge, I get off the back of the truck as well. The soldiers are busy working beside the vehicle, and I go over to look at what they are doing. They have some bricks of explosive wrapped in black plastic that they are rigging with a cable of some kind.

"So does that stuff have a trigger or a timer or what?" I ask.

Hoff glances at Hernacki and then smirks.

"Well, this is a fuse, but I could use a detonator," Hoff says. "Why?"

"What if we waited around awhile and took out the bridge while they're on it?" I ask.

"We could do that," Hoff says. He pauses as he cuts a span fuse. "But I don't think Lorento is willing to wait around. Besides, there is no guarantee this will be enough to bring down a section of the bridge."

"It won't?" I ask.

"It should. Probably. Would be sure if we had twice as much as we do, but I think fifty pounds will be enough for a bridge this old."

"But even if it doesn't take out the bridge, we could use it to take them out."

"Some of them, probably. One or two of their trucks. Then the rest of them would be all over us. That's assuming they even come this way at all. For all we know, they might have given up and turned around."

Hoff returns his focus to the explosives that he is rigging and scratches his head and scans the supplies as though he has lost something. Then he notices the wire clippers he is still holding in his hand and returns to cutting another span of fuse. I decide I should probably leave the two soldiers to focus on setting the charges, so I return to the truck. After I climb into the back, I retrieve another bottle from my pack and drink the lukewarm water while I keep an eye on the other end of the bridge. A number of the corpses from town shamble down the middle of the overpass. The main horde, however, is still about a quarter mile away, so it will still be a while before they get too close. If it takes much longer than ten minutes to prepare the explosives, we might have a hell of a time holding them off. I grab a few extra magazines and set them down in the seat next to me, and then I wait and listen to the sound of the river rushing below.

Lorento appears at the back of the truck and asks how I am doing.

"I'm hanging in there," I tell her.

She looks away from me and watches the approaching corpses.

"Just a couple more hours to go," she says. "Most of the towns the rest of the way up are smaller. It should be easier."

"Should be," I sigh.

"It was a good idea," she says. "Taking down the bridge."

"If it works," I say.

"Even if it doesn't it's still a good idea." She swivels around to face me and studies me from behind her aviator sunglasses. "Might just save our asses."

"Maybe," I shrug. "But we still got a long way to go."

"We'll make it," Lorento tries to assure me. She doesn't seem certain at all herself, though. The agent turns again and glances back at the road behind us. Steven returns from checking on his son and Lorento steps to the side to let him climb onto the back of the truck.

"They're getting close," I say, and jerk my head in the direction of the approaching corpses.

"You want help?" Lorento offers.

"We got it," I say.

"I could use the extra practice anyway," Steven adds.

"No kidding," I tease him.

"Suit yourselves," Lorento nods and leaves to check on the progress of the soldiers.

"Seems like you got a new best friend," Steven smiles as soon as Lorento is out of earshot.

"I guess," I scoff.

"Never thought we'd come across somebody that actually likes you," Steven teases.

Steven flinches when I pull back my fist to slug him in the arm, but then I remember his injury and stop myself.

"If you weren't hurt, I'd kick your ass," I tell him.

Steven lets out a laugh, and then clutches his shoulder in pain.

"Shit," he grimaces.

"Serves you right," I tell him. "How is Stevie doing?"

"Good," Steven says. "That girl, Valerie, she seems pretty good with him."

"That's good," I say.

"Wish I had a babysitter that looked like that before," he adds.

"Gross," I cringe. "She is like half your age."

"Oh, don't be jealous," Steven laughs.

"I'm not," I sneer. "Believe me. She can have you."

Steven's smile falters for a moment. He lowers his head and stares at his boots. An awkward moment passes, and I feel guilty for hurting his feelings. I was never good at joking around. I'd always be the asshole that took it too far and said something a little too harsh. Steven recovers a few seconds later and chuckles to himself.

"What?" I ask him.

"So, you think she'd have me?" he asks me.

"Gross," I say and roll my eyes. I pick up my rifle and take up a shooting position at the rear of the truck bed. I bring my eye to the scope and center the target on a dead woman in a bloody hospital gown behind a Buick about fifty yards down the road. When she steps around the hood of the car, I notice her round belly. I close my eyes and open them again but the sight of her is just as traumatic. My finger shakes as I pull the trigger.

"Maybe I'll ask Val for her phone number," Steven cracks.

"Shut the hell up and help me shoot some of these things," I tell him.

Steven begins firing alongside me and curses in pain from the recoil of the rifle between each shot. I take out two more stiffs, and then I pause to scan the road again and get an idea of their numbers. There must be a couple hundred between here and the town. I find another target and am about to squeeze the trigger again when I hear automatic weapons in the distance. I sweep over the bridge and notice some corpses at the back of the group turning back toward town. Then I see that damn yellow flag again.

"Shit," I growl. "It's Bishop."

I grab the radio from my pack to warn the others we will soon have company.

"We're good," Hoff transmits back. "Ready to roll."

I keep firing at the dead that are beginning to close in now. I don't even use the scope, but just quickly point and shoot the way James had taught me. Steven drops the rifle and pulls out a handgun from his waistband and fires at the closest corpses. The Humvee engines fire up as Bishop and his convoy arrive at the other end of the bridge. I try to get a count of the vehicles but quit when I get to ten and the Humvee lurches forward. I lose my balance but luckily Steven grabs onto my arm just in time to keep me from falling out into the waiting arms of the undead. A couple of the corpses manage to grab onto the truck as it pulls away. They clutch the bumper for a hundred yards or so, their bodies dragging along pavement and leaving trails of coagulated blood behind us.

Once I steady myself, I lift the rifle and peer through the scope again to see Bishop and his men firing on the dead to clear a path down the bridge. I lower the rifle as the Humvees clear the bridge and pick up speed on the open road. Time slows to a crawl as I wait for the explosives to detonate. I watch as pickup trucks make it halfway across the bridge. I wonder what the hell is taking so long. If the trucks make it across before the bombs detonate, we will really have no choice but to fight.

An explosion rocks the bridge. A grey haze fills the air and a split second later I hear the massive boom. The shockwave knocks off one of the dead clinging to the truck and it skids to a stop in the road. The Humvees slow down as a plume of smoke drifts up in the sky above the bridge. My ears ring from the deafening blast so that everything sounds muffled. I stare at the road and wait for the visibility to improve, half expecting the armada of pickups to emerge at any moment.

As the dust settles, I spot the new gap in the bridge. On the other side, I can see the pickups stopped on the overpass. I glance through the scope once more and watch the chaos as the men scramble to fight off the dead while turning the vehicles around. The corpses have them pinned down with only a forty-foot drop into the river for an escape. The bridge now seems to be loaded with every poor dead bastard from town, too.

I lower the rifle and nod to Steven to let him know the bridge is down.

"All clear back here," Steven transmits over the radio. "The bridge is down. Good work, guys."

"Woo!" Hernacki cheers.

I notice the corpse that is still hanging off the back of the truck and take the butt of the rifle and repeatedly smash the thing in the face as it snaps and hisses at me. Somehow it still hangs on. Steven steps over and pulls me out of the way and fires off the nine-millimeter. The thing releases the bumper, bounds along the pavement, and lands limply in the tall weeds beside the road. As the Humvee rounds a curve I fall back into the seat and let out a deep breath.

"I still think I'm going to ask Valerie for her number," Steven grins.

I shake my head and resist the urge to punch his dumb ass again.

CHAPTER FOURTEEN

I can only guess how much more time we might have bought, but I am starting to feel able to relax a little. I collapse into a seat and open my pack to grab a full water bottle and a bag of potato chips I've been thinking about all morning. The view alongside the road turns again to open fields and small farms interspersed between swathes of thick, leafy trees. The sparse clouds occasionally cast a shadow from the warming sun, but I start to feel my shirt and pants getting damp with sweat. I take off my jacket and shove it inside my backpack.

"Don't suppose I can talk you into sharing those with me?" Steven asks.

"You can try," I smile. I pop a salty chip in my mouth and crunch it loudly with my teeth. "Probably isn't going to do you much good, though."

"You going to make me beg?" he asks.

I shrug and let him watch me remove another chip out of the crinkling bag and slip it between my lips before I respond.

"Didn't your mom ever teach you how to ask nicely when you want something?" I tell him. "I mean, you didn't even use the magic word."

"To hell with you," Steven laughs. "Give me a goddamn chip already."

He reaches out to try and grab the bag out of my hand, but I move the bag away from him in time. Steven tugs at my arm and reaches for the bag again and I swat his hand away and clutch the bag to my chest.

"Get away, you asshole!" I yell at him.

Steven eases back into his seat with that stupid smirk on his face. He definitely isn't getting any chips now.

"You stay over there," I warn him. "I'm serious."

He raises his hands in surrender, then sits back and allows me to eat in peace. Even if he is being annoying, it still makes me feel better just to act like everything is still normal every now and then. But everything is not normal. This is not normal. I feel like the minute I let all of this feel normal, there will be no chance of ever going back again.

A memory from last year suddenly comes back to me. I was sitting next to Kevin on the couch in a tiny office talking to a psychologist. I had been depressed or whatever for a while and thought maybe marriage counseling might help bring us together again. Kevin agreed to go, but he mostly just sat there sighing and insisting things were okay.

"This is normal," he said over and over again.

That just pissed me off like most of the other inconsiderate things he did. I started to cry. At the time, my world felt pretty far from okay. My life felt pointless, unfulfilling, and just… empty. It all seems so silly now, but I couldn't see past it at the time. I was too busy wishing things were better to see how good I already had it.

The trucks slow to a stop and I swivel in my seat to see a school bus with a flat tire abandoned in the road. Hernacki gets out and walks over to check the vehicle. He steps inside the open door of the bus and looks around the cabin. A moment later he emerges.

"She's out of gas," he announces. "Can probably move her if we give her some juice."

"Hurry it up," Lorento urges him.

"Top off our tanks too while you're at it," Hoff adds.

The young soldier nods and jogs back to the truck and retrieves a container of fuel. I scan the woods for any sign of movement, but all seems quiet. My eyes drift upward, and I watch the wispy clouds float across the sky. If it weren't for the whole end of the world thing, today would be a beautiful day. My mind slips back into remembering, and I try to latch on to some nice memories of days like this from my old life, but I can't. It's already getting harder to block out the horrors long enough to find something pleasant that still remains in my mind.

"You okay?" Steven asks.

I realize he must have been watching me staring at nothing for several minutes while I was lost in my thoughts.

"Just tired," I lie. "Spacing out a little."

"I hear you," Steven sighs. "It's just, you were doing that thing you do when you're worried."

"What thing?"

"Biting your bottom lip," he says and brings a finger up to his lips, as if to clarify what he means.

"I don't do that," I insist. "Do I?"

Steven nods.

"I'm kind of alarmed that you've been studying me enough to know that," I chide him.

"I can't help that I'm observant," he laughs.

"No, really, it's kind of creepy, Steven."

"You also have a way of changing the subject whenever something is bothering you."

I break eye contact with him and stare back at the country road behind us as though I am checking for signs of trouble.

"What is it?" Steven presses me.

"The day this whole thing started I told my husband I didn't think I loved him anymore. That's the last thing I said to him. He stormed off to the bar and just never came home. I don't think I can ever forgive myself for that."

"Scout," Steven interrupts.

"No," I continue. "You don't understand. I did love him. I just wanted to, I don't know, get a reaction out of him, I guess. It was so stupid and selfish of me."

I stare down at my shoes and try not to cry. There are good reasons I don't bring up the past. I already regret bringing it up now. It just came pouring out of me. Maybe what happened to James brought everything boiling up to the surface. Since it's out there now, I might as well finish it.

"For a few days I kept hoping that maybe he would come back. I couldn't eat or sleep. If I could have gone out looking for him, I would have, but I knew I'd have no chance out there with the kids. When I finally did sleep, I was so tired, it just happened. My eyes wouldn't stay open any longer. I should have locked up the gun."

"Jesus," Steven sighs.

"Zack was so terrified when the gun went off. I jumped up and grabbed him and snatched the gun out of his hands. He started crying so hard. For a couple minutes, I hugged him while he sobbed and told him everything was okay. I had no idea anything was really wrong until I heard Kyle let out a moan behind me. I turned around and saw the blood on his shirt as he got to his feet. Before I even realized he was already dead he bit Zack on the arm. Three days later, Zack was dead, too."

"I'm sorry," Steven says.

"It was all my fault," I admit. "All of it. If I hadn't fought with Kevin that morning it all might have turned out differently."

"It's not fair to beat yourself up over that, Scout," Steven says. "You've got to let it all go."

"I don't think I will ever be able to do that."

"It's not what they'd want for you," Steven says. "You have to know that."

"What you're saying should make me feel better, but it doesn't."

"I wish I had done a lot of things different, too," Steven adds. "But nothing good comes from wishing you can change the past. Nothing."

The door of the Humvee slams shut, and Hoff starts the truck up again. The tires churn over the pavement as we continue down the road. I force a smile to let Steven think I feel better just so we can stop talking about it now. It is a relief to finally tell someone. I've carried the weight of it alone for too long. But even after getting it off my chest, I still don't feel any less guilty for being alive.

CHAPTER FIFTEEN

For the next hour, I watch as farmhouses and pastures slip by alongside the road. The Humvees cruise over the hot pavement beneath the scorching summer sun. Eventually, the vehicles pull into a gas station alongside the highway. The area surrounding the gas pumps and the convenience store is deserted, so we stop to refuel. I get out of the truck to stretch my legs and look around for a spot to go to the bathroom. For some reason, even during the apocalypse, I always have to pee whenever I am stuck in the car too long.

"I'm going to have a look around inside," I tell Steven.

"You want me to come along?" he asks.

"I'll be all right," I tell him and sling my rifle over my shoulder before heading for the shattered glass doors of the convenience mart.

"Check the liquor aisle for me," Nick calls. I pause and look back over my shoulder to see him finishing off the last swig of a bottle of whiskey and tossing out the window of the truck. The bottle makes a popping sound as it shatters on the pavement.

"Watch it, asshole," Lorento snaps at him as she steps around the front of the Humvee.

The inside of the store is dim and reeks like an outhouse. After coming in from the bright sunlight, it takes a moment for my eyes to adjust to dark. I hold the rifle low, but ready, with my finger poised over the trigger. As my vision adjusts, I scan the empty racks and refrigerators. There are hundreds of empty wrappers scattered on the floor. I locate the restrooms at the back of the store and push open the door of the ladies room. The scent of urine and feces rushes outward and causes me to take a few steps back as the door swings closed again. I'm definitely not attempting to go back in there. Reluctantly, I push the door to the men's room open a crack to discover the same horrific smell.

"What the fuck?" I shudder. I guess I will have to go outside, again. I turn to leave the building when I hear the sound of a glass bottle rolling along the floor. My eyes dart around the store but everything is still. The voice inside my head is screaming for me to get the hell out of there. I take a step toward the front door, but then I notice the open door to the cooler behind the beverage case along the back wall.

"Hello?" I call.

No response. Fuck. That's never good. If a stiff is back there, it would have started going nuts at the sound of my voice. Whoever is in the cooler is probably still alive. They're either afraid, or they're setting a trap to kill me. So, I raise the rifle and approach the door. I step on an empty bag of potato chips and the crunching noise makes me freeze for a moment. I try to peer through the empty beverage cases but can't see anything in the darkness behind them. Since no one has shot at me yet, I decide to take a chance and rush the doorway.

"Don't move," I bark as I peer around the edge of the cooler door. There is a human shape cowering in the dark corner of the room. I keep the rifle raised.

"Just go away," a voice pleads. The guy has a thick accent. India, maybe.

"I'm not here to hurt you," I assure him. "Do you have a weapon?"

"No," the man says. "I don't have shit!"

"Come out here where I can see you," I urge him.

"Fuck," the man whines. "I don't want to die."

"Good," I say. "I don't want to have to kill anyone else today. So, just come out here and let me help you."

A pause.

"All right," the man agrees. "I'm coming out."

Even though he doesn't seem like a threat, I step back from the doorway to keep a safe distance anyway. I've been through enough already to know it's not a good idea to trust anyone right away these days, no matter how harmless they might seem. The young, dark-skinned man emerges from the cooler.

"Who are you?" I ask him.

"My name is Midhun," he says. "Please don't point the gun at me."

"Not until you tell me what the hell you were doing hiding back there?" I ask him.

"I'm waiting for my brother," Midhun explains. He lowers his eyes to avoid looking at the muzzle of the rifle. "This is his store."

"Where is he?" I ask.

"I don't know," he says. "I came here the first day looking for him, but he never come back."

"Jesus," I say. "You've been here since this all started?"

He nods.

No wonder the store smells like it does.

"Please don't shoot me. There's nothing left here anymore. Thieves have come and taken everything from me, you see?" He sweeps his arm in an arc to indicate the empty store.

"I'm sorry," I tell him.

The man waves his hand dismissively.

"Just go," he sighs. He turns his back to me and walks over to sit on a stack of empty milk crates. "There is nothing left for you to take. Go!"

I lower the rifle and take a step toward him.

"I'm not here to take anything," I assure him. "Why didn't you ever leave here?"

"Because," he says. "I wait here so that my brother can find me."

"You want some water?" I ask him. "Maybe some food?"

Midhun looks at me skeptically.

"I have plenty outside in the truck," I say.

"I have no way to pay you," he sighs.

"You don't have to," I say. "Come on."

He turns his head to look at the Humvees idling outside the store. I leave him to decide and walk back out through the shattered door frame. When I get halfway to the vehicles, I pause and look back over my shoulder to see the man emerging from the doorway. In the daylight, the accumulated grime and stains on his clothes make him seem even more forlorn. He lifts a hand to block the sun from his eyes.

"Who the fuck is that?" Hoff asks as he finishes topping off the tank of the Humvee.

"Jesus Christ," Lorento mutters and shakes her head.

"He needs our help," I tell her.

"He's not coming with us," Lorento says.

I ignore her and climb into the back of the truck. I pry open a case of MRE's and grab a couple plastic bottles of water. With a grunt, I hop back down and wave Midhun over to the truck and twist off the cap of a water bottle and hand it to him.

He smiles and clasps his hands together and mumbles some kind of thanks in another language, at least that's what it sounds like. He gulps eagerly from the bottle, the water trickling down his cheeks as he tilts the bottle upward.

"Does he even speak English?" Lorento asks.

"Yes, he speaks English," I growl.

"I speak seven languages," Midhun says after wiping his mouth dry with a filthy sleeve. "English, Hindi, Bengali—"

"I don't give a shit, Apu," Lorento interrupts him.

Hoff lets out a chuckle but falls silent when he notices the look on my face when I stare him down.

"He's not coming with, Scout," Lorento insists and folds her arms across her chest.

"We need all the help we can get," I remind her.

"You know how to use a gun?" she asks Midhun. "Can you fight?"

"I'm a peaceful man," Midhun says.

"That's great. He is not coming with us, Scout," Lorento repeats.

"Then neither am I," I tell her.

"It's okay. I will wait here." Midhun gestures at the remnants of the gas station. "For my brother. He will be coming."

"See, he doesn't even want to come," Lorento argues. "Let's go."

"You can't stay here anymore, Midhun," I explain. "If your brother was alive, he would have come back already."

"This is a waste of time," Lorento interrupts.

"My brother is most definitely alive," Midhun says. "I am certain of it."

"So come with us," I tell him. "We will help you look for him."

"No, we won't," Lorento says.

"I will," I insist. "I will help you look for him. Once we finish every-thing."

"We're not taking a goddamn gas station clerk along for the ride," Loren-to growls at me.

"Engineer," Midhun corrects her.

"What?" Lorento asks.

"You said I was a gas station clerk, but that was my brother's job. I am a mechanical engineer," Midhun says.

Lorento pauses for a moment to consider this new bit of information.

"Whatever," Lorento sighs. "If you're coming, hurry it up. Everybody get back in the damn trucks. We already wasted enough time here."

Midhun turns and begins to climb into the back of the truck. As I wait for him to get out of the way so I can haul myself back into the bed of the Humvee, I see Lorento glaring at me out of the corner of my eye. I've never been one to argue with someone. Even when they piss me off. Even when they deserve it. Seeing my disinterest, she turns her attention to Steven and waits until he makes eye contact with her.

"Is she always picking up strays like this?" Lorento asks him.

"Everywhere she goes," Steven smiles.

"She should know that someday it will get her killed," Lorento says.

I look over and see her scowling at me. She waits for me to respond for a moment before she shakes her head again and heads for the lead truck.

"Looks like you already pissed off your new friend," Steven smirks as he climbs into the back of the truck behind me.

"I guess," I shrug.

The loud engine of the Humvee starts once more, and I gaze off into the sky. As the trucks pull onto the highway, I watch Midhun smiling at the trees we pass as if he suddenly had no cares in the world. It makes me feel better about everything, even if I did piss off Lorento.

CHAPTER SIXTEEN

As the afternoon drags on, I spot charred trees along the horizon. Ashes float around in the air and cover the road in a thin layer as we get close to the scene. There isn't any smoke, so the fire must have died out, but the town is nothing more than scorched earth now. The highway passes along the outskirts of town, but close enough that I can spot a charred corpse here and there crawling among debris. As we leave the town behind us, I notice the tire tracks in the ash we left in our wake.

For the next hour we ride in silence through the open farmland, a sure sign we were getting close to Iowa. A river comes into the view off to the right that I guess is the Mississippi, but I can't be sure. I'm not that familiar with this area. I feel the burn from the afternoon sun on my skin. It will probably hurt like hell tonight and keep me from sleeping. Not like I'd been sleeping that well to begin with.

Finally, we reach the Des Moines River and the state line. By the angle of the sun in the sky, I guess it to be around five or six in the evening already.

We pull off the road at the entrance to a rock quarry. Lorento gets out of the truck and checks the GPS device alongside a map of the state. Hernacki and Hoff gather around her— the younger Navy Seal kicks at the rocks half-heartedly with his boots, while Hoff gazes at the rock quarry and frees sunflower seeds from their shells in his mouth.

"I'm going to see what's going on," I tell Steven.

"I'm going to wait until you're gone and see if there is another bag of chips in your pack," he grins.

I give him the finger before I squeeze by Midhun and climb off the back of the truck. The bastard is still going to go through my stuff anyway. I'm sure of it. There isn't much left to take in there anyway, unless he needs a tampon, a sports bra, or my Lady Speed Stick deodorant.

Hoff looks over and smiles as he sees me approach.

"How much farther?" I ask.

"They look to be close to Iowa City," Lorento says. "If the satellite signal is still viable."

"We can probably get there before nightfall," Hoff says. "Couple hours. Maybe three if we hit traffic."

"Iowa City is a lot bigger than any place we've been," I say. The thought of going into an area with upwards of fifty-thousand undead makes me anxious. "It's not a good idea to rush into a city that size after dark."

"We may not have much choice," Lorento tells me. "Although we may have slowed Bishop down, I am pretty sure we pissed him off, too. He'll be coming."

"Then there's no time to lose," Hoff agrees. "Let's get this show on the road."

Lorento nods and avoids making eye contact with me as she folds up the map and slides back into the driver seat. I roll my eyes and turn myself around to head back to the other truck with Hoff.

"You sure about this?" I ask Hoff.

"Nope," he pauses to spit out a sunflower shell. "We got a saying in the Seals... Don't run to your death. Kind of feels like that's what we're about to do."

"It does."

"You got a better idea, though?" he asks.

"No," I sigh.

He pauses at the Humvee with his fingers around the door handle.

"I'm not going to bullshit you and say it will be okay. Most of my team is gone already. More people are going to die, and you should always be uncomfortable with that. So, get comfortable being uncomfortable."

"That's another saying, isn't it?"

"No, I just made that up." He gives me a wink as he pulls open the door of the Humvee. "Get in the damn truck, Scout."

I squeeze back into the rear of the Humvee and settle myself back down between Steven and a row of fuel canisters.

"Everything okay?" Steven asks.

I nod and bite my lip. I'm afraid if I say anything, my voice will be shaky and then he'll know just how worried I am.

"They figure out exactly where we're going?"

"Yeah," I manage to whisper and nod again.

"Where?" Steven presses me.

"Iowa City," I tell him.

"Fuck me," Steven sighs. He tilts his head back against the cab of the truck and closes his eyes. The vehicles start up again and pull back onto the highway toward Iowa City.

I close my eyes and try not to think about what lies ahead. The vision of thousands and thousands of the dead in the streets of Iowa City is still all I see. I take a deep breath and try to relax like I used to when I could sit around and meditate. But an unsettling scent fills my nostrils and snaps me back to reality.

"Damn it," I mutter as I open my eyelids. "You smell like Lady Speed Stick, Steven."

Steven slaps his knee and starts laughing his ass off. He coughs a moment later and grabs his shoulder in pain, but still can't stop himself from grinning.

"Son of a bitch," I scold him. I try to act mad, but my lips crack a smile.

"Smells very nice," Midhun adds. He fans his armpits with his hands. "Very fresh."

"You too?" I say and can't help laughing. "To hell with both of you."

"He needed some," Steven says. "Desperately."

The truck lurches forward with a growl and we head into the vast farmland of southern Iowa. The two-lane road we'd been traveling on expands to a four-lane highway with a grass median separating the northbound and southbound lanes. It rolls on in an endless straight line into the horizon. On either side of the road lie countless rows of untended crops that will all likely rot in the field when no one is there to harvest them. Out here the dead are few and far between. I spot one here and there, wandering through stalks of corn or shuffling along the highway. We pass by a cattle farm with a pack of feral dogs feasting on the carcass of horse in a pasture. For the most part, the countryside is desolate.

Steven nudges my arm and when I turn my head to look at him, he gestures at the road behind us. I notice a couple of specks on the road in the distance. After glancing through the rifle scope, I can make out the yellow flag flying above the pickups in the distance.

"Damn it," I say. "It's them."

"Unbelievable," Steven shakes his head.

I pick up the radio and notify Lorento.

"How far away is the city?" I ask.

"Maybe ten miles," Hoff says.

"I think we can make it," I say as I look back at the trucks in the distance. "They're going to be right on our ass, though."

"Maybe we can lose them going through town again," Hoff suggests. "Buy ourselves a little more time."

"It might be our only shot," Lorento says. "Either way, we're not going down without a fight."

I grab the duffel bag full of ammo and locate a couple of magazines for my rifle before I hand the bag to Steven. The pickups in the road behind us seem slightly larger as they begin to close the distance. We pass a sign that says it is six miles to Iowa City. Even if we make it there before Bishop manages to catch up to us, we're probably in for a fight with the dead. The sun is beginning to set, we have dwindling supplies, and we don't even know the exact location of the pilot. It will probably take a miracle for us just to make it through the night.

As we exit the highway at Iowa City, Bishop and his men close the distance to half of a mile. There is nothing we can do to keep them from catching up within a few minutes. I keep my eyes open for anything in the surroundings we might be able to use to lose them or gain the upper hand. On the right we pass by an auto scrapyard with rows and rows of demolished cars. Across the road is the Iowa City airport. The wreckage from several crashed planes and hundreds of corpses covers the runways. We go round a bend and a river appears along the right side of the road. As we continue toward the center of town, the road becomes congested with abandoned vehicles and the dead.

Hernacki opens up with the big gun in the turret of the lead vehicle to help clear a path. I keep an eye on the trucks closing in behind us. I wave an arm to tell Midhun to duck down. As I raise the rifle to peer through the scope, a bullet clangs off the back of the truck. I dip my head down instinctively, then raise the rifle again and take aim and fire. In the dwindling light, I still count eight or nine trucks in the convoy behind us, with at least four passengers in each of the pickups. I try to aim, but the Humvees begin to swerve from side to side to navigate the treacherous traffic on the street. After I steady myself, I fire off a few more rounds that miss wildly. Realizing I am better off saving the ammunition, I turn and glance back toward the front of the vehicles and see the street signs for different buildings of the college campus. Left to the hospital and the football stadium, right is a bridge over the river toward the library and downtown campus. The road beyond the intersection is jammed with a sea of cars and corpses.

The vehicles swerve to the right at the intersection. We cross over the bridge and pass some kind of power plant and then we run into another massive traffic jam. Lorento turns the lead vehicle down a side street to the right and the tires squeal as she takes a hard left at the next turn. We speed up three more blocks and Lorento takes a left to try and get back to the main road. I spot a parking garage up ahead attached to some big building.

Maybe we can slip inside the garage and hideout until they pass. It might be our best shot. I grab the radio and click the mic.

"Lorento," I say. "Duck inside that parking garage!"

She doesn't respond, but speeds through the intersection and swerves into the entrance to the parking garage on the left. I watch the road behind us to make sure none of the pickup trucks pursuing us round the last turn in time to see us enter the parking structure. The Humvees pull to a stop at a set of glass doors. Everyone hurries to grab what they can and get out of the vehicles. I grab Stevie out of the backseat and take cover behind a van parked next to the access doors and keep my eyes on the entrance ramp. A handful of corpses from the street begin to wander up the embankment behind us. I look down at Stevie and raise a finger to my lips, so he knows to keep quiet. Tires squeal and gunfire rattles in the streets nearby. Several seconds later, I hear more gunfire. This time it sounds farther away, but it's impossible to be sure inside the concrete walls of the garage.

Hoff cups a hand to the glass doors and peers inside, then he pulls on the handle. The door opens and Hoff waves Hernacki inside to check out the inside of building. A few seconds later Hoff waves everyone through the doors. I linger outside a few moments longer, keeping an eye on the street. Even if we lost Bishop for the moment, it doesn't mean they won't figure out what happened pretty quick and come back to look for us. We can only hope they run into plenty of trouble on the downtown streets.

CHAPTER
SEVENTEEN

The building is dark inside, with just enough light from the long skylights above to see. It's some kind of mini mall. Our group gathers near a bench and some fake potted plants by the entrance. Lorento clicks on a flashlight and examines a map of the mall as Hoff and Hernacki hover behind her. There's a movie theater, a few clothing shops, and some restaurants spread out along two floors.

"We need to check out the building," Lorento whispers. "I don't plan on staying here long, but I want to check every way in and out of this building and make sure we don't have any surprises."

"It seems pretty quiet in here," Hernacki offers.

"There's another exit on the east end of the building near the coffee shop," Lorento points. "One in the pharmacy to the north. Two in these restaurants on the south side of the building."

"We'll check them out," Hoff says.

"No," Lorento says. "I'll take Hernacki. Keep this entrance secure. Let me know the second there is any trouble." Her eyes scan the rest of the group for a moment. "Make sure nobody goes wandering off."

"Got it," Hoff confirms.

Lorento reaches for the bag of weapons and pulls out a pair of silencers and hands one to Hernacki and attaches the other to her pistol. Lorento then retrieves the GPS device from her satchel and examines the screen. I step closer to the group and wait until Lorento looks at me. She seems to have forgotten all about the argument earlier, or at least, she has put it aside for now.

"What is it, Scout?" she asks.

"Maybe we should think about staying in here for the night," I say.

"We still have to see just how safe it is here," Lorento says. "Then we will make that call."

"It's getting dark," I remind her. "And there's too many of those things to deal with out there right now. We don't have a choice."

As if to punctuate my point there is a thud on the doors to the garage. A corpse presses against the entry and slaps a palm against the barrier as though it believes it might reach right through the glass. Luckily, these things don't have such an easy time with doors that have to be pulled open.

"I'm not saying no and I'm not saying yes," Lorento sighs. "We are going to see what happens."

"Fair enough," I agree.

"Damn it," she growls at the GPS screen.

"What is it?" I ask.

"Our asset is about thirty miles away still," Lorento seethes. "Or this piece of crap is malfunctioning now."

She pulls a pen and the map out from her satchel and flattens it out over the map for the mall. For several moments she compares the screen to the map then marks an X to the northeast of the city.

"Tipton," she says.

"That makes sense. Looks like there's a small airport," Hernacki notes. "That means he could be airborne soon."

"Nah," Hoff interjects. "Without daylight or reliable satellite data for guidance it'd be like flying blind. He might be crazy, but he ain't stupid. No way he'll move at night."

"Neither should we," I repeat.

"Either way, I want to be at that airfield at sunrise," Lorento says. She folds up the map and tucks it and the GPS device back in her bag. "Now let's make sure this building is secure."

"I can help," I offer.

"Me too," Steven chimes in. I glance back over my shoulder and find him hovering like a vulture as usual.

"All right," Lorento says. She shines the light back on the map. "Down this hall is the mall office and service area. You two check it out and see if you can find some keys to the building. If we're going to stay here tonight, we might need them."

"We got it," I assure her.

"Just keep quiet," Lorento says. "No shooting unless you have to."

"I can help, too," Nick offers. He runs a tongue over his lips as he examines the map. "I'll check the sports bar over here. Make sure it's clear."

"You're a big help as usual, Nick," I groan.

"What?" Nick shrugs and raises his palms in a display of ignorance.

"Actually, that's not a bad idea," Lorento agrees. "There is an entrance to the bar inside the mall, but there is an exit to the street on the other side of the restaurant, too. Check it out and make sure it's locked up tight."

"See?" Nick boasts. He taps his forefinger against his temple several times.

"Hernacki," Lorento says. "You're with me. We'll check out the pharmacy on the far side of the mall. Make sure the street entrance there is secure. I don't want to be caught by surprise if Bishop figures out our location."

"Here," I say. I fish out the list of supplies Fawn gave me when we left the farmhouse. "Maybe you can find some of this stuff in there."

Lorento stares at the paper in my hand but doesn't move to take it.

"We're not going shopping, Scout," Lorento says.

"It's for Piper," I tell her.

"I'll take it," Hernacki says. He reaches over and grabs the list from my hand and glances at it quickly. "I'll see what I can find."

Lorento jerks her head and leads Hernacki away down the main corridor of the mall. The two of them break into a jog as they hustle to secure the building. Nick follows behind them, strolling casually along the storefront windows with his hands in his pockets. He whistles a few cheerful notes that almost resemble a song as he walks.

I pull the strap of my pack off my shoulder and set it down on the bench beside Stevie.

"Me and your dad are going to have a look around real quick," I tell him.

"Can I come with you guys?" he asks.

"No," Steven says. "That's not a good idea, kiddo. Just stay close to Val and keep an eye out for trouble, okay?"

Stevie looks at the young girl with a gentle smile and nods his head. I bend down and kiss the top of his head and then he holds out his hand for a fist bump.

"You got the radio in case you run into trouble?" Hoff asks as he hands me a flashlight.

"We'll be fine," I say as I take the flashlight from him. I reach down and retrieve the radio from my pack. "We can handle ourselves."

"I know you can," Hoff smiles. He glances at Steven for a second then steps aside and watches as we head for the dark hallway.

I flick on the flashlight as we pass a ticket window for the movie theater. The last film that was played was called "*End of Days*." How ironic. The echoes from our shoes on the floor fill the hallway as we head for the mall office. I shine a beam of light on a retail vision center with a bunch of spectacles eyeing us through the display windows. The smiling people wearing brand new glasses on the posters will never have to see how bad the world has become.

Just beyond the eyewear store we reach a set of three doors at the end of the hall. The one on the left leads to the loading dock. The one on the right is a door leading to the mall office. The third door is marked as a staircase, which probably leads to the second floor. I shine the beam of the flashlight through the glass doors of the mall office and scan the interior of the room. Several chairs, a pair of potted plants, and a coffee table compose a waiting area in front of the reception desk. A hallway behind the desk leads to darkened offices. Nothing inside the room stirs. I give the handle a push and the door eases open quietly.

Steven readies his machete as we step inside. I check behind the front desk as quietly as I can while Steven keeps an eye on the hall. I look up when I hear a crash coming from the other room.

"Get that light over here," whispers Steven as he squints into the darkness. He clenches his bandaged fist around the handle of the machete.

I hurry around the desk and shine the light in the hallway. We inch down the hall, the beam of light shaking in my hands. It would be one thing if we could shoot the thing but making that much noise isn't an option right now. Steven raises his machete, ready to strike at whatever we might find. I pull out the knife from my jacket pocket. At the end of the hall there is another small room with a pair of cubicles on either side of an aisle. I scan from one side of the room to the other with the flashlight, but I don't see anything. Steven glances over at me and shrugs. We creep into the dark room, peering around the corners into each of the cubicles in the first row. Both are empty except for the family pictures and personal belongings that seem to stare back at me. I try to avoid noticing these things, but I still can't help but see them when they are there.

As we move toward the second set of cubicles, I hear a soft moan on our left. The sound causes me to freeze for a moment. I shine the light on the opening of the cubicle. A horrific face appears a moment later. The thing snaps its jaws and lunges and then falls to the floor at our feet. Its hands are cuffed to the back of the office chair. I stare at the lifeless eyes at what used to be a security guard as it struggles to free itself from the toppled chair.

Steven swings the machete, and it glances off the skull of the thing, slicing away a chunk of its forehead and hair.

"Shit," Steven grunts as he brings back the machete again.

I keep the flashlight steady, but I avert my gaze until the only sound is Steven gasping for breath. When I open my eyes, the severed head is still blinking up at me beside the body on the floor.

"Christ, Steven," I complain. I sweep the flashlight around the workspace and notice a set of keys on the desk. I step over the body in the chair and inside the cubicle. As I reach for the keys, I notice a handwritten note sitting beside them. I resist the urge to pick it up and read it. Nothing good could be written in there. After I grab the keys, I glance around the shelf and the walls for anything else of use. There are just a few procedural binders, a calendar, and a photo of the security guard and his wife and three children wearing Mickey Mouse ears at Disney World.

"Find anything?" Steven whispers.

"Yeah," I say. "Got the keys."

"Come on then," Steven urges me.

When I turn to go, I can't help looking at the head on the floor again. The taste of bile creeps into the back of my throat.

"We can't just leave him like that," I say.

"Him?" Steven says.

"It ain't right," I shake my head.

Steven sighs and looks around the dark room. I slide the knife out of my jacket pocket and hand Steven the flashlight to hold before I crouch beside the head. I hold the thing steady beneath one of my boots and plunge the knife into the brain through the eye socket. The mouth of the thing goes slack, and I remove the knife and wipe the black blood off on the jacket still worn by the body on the floor.

"Let's go," Steven hisses.

I follow him out to the hallway, and we head back toward the entrance of the mall.

"You think someone did that to him?" Steven asks. "Tied him up like that and left him to die."

"I don't think so," I say. "He knew he was going to die. Probably just didn't want to hurt anyone else."

"Could have had the decency to shoot himself," Steven complains. "Some people."

"Some people just don't have it in them to do that," I remind him.

He glances back at me and remembers that I am one of those people.

"I didn't mean it like that," he apologizes.

"I know," I say.

"Hoff" Lorento whispers urgently over the radio. "Get everyone out now."

The radio is silent for several seconds as Hoff fails to respond. My heart begins to pound.

"Hoff!" Lorento whispers again. "They're in the pharmacy."

CHAPTER EIGHTEEN

Gunfire erupts down the hall near the parking garage entrance. Steven lopes along beside me, hunched over in pain from his shoulder. I could run right past him, but I don't want to leave him behind. We pass the box office for the movie theater and round the corner in time to see a mob of corpses pouring in through the parking garage.

"Where the hell are they?" Steven panics. He sweeps the flashlight by the benches where we left the rest of the group. They're all gone. The corpses stumble toward us from the garage entrance. Their moans echo loudly in the vast building.

"We'll find them," I say and push Steven so he will run away from the doors.

"I have to find him," Steven pleads.

"Go, Steven!" I push him again until he turns and begins to run as fast as his injured body is able.

A muzzle flash appears up ahead of us, followed by several more. The mall fills with the sharp crack of weapons firing. Bullets whiz by us, striking the horde of dead behind us.

Steven clutches his shoulder as he quickens his pace beside me but struggles to keep up. We weave through the seating area of the food court and the silhouettes of the group become visible in the moonlight. They have taken up a position outside the sports bar.

"Hurry your asses up," Hoff barks in between shots.

We are panting as we reach the entrance and Steven rushes to grab his son who is cowering in the doorway beside Val.

"You get the keys?" Hoff asks me.

"Yeah," I gasp.

"Get us inside!" Hoff screams and resumes firing at the dead.

I fumble with the set of keys and try a couple of random ones on the door. My hands are shaking so much I can barely keep the key steady enough to stick it in the cylinder.

"We're running out of time," Hoff reminds me.

"Working on it," I tell him.

There must be thirty or forty keys. I know I can't sit here and try them all. I glance around at the door and notice the address is listed next to the hours. Unit 31. I shuffle through the keys until I notice the one engraved with the number 31. I shove it into the lock and twist it until the bolt clicks. I push open the door and hold it while everyone rushes inside. Hoff is the last person in, backpedaling into the bar as he continues to fire. We push the door closed and I twist a knob to lock the deadbolt back in place. The dead fall onto the glass doors and windows and throw their fists and bodies into the glass. We bought ourselves a few minutes, but it won't hold them forever.

"What the hell happened?" Steven asks.

"I'm not sure," Hoff shakes his head. "Some more of them showed up. The doors were holding up fine, though. Thought I heard some shots fired outside. Maybe someone took out the glass."

"Where's Lorento?"

"Never made it back," Hoff sighs.

"Damn it," I curse. "What do we do now?"

Hoff shrugs. The big soldier collapses into a chair and wipes the sweat from his brow.

"We're all gonna fucking die in this shit hole now, that's what," Nicole says.

I glance over to see her standing in front of the bar next to Midhun. Nick is behind the counter twisting off the cap of a bottle and nodding in agreement. He sets a shot glass on the bar and pours himself a shot of whiskey. Nicole taps her index finger on the bar and Nick locates another shot glass and fills it.

"What about you, Habib?" he asks.

Midhun waves a dismissive hand and wanders over to a seat next to the windows. He stares curiously at the infected pressed against the glass.

"At least we picked the right spot to die," Nick says and lifts his glass.

I storm over to the bar and smack the glass out of his hand and send it flying across the room.

"Are you fucking kidding me right now?" I snap.

Nick stares at me in shock. I've always been the one willing to put up with his shit, but I am tired of waiting for him to get it together.

"Fucking get control of yourself and quit being an asshole," I scream at him. "I'm sick and tired of waiting for you to get your shit together. Help us for once in your miserable life."

Steven grabs me by the arm and pulls me away from the counter.

"Everyone just calm down," Hoff soothes. "Give me a minute to think."

Steven leads me to a booth across the dining room where Valerie hugs Stevie, and I pretend not to notice when Nick grabs another shot glass behind the counter and pours himself a drink anyway. It's not that I am pissed because Nick wanted a drink. Heck, I could use a stiff shot right now, too. I just can't understand people that don't give a damn, even when their very lives depend on it. Not to mention the lives of everyone around them. I let out a long breath and look away from the bar and notice Stevie with tears in his eyes.

"You doing okay, kiddo?" I ask him.

"I'm scared," he says. His eyes keep checking on the door to the mall where the crowd of the dead continues to grow.

"Everything's gonna be fine, champ," Steven says.

"Don't worry," I smile. "I locked it up good. They can't get in here."

Stevie nods and then tilts his head to rest it against Valerie. She wraps her arm around him and tries to smile, but she seems pretty scared as well. While I am glad to see that Stevie seems to like her, a part of me resents her, too. I would much rather be the one who had nothing to do but look after a sweet little boy. To hold someone and tell them everything is going to be okay is so much easier than making sure it actually will be.

"Lorento," Hoff whispers. I turn and see him hunched forward in his chair with the radio pressed to his lips as he stares at the floor. "Hernacki? You read me?"

A long silence follows.

"I'll be damned," responds a voice. At first, it sounds like it could be Hernacki, then I realize it's actually Bishop.

"Son of bitch," Steven whispers.

I walk towards Hoff to hear the transmission over the sounds of the dead outside.

"You people are really hard to kill! I'll give you that much," Bishop laughs.

"Maybe you ought to give up then," Hoff responds. "Just walk away while you still can. There's no way this ends well for you."

"Did you really just threaten me?" Bishop says. "Wow. You got some balls, man. I could have used a guy like you. What's your name anyway?"

"Fuck you," sneers Hoff.

More laughter. Several other voices in the background join in.

"You better watch it," Bishop says. "Or I might just get mad and put a bullet in blondie's pretty little head."

Hoff lowers the radio and glances up to meet my gaze.

"At least she's alive," I whisper.

"So, he says," Hoff mumbles. "Not sure I believe him, though."

"Now, in spite of what you might think, I'm a fair and reasonable man," Bishop says. "I'll give you all five minutes to surrender before I knock the hell out of little miss secret agent here."

"How do we even know she is okay?"

"Say something," Bishop says.

There's a long pause and the sound of a struggle at the other end of the radio.

"Talk!" Bishop barks.

"Just get out of here, Hoff," Lorento says. "Follow the plan."

"That's enough of that," Bishop growls.

"You have to give us more time," Hoff says. "Those things are all over the mall now."

"This ain't a goddamn negotiation. I don't care how you do it," Bishop says. "Five minutes. Don't keep me waiting."

The radio goes quiet, and Hoff slams it down on the table in frustration. He gets up from his chair and paces several steps toward the door, then turns and walks back to the table. I look through the restaurant windows at all the dead in the mall. A few dozen are still crowding against the glass and hundreds more are now wandering the building.

"We can't possibly get through the mall now," I say. "Not with all those things out there."

"That's not an option," Hoff says.

"What about Lorento?" I ask.

"Jess can take care of herself," Hoff sighs. He walks across the restaurant to the doors that lead outside the mall. At the street entrance, Hoff cranes his neck to peer up and down the block in each direction. After a long moment, he turns and walks back to the table and starts pulling out magazines from the pack and loading them into his ammo vest.

"What's the plan then?" I ask.

"Tipton," Hoff says. "We can make it there."

"On foot?" Steven interjects. I glance back to find Steven has crept up right behind me again. "You can't be serious."

Hoff lifts his eyes and shoots Steven a serious stare. He returns to filling up his ammo vest.

"Staying here is suicide," Hoff says. "We have to get out of town. That's our only chance. There are a lot of houses on the westside of the city, maybe we can find some transportation once we get out there."

"If we get out there," Nick scoffs. He grabs the bottle of whiskey off the counter and refills his shot glass.

Midhun turns from the window and approaches Hoff. The soldier looks up at the engineer with an impatient scowl.

"What?" Hoff asks.

"May I have a weapon?" Midhun asks.

Hoff glances at me and then cocks an eyebrow at Midhun.

"Sure," Hoff agrees. He reaches down into the duffel bag and pulls out a handgun and a couple clips. "What about all that non-violence crap?"

"To destroy one of those beings is not violence," Midhun says as he takes the weapon. "That is an act of mercy."

"You know how to use that?" Hoff asks.

"I will manage," Midhun smiles. He pulls back the slide and chambers a bullet. The man turns away from Hoff and walks toward the windows along the street.

Hoff shakes his head and then he hoists the duffel bag and dumps the contents out on the table. There isn't much ammunition left. Not compared to what the soldiers had yesterday.

"Everyone load up," Hoff says. "We will need to move fast, so leave behind anything that isn't essential."

Nick pours another shot down his throat and wipes his lips with the back of his hand. He notices Hoff giving him a hard stare. The soldier grabs his rifle and stalks over to the bar. I trail behind Hoff in case there is trouble between the two of them.

"Mind pouring me one of those?" the soldier asks to my surprise.

"See, Scout," Nick smirks. "Nothing like a little liquid courage. Right?"

Hoff grunts and twirls his index finger a few times to get Nick to hurry it up.

Nick grins and nods and sets a shot glass on the counter and fills it. He moves the bottle to fill his glass, but Hoff grabs his hand.

"No more for you," Hoff tells him. "If you ain't sober enough to keep up, I'll leave your ass behind. That's a promise." He shoves the hand back at Nick, causing him to spill some whiskey on his filthy dress shirt. Hoff picks up the glass and tosses it back and squints at the harsh taste. He clearly isn't used to drinking like that. He sets the shot glass back down on the bar and heads for the door.

The rest of us divide up the remaining ammunition. I only have two mags for the assault rifle, and three for handgun. A couple minutes later we all assemble near the doors.

"I want everyone single file," Hoff instructs. "Leave a few paces between the person in front of you." He glances at Stevie, then at his dad.

"He going to be able to keep up?" Hoff asks Steven.

"We'll try," Steven says.

Hoff spits a sunflower seed shell onto the ground and stares at it as he scratches his temple with his index fingers a few times. He sighs and crouches down to look Stevie in the eye.

"Your dad ever give you a piggyback ride?" he asks.

Stevie looks up at his dad, then back at Hoff and shakes his head.

"Seriously?" Hoff cocks an eyebrow at Steven.

Steven shrugs and averts his gaze. Hoff shakes his head and returns his focus on Stevie.

"How about I give you one today?" Hoff grins. "That be okay?"

"I guess so," Stevie says.

Hoff lets Stevie climb on his back. The boy clutches his hands together around the soldier's neck and wraps his legs around his midsection. The soldier leans forward slightly so that his back does the job of carrying the weight away from the little boy's tiny arms.

"Hang on real good," Hoff tells him.

"Good job, son," Steven adds.

Hoff gives me a nod and I turn the key and unlock the door to the street. I push through the doorway and hold it open as Hoff leads us out into the darkened town.

CHAPTER
NINETEEN

With all the dead swarming into the mall, navigating the streets outside is a little more manageable than when we arrived. After everyone clears the store, I take up position at the back of the column. Hoff leads us across the street and into an outdoor courtyard mall. In the faint moonlight, it's hard to make out many details. I just do my best to dodge the lurching shapes in the darkness. We weave between benches and food carts containing melted Italian ice and stale churros. Within moments the dead become aware of our presence and close in around us. We have to open fire at the ones that get too close.

The brick plaza angles to the left and Hoff pauses at the corner of the building, pressing his shoulder up against the window of a candle shop. He pivots around the building and fires off several rounds into the crowd of corpses shambling in our direction. The soldier swings back around and glances to make sure everyone is still with us. He rounds the corner and runs ahead, firing with one hand as he moves and gripping Stevie's wrists with the other.

I swivel back around and open fire at the dead that are closing on us from the rear. At first, I try to carefully aim my shots to conserve ammunition, but in the darkness, I might as well be firing blind. It takes several shots just to stop one of the things and they close in faster than I can take them down. To my right, one of the things lunges forward after I'd already shot it twice. It latches on to Nicole and shoves the woman up against the window right beside me.

I look for someone to help, but everyone else has already moved around the corner of the building. The corpse sinks its teeth into the side of her face as she lets out a scream. I bring the rifle up to shoot the thing in the head when several more bodies crash into me. The rifle fires wildly and the last thing I see before I crash into the store window is Nicole's head exploding as a round pierces her skull. The window gives way and I topple over a glass shelving unit full of candles. I scramble to my feet and spend the rest of the bullets in the magazine blasting holes in the adjacent window. Even though the glass doesn't give way, I don't have a choice but to try and throw my body into the window and hope I bust through it. I lead with my shoulder and jump at the window. The pane shatters and I hit the ground hard. My body scrapes along the sidewalk but I scurry to my feet and take off running again.

The rest of the group has already reached the street at the end of the mall. They are positioned at a clothing store at the corner. At least I hope it is them. The darkness makes it impossible to be sure. Someone fires off several rounds into the dead before they move around the building and out of sight. I eject the magazine from the rifle and reach into my pocket for a fresh one as I sprint. Sweat streaks down my face and my lungs hurt from panting. It feels like there must be slivers of glass buried in my skin, but there is no time to check. There is no time for pain. I try not to think about the fact that I just shot Nicole in the head. I'll have to deal with that shitty feeling later.

I reach the clothing shop and round the corner. The street is congested with the remains of cars and people. Within moments, I have to stop when the cluster of the dead on the sidewalk leaves no room to maneuver around them. I raise the rifle and I take down one with a pair of shots. Once it falls, I sprint forward again and leap over the body before the gap closes between the other corpses. Up ahead, hunkered down along the parked cars, I spot the others. Hoff peers over the hood of the car, fires a trio of shots and then scrambles a few parking spots further down the road to crouch behind another car.

The racket we are making as we fight our way through the city draws out more and more of the dead. Bishop must have figured out by now that we won't be surrendering. It will just be a matter of time before he comes after us. I can only wonder what might have happened to Hernacki and Lorento.

Not now, Scout. Focus.

I catch up to the others, and Hoff glances back briefly to make sure I'm okay. His eyes squint into the darkness, and his eyebrows raise slightly in surprise. With a nod, I let him know I'm good to go and he turns away and advances across the intersection to the next block.

"I'm out," Valerie tells me.

I reach down to my waist and grab the handgun and shove it at her chest. She fumbles with it awkwardly and for a minute I worry that she is going to shoot herself or me.

"Go," I urge her and push her shoulder to get her moving again. I pivot around and fire several shots at a dead barista just as he falls on top of me. His head explodes and skull fragments and brain tissue come down on me in a shower of blood. I squirm out from beneath the body and crab walk a couple of feet away to collect the rifle while trying to blink the blood out of my eyes enough to see. The hot barrel burns my hand when I grab it and I yelp in pain. Finally, my vision clears, and I quickly scan the area around me. Several dead bodies are lying on the ground nearby that weren't there a few moments ago. Then I happen to glance down at my jacket and notice it's spattered with blood and there are a few teeth resting on the fabric. I flick them away with a shudder. I scramble to my feet and turn to run when I notice Nick standing in the intersection with a rifle pointed in my direction. He fires off a shot and I flinch in terror. The bullet whizzes past my head. Several feet behind me the corpse of a kid wearing a blood-stained Hawkeyes sweatshirt collapses on the ground.

"Come on, Scout," Nick screams and beckons me to move with a wave of his arm.

The drunk bastard actually stopped to help me. I can hardly believe it. Despite everything going on, the moment actually makes me smile as I begin to run forward again. Nick stands at the rear doors of a white van in the road and waits for me to reach the intersection. As I step in the street, he turns to move forward again but a corpse stumbles at him from the side of the van and latches on to his jacket. Before I can even raise the rifle, the thing sinks its teeth into his neck. I hurry over and slam the butt of the rifle into the skull of the thing as hard as I can and knock it to the ground. Nick grabs at the blood trickling from his neck and looks at the red fluid soaking his fingers.

I grit my teeth, raise the rifle, and fire several rounds into the corpse that bit him. I grab his hand and pull him up to his feet. He hobbles along beside me in a stupor, but I can't tell if it's because he is losing a lot of blood or because he is in shock. We dash along the sidewalk to catch back up to the others, but I have already lost sight of them.

As we approach the edge of the downtown district, the swarm of the dead begins to thin out. Nick suddenly pauses next to an ATM machine, leaning his body against the side of the box.

"Nick," I plead. "We have to keep moving."

"Just leave me," he moans as he slumps toward the ground.

"Like hell," I say. I reach down and grab the collar of his suit jacket. He swats my hand away.

"Just go," he says. "We both know I'm dead already."

"Get the fuck up!" I scream and pull him as hard as I can.

He reluctantly straightens up and stumbles along beside me, clutching at his neck. At the end of the block, we cross another intersection and into a large open field. I glance around to see where the others have gone, but I don't see them anywhere. There are just a bunch of dark figures shambling through the tall grass. We've fallen too far behind and now we have lost them.

"Come on," I whisper to Nick and grab his arm to lead him into the dark field. The overgrown blades of grass brush against our legs as we churn through them. The dead are spread out enough that we can maneuver through the field without fighting. With only one magazine left, every bullet is going to have to count now. We cross a baseball diamond at the edge of the park and emerge on residential street. There are still no signs of life anywhere.

Nick pauses and leans his body up against the side of car parked in the road. His knees buckle and he drapes an arm over the roof to keep from falling to the ground. Blood soaks the front of his dress shirt and dribbles down the grey fabric of his pants.

"I need a minute," he gasps.

"We don't have a minute," I tell him.

"Just let me get a drink," he growls. His hand slips into his jacket and he fumbles with the silver flask inside.

"Seriously?" I ask him. I yank him forward again.

"Fuck," Nick spits. He loses his grip, and the metal container clangs against the street. "You made me drop it."

"Come on," I hiss.

I grab his wrist and drape his arm over my shoulder and let him lean on me as we walk down the street. Even though he always seemed thin, he stands a good six inches taller and must weigh a good forty pounds more than me. I start to breathe heavily with the added weight on my frame. Panic grips me as I realize that I can't keep going on like this for very long. If I leave Nick, I can possibly save myself. I'd still be out here alone. The fear of being alone helps me find the strength to drag Nick along beside me.

"Don't quit on me," I whisper to him.

He lifts his head for a moment and looks at me out of the corner of his eye. He tries to smile but coughs up blood that trickles down his chin.

"I'm gonna die, Scout," he says.

"No, you're not," I lie.

"It's okay," he grunts. "Bound to happen eventually."

"You saved me," I tell him. "I'm not giving up on you."

A burst of rifle fire echoes off the aluminum siding. Hoff and the others must still be close by, but it's hard to tell exactly which direction they went. We reach an intersection and I pause to look down the street in each direction. I notice a faint blinking light for a moment down the street to our right. I squint my eyes and can just barely make out Hoff hunched behind the wheel of a pickup truck. A second later the interior light shuts off and I lose sight of him.

"I see them," I whisper to Nick.

He groans. His head lolls forward and his eyelids stay closed. The man is out on his feet. It won't take long before he completely collapses. Somewhere deep inside, I wish for it to happen. Not out of malice. Just so I don't have the burden of carrying him any longer. I push the feeling away and move down the block. My legs ache from the strain.

We pass several houses before Nick's legs give out completely and he collapses onto a driveway. I squat down and grab him by the collar and shake him. His eyelids open but don't seem able to focus on me. He stares up at the stars behind me in the sky.

"Reason," he gasps. His hand locates my arm, and he digs his fingers deep into my wrist. He lifts his head off the ground and bares his teeth like a snarling dog. "I had a reason."

"Stay with me," I urge him. Seeing no choice, I call out to the others for help. The sound of my voice seems so loud in the quiet of the night.

"I'm sorry, Scout," he chokes. Nick loosens his grip on my arm and lays his head back on the concrete.

"It's okay," I tell him. I know he isn't going to make it.

"This is me," he says. "This..."

His hand flops down on the ground as a long final breath escapes his lungs. I lower my head and my vision blurs as my eyes fill with tears. Sure, he was a piece of shit since I had met him, and had almost gotten me killed just yesterday, but today he had actually came back for me. He finally tried to be a good person and it got him killed. It just feels so terribly wrong.

"Shit," Steven cusses.

I turn my head to see him and Midhun coming toward me through the tall grass. They both reach down and help me get to my feet.

"You okay?" Steven asks.

"I think so," I tell him. My legs still feel tired and weak. The two of them begin to lead me back toward the truck but I shrug loose and turn around.

"We got to go," Steven pleads.

"I'm not going to let him turn into one of them," I growl. I point the rifle at Nick and stare at his lifeless face for a second, and then I pull the trigger with a trembling finger.

Another gunshot follows as Midhun puts a bullet in the corpse of a mailman that staggers across the front lawn of the house. I shoulder my rifle and jog behind them toward the pickup. As we approach, the engine turns over and the running lights illuminate the dark street. I see the shaggy red hair on the top of Stevie's head beneath the dome light in the cab. Hoff wheels the truck around and the three of us hop into the bed and drive off into the night.

CHAPTER TWENTY

After we set out with fourteen of us yesterday, there are just six of us remaining. I am smart enough to know we should just walk away. If the last two days have taught me anything, it's that we can't possibly win. But to give up now would mean that we lost all those people for no reason at all. I just can't live with that.

"What happened back there?" Steven asks.

I shake my head, unsure how to answer and not wanting to think about it. It feels like it was somehow my fault.

"Scout," Steven begins.

"I don't want to talk about it," I cut him off.

"No," he says. "You got a hunk of glass in your face."

I reach up to touch my face and feel the sharp edge of a shard of glass embedded in the skin over my cheek bone. The sudden pain from the slight touch makes me hiss. If it had been up another inch, I would have probably lost an eye. I pinch the glass and tug it slightly. The truck rolls over a pothole and the movement causes me to accidentally shove the piece farther into my skin.

"Fuck!" I curse and let go of the glass.

"You want some help with that?" Steven offers. He reaches a hand toward my face, but I swat it away.

"Just leave it," I shake my head.

Steven stares at the side of my face, his mouth agape.

"Quit it," I growl.

He shifts his gaze to the road behind us. I notice Midhun staring at my face as well. I must look horrific. It will probably leave a scar for the rest of my life, however long that may be. Even now, I'm still worried about how I look and what other people will think when they see me. I feel stupid for even feeling like it matters, but I can't help it. In the back of the truck, I prop my knees up and fold my arms across them. I rest my forehead on my arms, partly to hide my face but mostly to rest. It's the middle of the night and I'm more exhausted than I have ever been in my life. After the stress of the last couple of hours, it feels like my body is ready to quit on me.

"Do not lose hope," Midhun says.

I raise my head slightly and try to smile. All it does is make my face scream in pain again.

"How do you stay so fucking cheery?" Steven gripes.

"When I despair," Midhun smiles, "I remember that all through history the ways of truth and love have always won. There have been tyrants, and murderers, and for a time they can seem invincible, but in the end they always fall. Think of it--always."

"What the hell is he talking about?" Steven asks me.

"I think he's quoting Gandhi," I say.

Midhun nods. He reaches into the vest pocket of his jacket and pulls out a small book of famous quotations.

"It was my brothers," he says. "Over and over, I have read it these weeks. It is all I have of him now. He would always be telling me these things, even when my ears did not want to listen. Only now do I truly understand him."

He tucks the book back into his jacket pocket and gives it a couple soft pats with the palm of his hand.

"How'd that work out for him?" Steven asks. "What ever happened to Gandhi?"

"Stop, Steven," I say.

"No, really," he says. "I don't know much about history. I'd like to understand."

"He was shot by a right-wing militant," Midhun says. "Terrible tragedy."

"You don't say," Steven shakes his head.

As the truck slows to ease around a corner, I notice a sound coming from my pack. It's a voice on the radio. I dig it out and listen again.

"I know you're listening," Bishop teases.

I rap my knuckle against the window of the truck. Hoff glances back and holds a finger to his lips to tell me not to respond.

"I have to admit, I'm a bit surprised that you'd leave your friend behind," Bishop rambles. "You probably thought you would make me look like a fool, but you're wrong."

He sure does love to listen to himself talk. I glance over at Steven and roll my eyes.

"See," Bishop continues. "People are always underestimating me. But I am going to win. You'll see. Just like your friends back at the farmhouse saw."

They must have found Fawn and the soldiers. I clutch the radio in my fingers and resist the urge to scream into the microphone by biting down on my bottom lip.

"Son of a bitch," Steven growls.

Hoff bangs a fist against the dashboard inside the truck.

"You might think you're getting away," Bishop says. "But I know where you're going. You'll all be seeing me again real soon."

The radio goes silent, and I glance up at Steven.

"He's just talking out his ass," Steven says.

"No, he isn't. Lorento had the map. She marked the location of the airfield."

"Crap," Steven spits. "He knows exactly where we're going."

"He has the GPS, too," I sigh.

"We're fucked," Steven curses.

"Really fucked," I agree.

"We can just go somewhere else," Steven suggests. "Get the hell out of here and never look back."

"No," I say. "We are not running away. Not after what they did."

"You're crazy," Steven snaps. "It's suicide."

"We can't run forever," I insist. "They aren't just going to leave us alone. Not after everything."

"Christ," Steven sighs. "You got some kind of death wish. That's what this is really about."

My eyeballs roll up into my skull.

"That's not it," I say.

"No, really," Steven says. "I get it now."

We fall silent as the pickup truck leaves the subdivision. Cornfields appear on either side of the road. Once we are a few miles from town, one of the tires pops as we run over some debris in the road. At first, it sounds like it will be okay. But after another few miles the tire runs flat, and the rims begin to grind against the pavement.

Hoff pulls the truck over to the side of the dark road and gets out of the cab.

"Just can't catch a break," he groans. He stares at the piece of glass in my face, then notices me watching him doing it and looks away. Hoff fishes a bag of sunflower seeds out of his chest pocket and pours a few of them into his palm.

"How far away are we?" I ask.

"Maybe ten miles at the most." He shoves the handful of seeds in his mouth.

Along the horizon to the west, I spot a flash of lightning. To the east, the sun already begins to lighten the color of the night sky. The cornfields go on for as far as the eye can see in either direction. For a long moment I listen to the night but only hear the buzzing sounds of insects in the fields. There isn't any sign of Bishop, at least for now.

"Guess we will not be having much luck finding a spare tire," Midhun notes.

"Not likely," Hoff shakes his head.

"We better start walking," I suggest. "If that pilot is still in Tipton, we need to get there and find him before Bishop does."

"You sure you're up for it?" Hoff asks me.

"Don't really have much choice," I say. I pull the straps of my pack over my shoulders and grab up the rifle.

"Of course, we have a choice, Scout," Steven says. He climbs out of the bed of the truck behind me and grabs onto my sleeve as I walk toward the front of the truck. I spin around to face him without meeting his eyes. "There is always a choice."

Valerie opens the passenger door and helps Stevie down from the seat. I watch his horrified expression when he sees half of my face covered in blood. I turn to the side, so he only sees the side of me that still looks normal.

"You know I always have your back, Scout," Steven says. He glances back over his shoulder at the dark shape of his son standing beside the truck. "But don't do this. Enough is enough already. We don't have to die."

"I have to finish this Steven," I say. "I'd rather die than live in this kind of a world."

Steven shakes his head.

"I don't expect you to understand. Hell, I don't even want you to fight," I cringe. The glass in my face makes it painful to talk. I grit my teeth and rip the chunk of glass from my skin and let it fall from my shaking fingers.

"Fuck!" I gasp as blood trickles down from the hole in my face. I shrug a shoulder out of my pack and pull the zipper open. After digging around, I locate my other shirt and press it to my face to try and help stop the bleeding.

"We can't do this," Steven says. "Christ, Scout, look at yourself."

"Just take Stevie and Val and get as far away as you can," I say, the fabric on my face muffling my voice. "I should have never gotten any of you involved in this."

Steven drags his palm down his face as though wishing he could wipe the slate clean with a simple gesture.

"You know I'm not going to do that to you," he sighs.

"You don't owe me anything," I tell him. "Just go, Steven."

Steven stares at the pavement and shakes his head. He moves his boot like he is kicking something around, even though there is nothing on the street.

I nod at Hoff and Midhun standing on the other side of the truck and turn to walk down the road. I resist the urge to look over my shoulder, because I am afraid that Steven will still be there. There is also the fear that he won't be. To be honest, I'm not sure what frightens me more. Finally, my curiosity gets the better of me and I glance back to see them following along twenty yards back.

"Damn it," I whisper. "This is no place for a kid to be."

Hoff glances at me out of the corner of his eye.

"There is no place for kids in this world. Not anymore," Hoff says.

"Hey!" Steven calls.

I stop walking and look over my shoulder and realize immediately why Steven called to get our attention. A faint light on the far side of the hill behind us can only mean that a vehicle is approaching.

"Shit," Hoff whispers. He waves an arm to urge everyone to get off the road and take cover in the stalks of corn. As we reach the ditch beside the road, the first set of headlights appears on the horizon. I use the hand that isn't clutching a bloody shirt to part the crops and disappear inside. Hoff creeps in right behind me and readies his rifle. More sets of headlights appear out of the darkness. The vehicles slow as they approach the pickup truck down the road. The first couple trucks roll by, but the third truck skids to a stop beside the truck. It backs up a few feet and comes to a stop again.

"Damn it," Hoff growls.

I prop the rifle against my shoulder and squint into the scope. Someone gets out the vehicle and I make out the silhouette of a man as he walks into the beam of the headlights. When he crouches down in the road to inspect something I can make out his face. It's Arkady. Light glints off the bloody piece of glass between his fingers. I dig my nails into the bloody shirt pressed against my face. Arkady stands up suddenly and scans the surrounding fields.

"What you got, man?" The gruff tone of Bishop's voice sends a chill down my spine.

"Blood," Arkady says. He wipes his hands on his pants and walks over and puts a hand on the hood of the abandoned truck. "Still warm."

A door of the lead truck opens, and beneath the glow of the interior light, I see Lorento sitting between Bishop and the blonde woman from the diner. Bishop gets out the passenger door, looks around the road, and turns back to the other trucks.

"Get those lights on," Bishop says. "They can't be far."

Spotlights on top of several of the trucks flip on and search the fields. I crouch down closer to the ground and lean back a few more inches until the plants partially block my view of the road. We are probably far enough up the street that they won't notice us, but there is no sense taking any chances.

"Was that Lorento?" Hoff asks.

"Yep," I whisper. "She's alive."

"Hernacki?" Hoff asks.

"I didn't see him," I say.

Hoff glances down at the dirt.

"Come on out!" Bishop howls into field. "I know you're hiding out there."

There's a long pause as Bishop waits for a response. He scans the dark fields for any sign of us.

"I tried to talk this shit out reasonably with you people," he hoists his shotgun and rests the barrel on his shoulder as he paces up and down the road. "But you haven't been fair with me. Instead, you sided with this crooked CIA agent."

The men in the truck jeer at the mention of Lorento. Bishop stalks up to the lead truck and stares at her in the passenger seat. He raises the rifle and points the barrel in her direction.

"That woman is a traitor. She has murdered a lot of my fellow countrymen, and I intend to see that she pays for those crimes."

"Kill the bitch!" somebody yells from the street. The men begin to clap and laugh. Bishop raises a hand to signal them to be quiet.

He cocks his head slightly and gazes back down the road toward town. A moment later, I realize what got his attention. The moans of the approaching undead drown out the sounds of crickets and June bugs.

"You hear that?" Bishop asks the night. He tilts his head back and closes his eyes as he savors the sound. "Just listen to it."

He stands in the road for a long, painful minute as the sound of the corpses grows closer and louder. We need to get the hell out of here, but if we try to move his men are sure to notice.

"Isn't it beautiful?" Bishop asks. He stalks back down the road along the line of trucks again.

"That's the sound of fate," Bishop says. "That's the sound of justice. That's the sound of God in the machine."

He looks around the roadside once more. The shapes of the dead emerge from the darkness into the glow of the brake lights behind the convoy.

"Maybe now you'll finally understand," Bishop muses. "This is the way all this shit is supposed to end for you."

Bishop opens the door of the pickup and climbs back into the seat beside Lorento. Hoff pulls me back into the field as the convoy rolls slowly toward us. The men fire their rifles into the air and into the cornfields to rile up the horde behind them. Bullets hack through the plants around us as we retreat from the road.

As soon as the last vehicle rolls away, the tide of corpses rushes at us, trampling the crops. We push ahead through the field and work our way back toward the road.

Stevie trips over the tricky terrain and drags Val down to the ground with him. The kid begins to cry, so Hoff scoops him up and cups a hand over his mouth as he runs with the boy in his arms. I help Val to her feet, and she grimaces as she hobbles along beside me.

We climb up the ditch and make our way back down the road ahead of the dead, although they follow just ten yards behind us. We can still see the taillights of the pickup trucks in the distance for a moment and then they vanish over a hill.

We trudge on managing to gain some ground on the corpses, but they always keep coming. With no sleep in the last couple of days, it is hard to stay ahead. After an hour or so, the sun peeks over the horizon. The brightness of the day hurts my tired eyes. I pause a moment to look back and see several thousand dead lumbering down the road.

"Just keep moving," Hoff says. "Try not to think about them. One foot in front of the other."

"What happens if we actually make it the airfield?" Steven asks. "Bishop is going to be waiting for us."

"It's a good thing we have backup then," I say and jerk my head to indicate the crowd of the dead.

"God help us," Steven sighs.

"I seriously don't think I can do this anymore," Val sighs. She stops in the road and hunches over with her hands on her knees. I glance down and notice the swelling on her ankle.

"I'm really sorry," Stevie whimpers.

"It's not your fault, sweetie," Val lifts her eyes and tries her best to smile.

The boy wraps his arms around his father's thigh and buries his face in the fabric.

"You can make it," I assure Val. I pull her arm until she stands up again. Midhun approaches her and she puts her arm over his shoulder, and we push on again.

We cross over the interstate a couple hundred yards ahead of the dead. If we had more time, we could have tried to locate another vehicle, but with the dead this close it would be suicide. I can feel my legs getting a little shaky beneath me. It won't be long before my body just gives up. At one point, the world starts to spin, and I have to reach an arm out to Hoff to steady myself again.

"Sorry," I mumble.

"Hang in there, Scout," Hoff says. He jerks his head toward the road in front of us and I spot a sign for Mathews Memorial Airport.

CHAPTER TWENTY-ONE

We're crouched in dewy grass alongside a three-way intersection. I look down the long road to the airport through the scope until I spot a pair of pickups outside the terminal building. A sentry is positioned in the bed of each truck.

"They're here all right," I say. I lower the rifle and eye the dead as they approach our location from the south.

"This road is a dead end," Hoff says. "If we can lead this herd down it, Bishop will be blocked in."

"We'll need somebody to be the bait," Steven says.

"I will do it," Midhun says.

"You sure you can handle that?" Hoff raises an eyebrow at him.

"Piece of pie," Midhun grins.

"Then what?" Steven asks.

"Was still trying to work all that out," Hoff says as he scratches at his beard as he stares down the long road.

I scan the area and realize a country club is just across the road from the airport. If it weren't for the golf carts and the occasional flag sticking up out of the tall grass, it would be hard to recognize it as a golf course anymore.

"We can go through that golf course," I point. "Swing around the back of the airport and hit them from the rear when they're focused on the corpses."

"That could work," Hoff says. He gazes over his shoulder at the dead as they close in on us. Then he looks down at Stevie in the grass beside him. "On the map I saw a campground across the road from the hangars, too. Someone can stay there with the kid."

The soldier glances at Valerie and she nods. A clap of thunder echoes in the distance. I glance up at the darkening clouds and spot the vultures circling above, like they can sense the coming carnage and the chance at fresh meat.

"I got a bad feeling about this," Steven says.

"I can't remember the last time I felt good about anything," Hoff says. "Let's go."

We creep along the brush until we clear the intersection, and then we cross over the street. The crowd of the dead is fifty yards away and closing.

"Take this in case you get into any trouble," I tell Midhun and hand him my radio. "Good luck," I add.

"When it comes to luck," he says. "You make your own."

"That more of your Gandhi wisdom?" Steven asks him.

"No," Midhun smiles. "Bruce Springsteen."

Steven grins and shakes his head before turning and pushing through the tree branches.

"Stay safe," I tell Midhun, and then I follow the others into the country club. We scurry along the fairway, scanning the surroundings for threats. Since Bishop got here hours ahead of us, his men probably searched the area already. He may have even gotten to Lorento's contact. There is just no way of knowing what kind of situation we might be walking into.

We reach the end of the fairway and enter the woods at the back of the country club. The camping area is thick with trees that conceal us from the airfield, but it also prevents us from getting a good look at what is going on over there.

"We have to get closer," Hoff says.

"Looks like the campground office over there," I whisper. "I point a finger at a small brown building just off the road."

Hoff nods and I follow him forward through the trees. Birds chirp a chorus of morning songs. The noise covers the cracking twigs beneath our boots. Thunder rumbles again in the distance. A soft breeze rustles the leaves in the treetops. We rush up to the back of the campground office and Hoff peers around the corner to the door on the side of the building. He nods and then pivots around the corner and hurries inside. Out of the corner of my eye, I detect movement in the trees near the back of the campground. I wait until the others have slipped inside and then

I frantically watch the trees. I might almost believe that I imagined the movement, until I spot a branch swaying a bit more than it should be. My heart starts to race as I look from one side to another. I spin around the corner and stop in my tracks when I notice something unexpected coming around the front of the store.

It's a dog.

I take a step back, but instead of growling or trying to attack me, the dog just wags its tail. The thing isn't feral at all. The sight of the scruffy terrier should have made me suspicious. It was such a pleasant sight. I couldn't help but start to smile. The joy only lasts about half a second before I feel a gun pressed against the side of my head.

"Don't scream," a man says calmly.

I hold my hands up slightly and let the rifle hang around my neck by the strap. I spot Hoff through the front window of the store. He can see me with the gun to my head but can't get an angle on the guy who is still partially behind the back wall of the building. Maybe I can lure him over a few feet.

"Don't move," he says as soon as I lean slightly away from him. "What are you and your friends doing out here?"

"What?" I ask. I try to get a look at his face, but he nudges me with the gun to keep me from turning my head. "Tell Bishop he can go fuck himself."

"Who is Bishop?" he asks.

The dog sniffs at the air and growls.

"Quiet, Stitch," the man says to the dog.

Hoff bursts out the door with his rifle raised.

"Let her go," Hoff says.

The man steps back, pulling me with him. He peers around my head to get a look at Hoff.

"Don't I know you?" the man says.

Hoff squints his eyes at the man, then he lowers the rifle slightly.

"You?" Hoff stammers. "You're the guy that kept puking in the helicopter."

"Not my finest moment," the man admits. He relaxes his grip on my neck, then lets me go.

"Where's Fletcher?" Hoff asks.

"Right behind you," the man says.

Hoff turns around and finds a man in camouflage fatigues positioned at the front corner of the building with a rifle fixed on him. The man lowers the rifle and gives Hoff a wink from beneath his cowboy hat.

"Holy shit!" Hoff gasps. He takes a hand off the rifle and walks over and bear hugs Fletcher.

"Easy big fella," Fletcher laughs. "What the hell you doing out here?"

"Looking for you," Hoff says.

"How'd you know we were here?" Fletcher asks.

"Lorento," Hoff says. "She planted a tracking device on you."

"No shit?" Fletcher asks. "That sneaky little bitch."

"Where's the rest of your unit?"

Hoff shakes his head.

"Shit," Fletcher says. "Wiz?"

"Sorry," says Hoff.

"I told you that whole mission was FUBAR," Fletcher complains.

I turn around to get a look at the guy that held me at gunpoint. He is also dressed in a military uniform, but something about him makes me think he isn't a soldier at all. Even though his face has a few scars, there is something gentle about his eyes that almost seem to apologize for pointing a gun at me. When I make eye contact with him, he flashes a reluctant smile before shifting his eyes away from mine.

"Sorry about that," says the guy that grabbed me. He takes a step back and pets the dog that pants and trembles beside him. "I'm Blake."

"Scout," I tell him.

Blake nods. His eyes scan the faces peering out the glass door of the building and I notice a slight smile when he spots Stevie.

Assault rifles clatter across the road. The swarm of the dead must have reached the entrance to the airfield. The scruff on the neck of the dog bristles as it growls again. Blake looks past me toward the airport.

Four other people run toward us from the back of the campground. A tall black man and a dark-haired woman are followed by a teenage kid with a short blonde-haired girl. All of them also dressed in fatigues and carrying assault rifles. Clearly, they aren't all with the military, but I have to wonder how they got all their gear. I start to feel like maybe we still have a shot at taking down Bishop after all.

The brunette woman sidles up beside Blake and places a hand on his arm as she looks me up and down.

"Everything's all right," he whispers to her.

"Would you mind telling us what the hell is going on over there?" Fletcher asks Hoff.

Midhun suddenly sprints around the front of the building. Fletcher spots him and whirls around raising his rifle.

"Get down," Fletcher yells. "On the ground, camel jockey!"

Midhun staggers backwards and falls on his back in the dirt. He holds an arm up in front of his face as he scoots away from Fletcher.

"It's okay! It's okay!" Hoff says and grabs Fletcher on the shoulder. "He's with us, too."

"Goddamn," Fletcher says. "I'm sorry, man. Nearly shot the damn turban off your head." He lowers the rifle and reaches out to help Midhun to his feet.

"I think we better go," I remind Hoff.

"Right," Hoff agrees. He turns and looks and Fletcher. "I'll explain everything later. Right now, we need your help."

"With what?" Blake asks.

"We need to rescue Lorento," Hoff says.

"You have got to be shitting me," groans Fletcher. He shakes his head and walks away. After a few steps, he turns and paces back.

"I'm not risking my ass for her," Fletcher growls. "Not happening."

"Are you fucking kidding me?" I seethe. I can't believe this Fletcher guy was so important we risked our lives to find him. The people I cared about died just to make it possible. What a selfish asshole. Before I realize I'm doing it, I start walking toward Fletcher. "You have no idea how many people died so we could get here. Good people. My friends."

Fletcher glances at Hoff who nods in agreement.

"I'm sorry about your friends," he says. "Truly, I am. But I..." Fletcher's voice falters and he turns and steps away again.

"Fuck these people," I tell Hoff. "We don't have time for this shit. Let's go."

"Wait," Blake says. He grabs my wrist as I try to walk away.

"Let go of me," I growl.

"Tell us how we can help," he says. He casts a stare at Fletcher who throws his arms up in a show of exasperation.

"Fine," I tell Blake. "Follow me."

CHAPTER TWENTY-TWO

The rain begins to fall as we circle around the back of the airport through the trees. Hoff moves along beside me followed by Steven. A few yards back, Blake leads the others with Fletcher lagging at the rear. Lightning flashes and thunder rumbles and within a few minutes my boots are sinking deep in the mud. We reach a clearing and sprint across the grass until we reach the back of a pair of small hangars across from the main terminal. I peer around the front corner of the building and can hardly believe my eyes.

The dead have completely overrun the entrance to the airport. A trio of pickup trucks form a barricade across the road between the hangars and the terminal. Corpses swarm the vehicles, tearing at the bodies of the men. I hear gunfire from within the terminal. We have to make a run for the terminal before the dead lose interest in the trucks and move on toward the back of the airfield.

I point to a door across the access road and then we take off across the slick pavement, splashing through puddles until we reach the door. The tall, black guy with the goatee reaches the door several seconds before me. He twists the handle, and then holds it open for everyone to run inside. Just before I run into the dark building, I take a look at the trucks and see the dead staggering toward us. We don't have much time to find Bishop before the dead swarm the entire airport.

The interior of the building is so dark that it takes a moment for my eyes to adjust. Rain pelts the corrugated roof and fills the building with a loud, steady noise. The smell of jet fuel hangs in the air. What I thought was the terminal was actually another long hangar. I can barely make out the shapes of small aircraft parked down the length of the building. There is no sign of Bishop or Lorento.

"Where the hell did the rest of them go?" Steven asks.

Suddenly daylight appears at far end of the building. It creeps across the floor as an access door lifts up toward the ceiling. Four pickup trucks are parked inside the hangar. There looks to be about a dozen people scrambling to get inside the vehicles. I try to spot Lorento among them, but I don't see her.

"Let's move," Hoff whispers as he raises the rifle and presses forward along the row of planes. Fletcher leads the other group along the rear wall on the opposite side of the aircraft. The sound of the rain helps to cover the noise of our boots on the concrete floor. Before we get close enough to attack, one of the men near the trucks happens to turn his head in our direction.

"Bishop!" the man yells as he raises the rifle and opens fire on us.

I dive behind the landing gear of the nearest plane as the bullets fly and punch into the glass of the cockpit above me. Hoff crouches below the belly of another aircraft and fires a burst into the door of the lead truck as the driver starts the engine. The head of the driver snaps to the side, and blood splatters across the inside of the windshield. The vehicle surges forward suddenly and smashes into a metal support beam.

The gunshots are deafening inside the metal building. I glance around the landing gear and try to find a target but just fire a few rounds at the trucks blindly before ducking back to safety. I don't have much ammunition left, and it feels like I'm just wasting it shooting like this.

I glance around the landing gear again and notice movement in the truck that crashed into the support beam. The driver side door swings open and then the body of the driver rolls out and falls to the ground. Lorento emerges behind him and collapses on the ground beside the truck. She gets to her feet and scurries toward our position.

I raise the rifle to provide some cover for her and fire a few rounds at Dom as she climbs into another one of the trucks. Dom spots Lorento escaping and raises a handgun to fire several shots in her direction. The bullets poke holes in the building behind Lorento as she crashes to the ground. I can't be sure if Lorento was hit or if she was just trying to make herself a difficult target by diving to the floor. Dom flinches as I fire a short burst in her direction. She hits the gas and the truck tires squeal as the trio of pickups speed out of onto the wet apron outside.

"Run, you little bitches!" Fletcher yells as he fires at the retreating vehicles.

I get back to my feet and follow behind Hoff toward Lorento. A massive explosion outside shakes the building as I am about to ask if she is okay. She lifts her head up to look at me and I notice the black eye and fresh bruises around her neck. There is a trickle of blood on the floor beneath her.

"She got hit," Hoff says. He quickly scans her body and locates a bullet wound near her thigh.

"I'm all right," Lorento mumbles.

"Remember me?" The brunette woman appears at my side and kneels down beside Lorento.

"Danielle?" Lorento asks.

"Good to see you again," the brunette says.

Lorento squints her eyes and looks around. Her eyes land on Fletcher and she smiles weakly. Danielle checks the wound quickly and takes out a bandana from her pocket. Lorento struggles to move, but Hoff places a hand on her shoulder to encourage her to stay still.

"You're not bleeding much," Danielle explains. She knots a tourniquet around the injured leg and looks up at Hoff. "She can't walk like this, though."

"I can walk," Lorento insists. "Just help me up."

Hoff shoulders his rifle and scoops her up and carries her over his shoulder.

"Put me down damn it," Lorento complains but Hoff ignores her and carries her outside.

When I step out of the building, I see one of the trucks crashed into a tank of jet fuel beside the tarmac. Fletcher must have managed to tag the driver as they left the garage. I gaze out at the runway to watch the remaining pair of trucks drive away from the airport. All we can do is watch as they reach the end of the tarmac and pull into the grassy field. We were so close to taking Bishop out and ending this whole thing, but he slipped through our fingers. At least we got Lorento back alive. I guess that's something.

"Quentin," Blake says to the black guy. "Did you see who that was?"

"No way," Quentin says. "Couldn't be."

"Dom?" asks Danielle.

"I'm pretty sure it was," Blake says. He turns and looks at me. "You ever seen her before?"

"Who?" I ask.

"The blonde that was with Bishop."

"Yeah," I nod. "She's been with him at least a couple weeks."

"We need to move," Hoff interjects. "Talk later."

We head toward the back of the airport and cross a strip of grass into a cornfield. We make our way through the slop as the rain continues to pour down from the sky. When we reach the woods again, I pause and look over at the airport. A plume of smoke still billows up from the far side, and the dead continue to filter through the hangars. There is no chance of us going back out that way now. We will have to head back to the road through the golf course again.

We stop to pickup the others at the campground office. Stevie runs out the door when he spots us and races to his dad and gives him a hug. The shaggy dog trails behind him and circles around us excitedly wagging his tail. It makes me smile to finally see the kid with a look of excitement on his face again.

"Looks like somebody has a new friend," I tell Steven. The dog pauses and looks up at me and I let him sniff my hand, then scratch at the fur on his head.

"His name is Stitch," Stevie tells me. "But Val calls him Fleabag."

"I'm more of a cat person," Val explains.

Stitch leads the way to the back of the campground where there are a couple of camouflaged tents set up behind some sparse bushes.

"College boy," Fletcher says to the younger kid. He points a finger at the tents. "You and Nat start packing this shit up."

The scrawny kid shoulders his rifle and rolls his eyes. The younger girl brushes the blonde bangs out of her face and grimaces as she bends down to yank a stake out of the mud.

"Looks like we're not going to be able to drive out of here now," Quentin says as he gazes back toward the road.

"Going to have to leave the trucks behind," Blake agrees. "Too many of those things on the road. We'll never make it through."

"That's a damn shame," Fletcher says.

For a moment I wonder what they are talking about, then I turn around and notice Fletcher pulling a camouflage net away to reveal a pair of black pickups. From a distance I'd had no idea the vehicles were even there. No wonder Bishop never managed to locate them. These people are clever.

The truck beds are loaded with supplies, weapons, and ammunition. We can't possibly carry all of it, and it seems like such a shame to leave it all behind.

"You guys have any vehicles nearby?" Blake asks me.

"No," I shake my head.

"Ain't got shit," Hoff adds. "Lost our vehicles, all our supplies, food, water, ammo."

"People," I add.

"Everything," Hoff sighs. He sets Lorento down on the open rear gate of the truck.

"You should have listened to me before," Fletcher says to Hoff. Fletcher spits on the ground and glances over at Lorento with a look of disgust.

"Are you trying to blame everything on me?" Lorento scoffs.

"You heard me right," Fletcher says.

"Maybe if the helicopter had a full crew we never would have crashed in the first place," Lorento hisses.

"Don't you try to turn this on me," Fletcher pokes a finger at Lorento.

"Maybe those soldiers would all still be alive if you just did your goddamn job," Lorento continues.

"Fucking unbelievable," Fletcher snaps. He tightens his hands into fists before burying them in his pants pockets.

"You two mind if we continue this discussion inside somewhere," Hoff interrupts. "Those things will start wandering over here soon enough and I am getting pretty sick of standing around in the rain."

Fletcher remains still for a few moments and gives Lorento a hard stare between the drops of water dripping from the brim of his cowboy hat. Lorento rolls her eyes and slides down from the back of the truck, wincing in pain as she puts weight on her leg again.

"Grab as much as you can carry," Blake says. He reaches into the back of the truck and grabs a case of rations and dumps it in my arms. "We'll head back to the golf course. Maybe we can wait this storm out in the clubhouse and come back for the trucks when those things clear out of here."

CHAPTER TWENTY-THREE

The nylon awning over the entrance to the golf course flutters in the heavy wind and sheets of rain that pour down in the grey afternoon. My clothes are soaking wet as we finally push through the glass door and step inside the lobby. I scan the darkened bar and the dining area to see if there are any threats. All I see are the white table clothes and place settings, and the rows of liquor bottles lined up behind the empty bar.

"Don't worry," Blake says. "If there was anything in here, Stitch would have sniffed it out already. Right boy?" He cocks his head down at the happy dog and shrugs the heavy pack from his shoulders. The dog shakes itself off and pants and wags its tail. Blake crouches down and pulls a piece of jerky from his pocket and lets the dog take it from his fingers.

Hoff steps around me with Lorento's arm draped over his shoulder. He helps her into the dining room and pulls out a chair for her to sit down. Danielle hurries over to the table and drops her pack and opens the flap to dig around for something inside.

"Is she a doctor?" I ask Blake.

"Well, sort of," he smirks. "Almost, I guess. She knows what she is doing."

I nod and a cold shiver runs down my spine. I wish I had something other than these wet clothes to wear. My body aches from pain and exhaustion and all I want to do is lay down and curl up in ball and cry myself to sleep.

"You guys look like you've been through hell," Blake says.

"We have," I tell him. "You have no idea."

"I've been there before," he says and puts a hand on my arm. "You're okay now. Get something to eat and get warm and tell me all about it after you rest a bit."

"Lorento can probably tell you more than I can," I say.

"Maybe," he says. "But I'm more likely to believe you."

"Thanks," I smile. He almost smiles back but just gestures to the boxes of rations and tells me to help myself. I watch as he moves across the room and talks quietly to Quentin, Nat, and the kid they called College Boy. As much as they seem like good people and I want to trust them, it makes me nervous to be around so many strangers that we don't know anything about. When this whole thing started, the only thing that scared me was corpses, but after the last couple of days I am more afraid of people than ever before.

I carry the box across the lobby and find Midhun sitting on a bench near the front doors looking outside.

"What's wrong?" I ask him.

His head turns in my direction, his smile returning. His eyes flick to the side to peek at Fletcher. He eyes our new friends in their military fatigues with some apparent apprehension. The soldier stares at him with only a mild interest. Midhun lowers his eyes, then leans closer to me.

"I am not sure I can go along with these people," he whispers. "I am not a soldier."

"You're fine here," I say. "Don't be ridiculous."

"No, no, it is true," Midhun says. "I do not belong."

"Of course, you do," I insist.

Midhun cocks his head away from me and winces as though the notion was a source of heat he needed to back away from. He rests his wrists on his knees and stares at his fingers as he rubs the thumb of his right hand along the digits of his left slowly.

"You know we might not have survived at the airport if it wasn't for you," I tell him. "If you didn't lead those things down the road and take out those guards—"

"You don't see," he interrupts me. "There is already blood on my hands. I do not want to add any more."

"They are thieves and murderers," I say. "They had it coming."

"Maybe you are right," Midhun shakes his head. "But I want no part of it."

I sit there with my mouth open for a moment, not sure what to say. In the short time I've been around him, Midhun has grown on me. Something about his presence and his stupid quotes help ground me when the entire world around me is going crazy. Maybe it's just that I've already lost so many people recently, but I don't want to see him go. I don't care if he refuses to fight. Just because he isn't violent, doesn't mean he isn't brave. In a way, that strong sense of morality makes me like him even more. Good people are getting harder and harder to find.

"Stay for me then," I beg him. "I don't care if you won't fight. Help me keep Stevie safe. You can do that, right?"

Midhun sighs and tilts his head.

"I will," Midhun says. "I would be a coward if I did not."

"Good," I smile.

Midhun returns the smile before he turns his head to the unfamiliar faces across the lobby. The smile slips from his face and he lowers his gaze to stare at his fidgeting hands once again. I pry open the box of rations and glance at the labels. I spot a vegetarian lasagna and pull the package out of the box and hand it to Midhun. He squints his eyes to read the package in the dim light and then gives me a smile and heads to the dining area.

I carry the rest of the box over to a lounge where Val sits with her arm around Stevie while his dad digs through the contents of his Captain America backpack. The kid shivers in his wet clothes, his soaking wet hair clinging to his head. Steven pulls out a pair of plastic bags with a dry change of clothes for his son inside.

"Got some food," I tell them and set the box on the table.

"Looks delicious," Steven smirks. He sets the bags of clothes down and begins to peel the wet shirt off Stevie.

"Better than nothing," I shrug.

"I want a hamburger," Stevie says. "And fries."

"Sorry, kiddo," I tell him. "No hamburgers. How about some mac and cheese?"

The boy's eyes light up and he nods.

"My boys used to love mac and cheese, too," I say as I pull the brown package out of the box and tear it open. "They would ask for it for lunch every day. I'd get so sick of eating it with them, but I miss it a lot right now."

"That doesn't look like the good kind," Stevie frowns. His dad pulls the dry shirt over his head and Stevie pauses until his head comes out the top. "The good kind comes in blue boxes."

"This kind comes with chili," I tell him.

"Gross," Stevie grimaces. "I don't like chili."

"And candy," I say and hold up a bag of Skittles. "But only if you eat all the chili mac and cheese first. Deal?"

He nods and stands up and strips out of his jeans. He watches me as I take out a water bottle and begin to prepare the food.

"How's the ankle, Val?" I ask.

"Sore as hell," she says. "But I'll live."

"These people have a lot of supplies," I say. "Maybe they have some kind of cold pack to keep the swelling down."

"A couple aspirin would be great, too," she says.

"I'll see what I can do," I tell her. "You just eat something."

"I'm fine, too," Steven says. "Thanks for asking, Scout."

I glance up from the glass of lemonade I am making and roll my eyes.

"That's unfortunate," I tease him. "I had my hopes up."

"Ouch," Steven laughs.

"You should have learned by now not to mess with me when I'm tired."

"The day you stop giving me a hard time is when I'm really going to start worrying about you, Scout," Steven smirks.

"Pfft," I snort. "I've been going easy on you until now."

"If I didn't know better, I'd swear you guys were brother and sister," Val says.

Steven and I look at each other. I pretend to gag and hold in vomit. Steven makes a face like he smells something terrible.

"Please, Val," I pat her softly on the knee. "Don't ever, ever say that again."

"No, really," Val smiles. She stares at the wilted flowers in a vase on the coffee table without actually focusing on them. "Me and my older brother were the same way. He could be such a jerk to me sometimes. I guess I was too. I can't tell you how many times I told him I hated him. Now, I just miss him so much. Even if he was a dumbass most of the time."

Val lifts her gaze and blinks a few times. She swipes her fingertips across her cheeks, seemingly a bit embarrassed about bringing up the past. Most people don't want to hear about it. No one wants to remember what life used to be like just a few months ago.

"Sorry," Val says.

Steven reaches out and places a hand on her shoulder. I wish I could say something to Val to make her feel a little better, but words don't seem to matter anymore. The only way to avoid the pain is to distract yourself with something else.

"Get something to eat, Val," I tell her. "You too, Steven."

"Thanks, mom," Steven smirks.

I flip him off and grab a ration package for myself and head for the dining room.

CHAPTER TWENTY-FOUR

"It may not feel that bad now, but in a few hours, it will be more difficult to walk on it," Danielle explains. "You will have to try and stay off it as much as possible over the next few weeks, so it heals."

"Well, that's not happening," Lorento says. She sits down on top the table, listening to Danielle. "You got more of those painkillers?"

"You really shouldn't take more than necessary," Danielle says. "On a scale of one-to-ten—"

Lorento snatches Danielle by the wrist and clutches her tightly. The sudden movement startles Danielle and she tries to pull her arm free, but Lorento pulls her closer.

"Just give me the bottle," Lorento growls. "I am a big girl. I can take care of myself."

"What's going on here?" Blake asks. He steps into the dining room with Fletcher beside him. Blake shifts his gaze from Danielle's face to make eye contact with Lorento.

"Everything is fine," Danielle assures him. She tries to pull her arm free again and Lorento finally releases her hold on her. Danielle reaches into a duffel bag on the floor and pulls out an orange bottle with pills rattling around inside the container and hands it to Lorento.

"You got a lot of nerve," Fletcher tells her. "Putting a goddamn tracking device on me."

Lorento rolls her eyes. She twists off the white cap on the bottle and removes a pill and pops it in her mouth. I hand her the rest of the water bottle in my hand, and she takes a swig from the container and washes down the pills.

"What gives you the right—" Fletcher rushes toward Lorento.

"Easy," Blake says. He holds his hand out to stop Fletcher from getting in Lorento's face.

Fletcher shoves his hand away but keeps his distance from the agent.

"Why don't we just give her a chance to explain what she is doing up here?" Blake says.

Fletcher scoffs and retreats a few steps away. He collapses into a chair at the adjacent table and drops his cowboy hat on the white linen cover.

"I don't really know where to start," Lorento says. She twists the cap back on the water bottle in her hands and then loosens it again as she thinks.

"How about the beginning?" Blake says. "What happened after you left the bunker?"

"We stopped at Fort Leonard Wood to refuel," Lorento begins. "We made radio contact and got the okay to land. Only the base wasn't under military control anymore. We were ambushed shortly after we touched down. After a brief firefight, we tried to fall back and get the hell out of there, but the helicopter took some damage, and we went down in a nearby forest. Lost the whole crew."

"Ambushed by the same guys that we saw at the airfield today?" Blake asks.

"Bishop," Lorento clarifies.

"Who are they?" Blake asks.

"A bunch of assholes," I mutter.

Blake gives me a smile. At least someone appreciates my smart-ass remarks.

"We don't know much," Lorento says. "Seems like they are some local militia along with some rogue military elements. Maybe even a few religious fanatics. They are looking to take control of a large portion of the state of Missouri and re-establish some semblance of government in the region."

"So, what the hell does all this have to do with us?" Fletcher asks.

"There is still an operable V-22 Osprey at Fort Leonard Wood," Lorento explains.

"But you don't have a pilot," Fletcher smirks. "Supposing, just for a second, that I agree to go along with you; where is it you're planning on going?"

"Once we recover Dr. Schoenheim from Bishop, we would proceed to New Mexico as planned."

"Jesus," Fletcher shakes his head and rises from his chair. "Not this bullshit again." He scoops up his wet cowboy hat from the table and plops it back on his head.

"Chuck," Lorento says softly.

"Count me out," Fletcher says. "I ain't going back into the shit." He waves a hand as if he could swat the sound of her voice away as he stalks to the lobby and heads for the bar.

"I've never met such a baby in all my life," Lorento complains.

"Same old Chuck," Hoff chuckles and scoops a spoonful of pudding into his mouth.

"He is coming with us whether he likes it or not," Lorento says. "Keep an eye on him, Hoff."

"Don't worry. He isn't going anywhere," Blake says. He pulls out the chair Fletcher had been sitting in and settles beside Hoff.

"I don't have the same faith in him as you," Lorento says.

"If the rest of us agree to help, he'll come with us," Blake says.

Lorento focuses her eyes on Blake and studies him for a long moment.

"Chuck isn't so bad," Danielle says. "Just takes a while to warm up to him." Her hand casually removes the pill bottle from the table as she picks up the duffel bag and moves it to a nearby table. Her eyes scan the room to see if anyone noticed her, and she pauses when she makes eye contact with me. She gives me an innocent smile, then removes some more supplies from the bag and sets them on the table.

"Let me take a look at that cut, Scout," Danielle says.

"It's fine," I tell her. "I'm okay. Maybe you can check Val's ankle?"

"Right after this," she says as she rolls her eyes and gestures to the seat next to the table. I shrug off my wet pack and jacket and collapse reluctantly into the chair. She dabs a bit of alcohol on the cut that makes me growl in pain. My teeth grind together.

"Sorry," she apologizes. "Tilt your head back."

Danielle opens a bottle of water and flushes it over the wound. Her hand dips back into the duffel bag and she fishes out a spool and needle. She takes a small spray bottle from the bag and covers my eye with her hand as she sprays a cool mist onto my cheek.

"You're going to need a few stitches," Danielle tells me.

I gaze up at the ceiling and try to ignore the sensation of the needle piercing my skin. The spray must have been a local anesthetic like Lidocaine because there is only the dull pain and the strange feeling of my skin pulling away from my face.

"You're doing great, Scout," Danielle says. "Hopefully, this will keep it from getting infected and minimize any scarring."

"Would hate to ruin my chances at a modeling career," I joke. Danielle smiles but stays focused on threading the stitches as gently as she can. I try to keep still and make it as easy as possible for her even though it's still pretty uncomfortable. It takes a little effort, but I manage to block out the bitter ranting from Lorento in the background. This Fletcher guy really gets under her skin. In the short time I've been around her, she's been through hell, but this is the only time she has really been unable to control her emotions. As Danielle ties off the stitches, Lorento lets out a big sigh and tires of her rant.

"I have to admit, I'm a bit surprised to see the rest of you again." Lorento says. "Chuck has a lot of survival training, but to see all of you still alive is a little surprising. Even this stinky dog survived," Lorento says as she looks down at the dog on the floor beside her.

She holds out her hand to let Stitch sniff her, but the scruffy dog pulls away from her and lets out a little snarl. Lorento pulls her hand away and looks up to find Quentin shaking his head.

"Sorry," Lorento says. "I meant that as a compliment."

"We been getting by okay," Quentin smiles. "Better than you guys by the look of it."

"I guess it does seem that way," Lorento concedes. "What were you doing out here anyway?" Lorento asks.

"Heading west," Blake says.

"Why?" Lorento wonders.

Blake sits quietly for a long moment. He reaches a hand down and unzips his pack beside the chair and pulls out some kind of device.

"Is that a Geiger counter?" Lorento asks.

"Things on the other half of the country are probably worse than you realize," Blake explains. "Most of the nuclear power plants in the states are east of the Mississippi. Apparently, the majority of them are already becoming unstable."

"I thought those were all supposed to safely shut down in a crisis like this?" Hoff asks.

"Guess some people must have decided we didn't need to know how scary the truth was," Blake shrugs.

"Fucking government," Hoff grunts.

"How do you know all this?" Lorento asks Blake. I notice she doesn't seem particularly surprised by anything Blake has to say.

"We ran into someone," Blake begins. He pauses and glances at Danielle. She lowers her eyes and drops her gaze. She clasps a hand over her mouth as her lip begins to quiver.

"He had traveled too close to a plant that destabilized several weeks ago," Blake says. "By the time we saw him his symptoms were pretty severe. There wasn't anything we could do for him except to make sure he didn't come back. Since then, we carry one of these with us." He gestures toward the Geiger counter on the table with his forefinger.

"Damn," Hoff shakes his head. "I think I'd rather be eaten alive. At least it's over quick."

"It's not just that, though. There are chemicals pouring into the air in the cities. All those manufacturing plants that had all sorts of dangerous substances in tanks don't have power to control the temperature anymore. The tanks are heating up and venting into the atmosphere or blowing up."

"Oh my god," I gasp.

"Sounds like the end of the world," Hoff remarks.

"That's about what it looks like, too. The Chicago River flooded without any people around to control it. The entrance to that bunker is in the middle of a lake now. Most of Illinois is quickly becoming a wasteland," Blake shakes his head. "Seems like even the animals have been fleeing the region."

The thought occurs to me that the increased population of vultures in the area could be due to a migration from the affected areas.

"What about the corpses?" Lorento asks. "Is the radiation killing them, too?"

"Radiation seems to have no effect on the dead," Danielle chimes in. "Neither does the mix of toxic gases."

"Even if we manage to find a way to stop the dead, civilization may already be on the brink," Blake says. "Things are just going to continue to get harder once winter comes around. Odds are that most of the people who survived this long will still be dead before the end of the year."

Hoff holds the last spoon of pudding in an unsteady hand. He stares at it in front of his face, but instead of eating it he drops it back into the container on the table. For the next minute, no one has anything to say. The news is terrifying.

"We were headed to the Rockies," Blake finally says. "It might be our only chance to make it through the next few months alive."

"We didn't see anything like that in Missouri," I say. "We've been out there for weeks, and we haven't seen anything like that at all."

"That makes sense," Lorento says. "Missouri has long been considered one of the safest regions in the country. Lot of survivalists and doomsday cults have been living out there for years, which has probably helped Bishop to recruit so many people."

"How many?" Blake asks.

"Several hundred," I tell him. "Though, that might be a conservative estimate."

Danielle and Blake exchange glances. Blake wipes a hand over the dark stubble covering his jaw and considers how to respond.

"How does a group that large survive?" Blake asks.

"They use a huge underground industrial complex," I tell him. "It's built into the rock just outside of Springfield."

"Like a big cave?" Danielle asks.

"Sort of," I shrug.

"I don't mean to be Mister Negativity here," Blake says. "But how do you think a dozen people are going to stop a guy with that kind of resources from doing whatever he wants?"

A rumble of thunder vibrates the floorboards beneath our feet. I watch as ripples appear in the glass of water on the table in front of Lorento. Stitch lets out a whimper and circles around my chair. I stroke the top of his head to calm him down. Blake looks over at him and retrieves a piece of jerky from his pocket and tosses it on the floor for the dog. The dog settles on the ground and starts to gnaw on the meat.

"I don't think most of the people there want anything to do with Bishop," I say. "They're just afraid to go against him. Maybe they won't even fight us."

"People that are afraid are the worst kind of people," Blake says.

"I'm not saying we have to take them all on," Lorento says. "All that I'm asking you to do is to help me get the doctor back. I don't care how we go about doing it."

"Man, I don't know about this," Quentin says skeptically. "Sounds like a suicide mission to me."

"We all gotta die sometime," Hoff shrugs. "Sounds like it's going happen soon no matter what we do."

"I ain't in no damn rush," Quentin scoffs.

"You got some kind of big plans?" Hoff asks. "Something more important to do?"

"Shit," Quentin waves a dismissive hand.

"I'm not going to lie," Lorento says. "This isn't going to be easy. But I think we can do it if we work together."

"I don't know," Blake sighs. He sits back in his chair and folds his arms over his chest.

"That blonde woman with Bishop," I say. It takes me a moment to remember her name. "Dom. You know her, don't you?"

"Yeah. We have seen her before," Blake says. "In Chicago."

"She got a few of our people killed," Quentin adds. "Left the rest of us to die."

"Sounds like a bitch," I mumble. The thought occurs to me that some of my choices might have also gotten people killed, and I left friends behind as well. I wonder what that makes me now.

"I ain't disagreeing with you," Quentin says.

"I can't believe she is still alive," Danielle shakes her head. "I never thought we'd see her again."

"Bishop seems to have taken a real liking to her," I tell them.

"She'd go along with anything as long as she thinks it will keep her safe," Quentin says. "She don't give a damn about anyone but herself."

"So, are you guys going to help us or not?" Lorento asks.

Blake looks at Quentin who gives him a reluctant nod, then at Danielle. She bites her lip, then nods as well. Blake stares down at his hands as he twists a wedding band around his finger. Then he slowly nods his head and locks eyes with Lorento.

"I'll talk to Fletcher," Blake agrees. "We'll get him on board."

"Good," Lorento smiles.

"How soon will you be ready to go?" Blake asks Lorento. He eyes the bloody stains on the fabric of her camouflaged pants.

"I'm good to go," Lorento says. She gets up from the chair and stands gingerly. She forces a smile to hide any indication that she is feeling the pain.

"You should really take it easy for a few days," Danielle says.

"Really, I'll be fine." Lorento sighs. "Just as soon as you give me back that bottle of painkillers."

"What?" Danielle begins. She takes one look at the expression on Lorento's face and decides not to play dumb. Danielle unzips the duffel bag beside her and removes the bottle and hands it back to Lorento.

"We'll rest up here tonight," Blake says. "Find transport and hit the road at dawn. Maybe we can get the trucks back from the campground if enough of those things clear out by then."

Danielle and Quentin follow Blake out of the dining area and the trio makes their way to the bar to look for Fletcher. Stitch lingers by my chair a few moments longer, and then runs to catch up with the others.

Lorento collapses back down in the chair. She opens the bottle of painkillers and pops another pill in her mouth and takes a swig of water to wash it down. Even though she won't admit it, she must be in a ton of pain right now to be popping pills like that.

The storm continues to rage outside. Wind and rain batter the exterior of the building as the sky gets darker and more threatening with each passing minute. In the bar, Stitch begins to bark and growl at the blustery weather until Fletcher tells the dog to shut the hell up.

"I still don't trust them," Lorento tells Hoff.

"They seem nice," I interject.

"Your character assessments need a lot of work, Scout." Lorento folds her arms across her chest. She listens to the soft voices coming from the bar, trying to overhear their conversation through the sound of the rain.

"They helped save your life today," I remind her. "Maybe you forgot about that."

Lorento ignores the comment and spreads her arms, laces her fingers together behind her, and rests her head. She closes her eyes and lets out a deep breath. The painkillers must be kicking in. It almost appears she has fallen asleep, but I still have a hard time believing that she actually needs rest. She seems like nothing more than some government robot programmed with a mission.

"You should get some rest," Hoff tells me. "No offense, but you look like hell."

"Thanks," I laugh. "You sure do know how to make a girl feel special."

"I'm just saying," Hoff shrugs.

"Yeah, yeah," I sigh. I get up from the chair and scan the room for some place to lay down, but there aren't many options. "What I wouldn't give for a hot bath and a warm bed right now."

"Sorry," Hoff says. "Neither one of those are in the cards tonight."

Suddenly I notice a strange sensation in my ears. A change in air pressure causes them to pop. Stitch begins to bark and whine again in the other room. An uneasy feeling settles in my gut as I walk over to the window and stare at the rain trickling down the glass through the condensation. With my palm, I wipe away the moisture and watch the wind whipping around the branches of the trees outside. I gaze into the dark clouds to the west and notice a funnel cloud drifting up to the sky.

"Holy shit," I gasp.

"What is it?" Hoff asks.

"There's a tornado coming," I tell him.

CHAPTER TWENTY-FIVE

L orento's eyes snap open and she hops up out of the chair. Hoff hurries over to help her. She loops an arm around his big shoulders, and he moves her toward the kitchen.

"Stevie!" I yell in the direction of the lounge.

"Get to the kitchen!" Hoff yells.

I look over to see Midhun standing in the doorway of the kitchen and waving frantically for me to follow him. I ignore him and race toward the lobby. The clubhouse begins to tremble as the tornado nears the building. The windows rattle in their frames and debris crashes through the glass. The sound is like a freight train roaring right at me. I try to call Stevie again but can hardly hear my own voice. There isn't time to get back to the kitchen anymore. I stumble down to the floor and find cover behind the counter at the front of the dining room. I cover my head with my hands and bury my face in my knees. The raging winds seem to go on forever, but in reality, it couldn't have lasted for more than a couple minutes.

When I open my eyes and look up, I expect to see the building gone, but to my surprise there is a roof still over my head. My eyes quickly scan the room to survey the damage, although I am afraid of what I might find. Leaves, glass, and all sorts of debris cover the floor now. I glance back out at the lobby and notice the wall on the far side of the building near the lounge is gone and a golf cart is sitting amongst the wreckage in the lobby. My heart races when I see the devastation in the lounge where I last saw Stevie.

"Stevie!" I call out. I scramble to my feet and stumble over a pile of menus, some golf clubs, and a potted plant on my way to the lobby. From the opposite direction I hear Hoff calling my name. I glance into the bar and notice Blake and the others coming out from behind the counter. He picks up Stitch and carries him over all the debris strewn about the floor.

"Is everyone okay?" Blake asks.

"I need to find Stevie," I say. "Stevie!"

"Hang on," Blake says as he stumbles over broken glass and boards and toppled chairs. "I'll help you find him."

The damaged building groans. Rain pelts the roof and the wind howls through the open windows. I try to block out the noises and listen for sounds to help locate Stevie. I move carefully across the lobby, so I don't lose my footing. Falling would mean landing in a pile of jagged sticks and sharp glass. I notice an arm amongst the debris and the sight causes me to cover my mouth with my hand. My eyes search the surrounding area for the body that the arm belonged to, but I don't see anyone nearby. I step over the limb and move into what remains of the lounge.

The roof has partially caved in along one side of the room and rain pelts me as I sift through the wreckage looking for any signs of Steven or his son or Val. A pile of insulation covers the couch that they had been sitting on when I left the room. I grab the pink padding and toss it to the side only to find nothing but Stevie's wet clothes on the floor. I pick them up and clench them in my fists and look around. I stare outside at the junk in the grass that was left behind by the twister. Maybe it carried them off too. The thought makes me so weak the wet clothes slip out of my trembling hands.

Just as I am about to completely lose it, I hear Steven's voice.

"You okay, Scout?" he says.

For a moment it sounds like it is only inside my head. Then I hear it again. I turn my head and find Steven pulling open the door of the restroom. I climb over the furniture that is in my way to get to him, a smile creeping onto my face as I see Stevie peering out through the doorway.

We all managed to survive, for now. Everyone moves into the dining room to get away from the cold air swirling into the building through the lounge. Water drips down on us from leaks in the damaged roof. The unstable building could still collapse on us at any moment. Even though it is still early afternoon, the massive storm blankets the skies and fills the world with an eerie deep green light.

"We need to get out of here," Blake says. "This building isn't safe anymore."

"What? There isn't anything around for miles. Are we supposed to go wandering around in this storm?" Hoff raises his voice just short of yelling to be heard over the sound of the wind.

"I can't believe this shit," Fletcher complains as he shoves a toppled dining table out of the way with his foot. He pauses and whirls around and jabs a finger toward the service counter where Lorento stands beside Hoff. "We were doing just fine until she showed up. Then everything went to hell again."

"What is that supposed to mean?" Lorento scoffs. "You're blaming me for the weather now?"

"This isn't helping," I speak up.

Fletcher waves a hand dismissively in my direction. I lower my eyes and spot Stitch cowering under a table.

"She's right," Blake backs me up. "We need to stop arguing with each other and figure out a plan."

"A plan? Yeah, sure. I got a plan," Fletcher says. "We all get as far the hell away from that bitch as we can before she gets us all killed."

Stitch sniffs at the air and lets out a low growl. The hair on the back of his neck stands up.

"Quiet!" Quentin urges everyone. "Listen."

At first, I only hear the wind whistling through the clubhouse. Then I notice the moans outside. The dead must have made their way over from the airport. Maybe they could even hear our voices. Glass fragments fall to the floor as the dead push their way inside the building through the damaged windows of the bar. I spot several figures pushing their way through the wreckage of the lounge and grab on to Stevie and pull him close to me. I look around the dining area, but the dead are already approaching the windows along the back walls, emerging from the darkness to swarm the glass. We might already be trapped inside.

"Holy hell," Steven gasps.

"We need to find a way out of here," I whisper.

"This way," Midhun says.

I turn my head and spot him near the entrance to the kitchen. We hurry through the swinging doors and Midhun leads us between the stoves and counters to a long dark hallway with tile floors. He reaches a steel back door and pushes the handle, but the door doesn't budge. He tries again and throws his shoulder against the door without any luck. The moans of the dead grow louder as they surge forward through the dining room. I feel around the dark hallway and find the handle for the walk-in fridge. We could get in, but we'd never get back out. On the opposite wall I feel around, and the wall falls away from me. It must be another swinging door, but I have no idea where it leads.

"In here," I say.

We rush into a big room with a large banquet table. Along the wall is a long row of windows that face the road, but no exit. The others follow me through the doorway as the dead push into the hall. Val finally hobbles in the room, but the dead grab onto her before Blake can get the door closed. She lets out a scream as she clings to the doorframe to avoid being pulled into the horde. Blake reaches out a hand and grabs hold of her wrist momentarily, but the corpses pull her back into the hallway as she screams.

Blake pivots and fires several rounds into the dark hallway before he slams the door shut and presses his back against it to hold the dead off. Stitch barks angrily at the dead on the other side of the door until Blake tells him to shut up.

Quentin scoops up a wooden chair and swings it up over his head and flings it through the large glass window. He waves Hoff over before he places a foot on the window frame and hops outside. Hoff uses the muzzle of the rifle to clear away some broken glass from the bottom of the frame then scoops Lorento up in his arms and passes her to Quentin outside.

"Give me the kid," Hoff barks.

Even though I hear what he said, my arms stay wrapped around Stevie as he clings to me.

"Come on!" Hoff urges me. He pries the boy free of my grip and hands him to Quentin through the broken window.

Gunfire erupts behind me as the dead push into the room. Stitch stops barking and turns and sprints across the room and leaps through the window into the night.

I step on the window frame and hop outside, but when I land on the muddy ground, I lose my footing and end up on my back. Steven crashes to the ground beside me and helps pull me to my feet.

"Shit," Lorento gasps as she raises a pistol and begins firing.

More of the dead appear around the corner of the building. A flash of lightning briefly illuminates the hideous faces of the dark figures shambling toward us. Stevie wraps his little arms around my waist and buries his face in my belly. I scoop him up in my arms and clutch him close to my chest. He had always seemed so heavy when he would ask me to carry him before. Now, I barely notice him in my arms. For some reason, at that moment I worry that he has not been getting enough to eat.

"Come," Midhun urges me.

He walks beside me as we follow Stitch toward the road. I resist the urge to look back at the country club and instead I peer over Stevie's shoulder to make sure I don't lose my footing on the tricky terrain. Midhun spots a corpse in the road and raises the handgun and fires a round into the thing. He twists around and fires a second shot dropping another one to his left. For a pacifist, the guy seems pretty capable with a gun.

"Wait," I urge Midhun. "We have to wait for the others."

I turn back to look at the building and spot Steven scrabbling up the embankment on the side of the road. Fletcher, Blake, and the rest of their group move through the grass behind him. A gust of wind blows my hair across my eyes. I push it away as a flash of lightning strikes and I spot the large silhouette of Hoff helping Lorento. A crowd of corpses trails them. Thunder rumbles across the sky and Stevie squeezes my neck.

"It's okay," I assure him. "I got you."

"Keep moving," Blake urges me as he reaches the road.

The dead stagger towards the street, stumbling into the ditch as I take one last look toward the building before following the others down the road.

"Let me take him," Steven tells me. He reaches out to lift Stevie out of my arms but the boy clings to me even tighter.

"It's all right," I say, as much to Steven as to his son. But the truth is, I am so exhausted that I am not sure I can go on much longer. Thick drops of rain pelt my face and I lean into the force of the fierce winds that push me backwards. I struggle to keep up with the rest of the group as they walk down the road. Steven slows down his pace to stay beside me and keeps glancing back over his shoulder to keep an eye on the dead. We walk in silence through the rain until the wind finally calms and the dark skies begin to clear.

"Yesterday, I didn't think things could get any worse," Steven complains. "Boy, was I wrong about that."

"It can always get worse," I remind him.

He looks at the boy in my arms, then shifts his gaze to the road ahead of us.

"Anyone got a clue where we're going?" Steven asks. "It's going to be dark soon."

No one answers him. We just keep trudging forward to stay ahead of the dead. I can't help feeling like we're trying to play a game of solitaire without a full deck of cards. No matter how smart we are or how hard we try, we can't possibly win.

CHAPTER
TWENTY-SIX

E ven though we are exhausted, we manage to gain some ground on the dead. We round a curve, and the corpses disappear for the time being, but I know they are still back there. Stevie relaxes in my arms and rests his head on my shoulder. After the road winds past a cemetery, we spot the overpass that crosses the expressway in the distance.

"Maybe we can secure some transportation up ahead," Hoff says.

"Might be a little risky," Quentin says.

"You not feeling lucky?" Blake asks Quentin.

"Not after what we just went through," Quentin shrugs. "But still, it's worth a shot."

"I can't believe I'm doing this," Fletcher complains.

"Chuck," Danielle groans in agony. "Get over it already."

"Get over it?" Fletcher scoffs. "We just lost everything."

"Here we go again," Danielle rolls her eyes.

"I told you all this was bullshit a long time ago," Fletcher points a finger at Blake. "Nobody ever listens to a goddamn thing I say."

"Are you finished?" Lorento sneers.

"Oh, I'm finished," Fletcher throws his head back and laughs. "We're all fucking finished thanks to you, doll."

"Look," Stevie says. His head lifts off my shoulder. "Scout, look, a rainbow!"

I don't know why but I pause and turn around. We all do. In the distance there is a rainbow arching above the road behind us.

"We better keep moving," Blake says. I notice he is focused on Stevie.

Stevie twists in my arms to stare at it for a few moments as I continue walking.

"Mom used to say if you follow it to the end you'd find a big pot of gold," he smiles.

His words leave a huge knot in my throat, so I just force myself to smile.

"Can we go look for it?" he asks.

"Sorry, champ," Steven says. "Not today."

"Come on, dad," Stevie whines.

"They're just illusions, son. Like a mirage," Steven explains.

I glare at him, but the idiot is too busy staring at the sky to realize he is about to traumatize his child by ruining one of the few goddamn decent memories his kid has left to hang on to.

"See," Steven continues. "The sun reflects off the water and sort of tricks your mind into seeing something that isn't really there."

"They're not real?" Stevie asks.

"Of course, they're real," I say before Steven has a chance to open his stupid mouth again. "But some people made up stories about how they aren't real to trick stupid people out of finding the gold. One day when we aren't so busy, we'll follow it. Okay?"

Stevie smiles and nods his head. We continue down the road and I can feel Stevie's chin digging into my neck as he stares at the sky behind us.

"I probably should have kept my mouth shut," Steven says to me apologetically. "I thought I should—"

"Shut up," I interrupt him. "I know you can't help being an idiot."

Steven lowers his eyes and stares at the pavement as he walks.

"You mean well, though," I say. "That's all that really matters."

The dead have fallen back far enough that we are able to stop to rest for a few minutes when we reach the overpass. I set Stevie down to give my arms a break, but he clings to my leg. He refuses to let me go until Stitch comes over and starts to lick his face and playfully pounce around. As much as I want to keep watching them, I turn around to scan the expressway in the fading light.

"Which way?" Blake asks.

Hoff raises his rifle to scan the road through the scope. The dead wander along the highway in either direction. Although I spot twenty or thirty of them immediately, they are pretty spread out down there. Still, we can't afford to waste more ammunition than absolutely necessary. We don't have much left. Hoff turns around and scans the vehicles in the other direction.

"Let's check out that delivery truck over there," Hoff points his finger down the highway to a large brown truck in distance. "Hopefully, it has some fuel in the tank."

We move down the ramp toward the interstate. Stevie reluctantly agrees to walk so I can keep my hands free in case we run into any trouble. Stitch trots along beside Stevie, and I can't help but stare at his tail that never stops wagging.

"I'm sad about Val," Stevie sulks. He stares at his shoes as they move beneath him. Other than his dad, I'm the only person left that he even sort of knows. Val was the first person he really seemed to connect with, aside from me or Steven, and now she is gone.

"She was really nice," I tell him.

Several corpses close in on us as we step onto the highway. Steven moves away from the group to meet the closest one and swings the machete at the neck of the thing and sends it flopping to the ground. Fletcher pulls out a Bowie knife and meets a corpse as it approaches from the median.

"Look at me," I tell Stevie.

His eyes look up to meet my gaze. He doesn't see it when his father swings the machete into the dead flesh of another zombie. He hears it though. The boy flinches slightly at the sound of the blades striking the dead, and the moans they let out the moment before they go limp and collapse in the street. I know it isn't anything he hasn't already had to see, but he doesn't need to see it again and again and again.

"Sometimes no matter how hard you try, you still lose people you care about," I tell him. "That is how it has always been."

He starts to cry and buries his face in my jacket.

"I don't want to lose you," he whimpers.

I clutch him tightly and try to say something to reassure him, but I can't bring myself to go on with it anymore.

"Someone will always be here to make sure you're okay," I tell him. "I can promise you that."

I let go of Stevie as we start down the road again and his eyes fall on the bodies on the ground around us. He reaches up a hand and wraps his fingers around mine.

As we approach the truck, I notice the cardboard parcels spread on the ground nearby. Some of them look to have been hastily opened a long time ago. The contents are scattered around the road. Items that used to have value, like an alarm clock, a laptop, a high-end food processor are left on the ground like pieces of trash. The rear door of the delivery truck is wide open and there are several bullet holes on the side of the chassis. Hoff climbs behind the wheel and goes to work trying to get the rig started. The remaining corpses along the stretch of highway gradually converge on our position. While it will take the first of them a few minutes to close the distance, if we sit out here too long it's just a matter of time before we draw more of them than we can handle.

"Not sure I can get her going," Hoff informs us. He reaches into his pack and pulls out a flat-head screwdriver, then climbs back into the driver's side door.

"Hurry it up, man," Quentin urges Hoff.

"Son of a bitch," Hoff grunts from inside the truck.

"Can you fix it?" Lorento asks the soldier.

"I need more time," Hoff says.

Midhun moves around the front of the truck, lifts the hood and studies the engine. He leans over and begins tinkering with something inside.

The scruffy dog moves in front of me and Stevie and lets out a low growl. As the dead encircle the truck, I position myself in front of Stevie and raise the rifle.

"Stay behind me," I tell Stevie. "Don't move unless I say."

"They're getting close," Fletcher warns Hoff as he raises his rifle. He begins firing to take out the corpses as they get close enough that we can smell the rot.

"Forget it," Hoff says. "Battery is dead or something."

"Come on," Lorento barks. She raises her pistol and fires into the dead. "We're out of time."

"Turn the key," Midhun says.

No one seems to be paying any attention to him. Everyone is getting ready to run again.

"Turn the key! Turn the key!" Midhun repeats as he slams the hood of the truck.

Hoff turns around at the sound of the hood closing, and then climbs into the truck and hammers the screwdriver into the ignition again. A minute later, the truck engine turns over and growls and coughs. Hoff gives it some gas and the engine revs before the truck settles to a steady rumble. The scent of diesel exhaust fills the air.

"Fucking A, man!" Hoff cheers.

"Piece of pie," Midhun smiles and gives the soldier a thumbs up as he heads for the back door of the truck.

I grab Stevie and climb inside the vehicle. We crouch down beneath one of the shelves on the wall and Stevie huddles close to me. I can feel him shaking in fear. Stitch hops in the truck and leans his body on the other side of Stevie and pants.

"Hang in there, kiddo," I tell Stevie.

Lorento climbs in the front of the truck beside Hoff and fires at the oncoming dead from the steps on the passenger side of the truck. Fletcher takes up a defensive position just outside the rear door and opens fire on the corpses. He keeps firing until the rest of the group is aboard the vehicle.

"Everyone in?" Hoff asks as he slides the front door closed.

Fletcher stops firing, but he lingers just outside the rear door for a long moment.

"Get in the truck, Chuck," Danielle urges the pilot.

Fletcher grabs on the door frame and lifts a boot onto the rear bumper, pauses, and then turns his head and stares back down the road from beneath the brim of his cowboy hat. It almost looks like he is considering heading off alone on foot.

"Damn it," Lorento growls through the opening into the back of the truck.

He looks back inside the truck and his eyes lock with mine for a moment. Then he shifts his gaze toward the kid pressed up against my side.

"For the record, this is still a terrible fucking idea," Fletcher grumbles as he climbs to the back of the truck.

"You think everything is a terrible idea," Danielle snorts and rolls her eyes.

The vehicle pulls forward and we roll down the highway watching the dead that straggle down the road recede into the distance.

Fletcher clears his throat. When I glance over at him, he fixes his gaze on me.

"So how did you folks end up with Ol' Spooky out here anyway?" Fletcher asks.

"It's a long story," I say. The fact that they are curious about us doesn't surprise me, but after the last few days of hell I don't really feel like talking very much.

"We got a long way to go back to Missouri," he says. "Might as well get to know each other a bit.

CHAPTER TWENTY-SEVEN

"That's a hell of a story," Fletcher says after I finish telling him about the last several days.

"You ever hear anything from the people at the farmhouse?" Blake asks. He reaches a hand up and strokes the head of the shaggy dog beside him. Stitch leans into his leg and stops panting and licks his tongue around his mouth.

"No," I shake my head. "Bishop told us he tracked them down. Maybe that was how he found out that we were headed this way."

"Can you tell us anything else about this cave or whatever it is that Bishop is holed up in?" Quentin asks. "You've been inside there?"

"I haven't been inside," I admit. "I just followed one of their trucks back there. I was trying to get an idea of the size of their group to see how concerned we needed to be. It's a huge facility called Springfield Underground."

"I've heard of that place," College Boy says.

"You don't know shit, College Boy," Nat laughs. She nudges his ribs with an elbow.

"No really," he insists. "It used to be a mine, but they made manufacturing and storage facilities inside and rented the spaces out to lots of different companies. I read about how all these data centers were moving into facilities like that because they are more secure against virtually every kind of possible disaster. The whole place is like a hundred feet underground. If that's where they are, they're pretty damn smart."

"Sounds like a good place to ride out the apocalypse," Fletcher says.

"Probably got all kinds of useful shit down there, too," Quentin adds.

"What about access?" Blake asks me.

"It looked like they only use one entrance," I say. "The smaller one. It's pretty heavily guarded. I found another entrance near a large parking lot, but they moved some semi-truck trailers to barricade the loading bay doors."

"No way we're getting in there," Fletcher shakes his head.

"There might be a way," I say. "In between the two entrances I noticed this big hole in the ground surrounded by a barb wire fence."

"How big?" Blake asks.

"Maybe thirty feet across. It looked like it must go all the way down into the facility."

"Why would they leave that open?" Nat asks. "That seems stupid."

"Ventilation, maybe," Danielle says. "They might have no choice but to leave it open."

"They didn't seem to have anyone guarding it on the surface," I say.

"It could work," Blake says to Quentin.

"It's a stupid idea," Quentin says. "A real stupid idea."

Blake responds with a smirk.

"Shit," Quentin mutters.

"Say we get inside," Fletcher pauses and jerks a thumb in my direction. "She said there is a least a few hundred people inside there. Probably with a hell of a lot more firepower than us, too."

"A lot of them are just people that are scared," I say. "Families. Children. They probably hate Bishop just as much as we do. They won't fight."

"You don't know that," Fletcher says and shakes his head.

The truck swerves to the left and rumbles over the rough surface of the shoulder, kicking up pebbles that pepper the undercarriage. I grab onto the shelf over my head to keep myself from sliding around on the floor.

"When people are scared that makes them even more dangerous," Blake says. "We all know that by now."

"Still," Danielle says. "There's innocent people down there."

"No one is innocent," Quentin disagrees. "Those people are just as guilty because they aren't doing anything to put a stop to it."

"That's not true," Danielle insists. She crosses her arms and leans her head back against the wall of the truck.

"If Scout is right," Blake pauses to consider his next words, "and some of those people are just there out of fear, don't we need to find a way to stop him? Isn't that the right thing to do?"

"I've dealt with psychopaths like this Bishop guy before," Nat says. She pushes the wispy blonde bangs out of her eyes to look up at Fletcher. "You know what I went through in that pharmacy. I've been held against my will and treated like no human being should ever be treated. So, I'm fucking in."

"We might even run into Dom again," Quentin says. "Get a little payback."

"That part sounds pretty good to me," Danielle says.

"Am I the only one here with an ounce of goddamn sense?" Fletcher asks. He holds out his hands and looks around the faces in the back of the truck. "You got to be kidding me." He sighs and slumps back against the wall across from me and covers his face with his cowboy hat.

"Fucking nutjobs," Fletcher mutters to himself, just loud enough so that his words could be heard by the rest of us over the sounds of the truck.

Hoff steers the delivery truck off the highway and onto a back road. I rearrange Stevie so his head rests in my lap, and I watch him as he drifts off to sleep. The muscles of his jaw twitch and he grinds his teeth as he clutches the hem of my jacket with his small fist. I comb my fingers through his greasy hair and watch him until his face relaxes. My eyelids ease closed, too, as the rocking motion of the truck lulls me to sleep.

I dream immediately about being back at my house outside of Memphis. I can smell the azaleas that grow wild in the nearby nature preserve. It's a summer day and the boys are playing football in the backyard. The sound of their laughter and squeals that used to make me cringe seems so pleasant now. I close my eyes and listen as the sun warms my skin. Then I hear a scream. I open my eyes and there are corpses coming at me from every direction.

"Ow!" Stevie yells.

My eyes open and I look down and notice I'm practically pulling hair out of his head. I relax my grip and he pushes my hand away from him.

"I'm sorry," I tell him.

"That hurted," he whimpers.

"I didn't mean to," I tell him. "Go back to sleep, kiddo."

He lets out a long breath and closes his eyes and quickly falls back asleep. I look over and notice Steven is staring at me with a concerned expression on his face.

"Bad dream?" he asks.

I just nod my head. The sky outside is black now. I glance up at the lights in the ceiling of the truck and the other tired faces that surround me.

"How long was I out for?" I ask Steven.

"Maybe half an hour," Steven shrugs. He yawns into his fist and squirms around to find a more comfortable position on the floor, eventually set-tling with the side of his head leaning against the wall of the truck. "Sure, hope he finds a place to stop for the night soon. Can't take much more of this," Steven says as he closes his eyes.

I close my eyes again, too, but I can't bring myself to fall back asleep yet. I am afraid of what I will see if I do.

The squeal of the brakes as the truck slows tells me to open my eyes again. Hoff pulls the delivery truck off the road. We rumble to a stop in a gravel parking lot, kicking up a cloud of chalky dust in the night. The engine turns off and Hoff appears a moment later in the opening to the front of the truck.

"Where are we?" I ask him.

"Some church," he says. "If it's clear we'll rest up here for the night. We'll have to find some more fuel in the morning."

"I'll take Stitch and check the church out," Blake offers. He gets to his feet and pats the dog on the head. The dog hops out the rear door of the truck and looks around. Stitch leans back and stretches his front paw out as he turns his nose up and sniffs the air.

Quentin groans as he hauls himself up off the floor and follows Blake out the door as well. He checks the magazine of his rifle and then glances around the darkness.

"You good?" Blake asks.

Quentin nods.

"Be ready to haul ass just in case," Blake tells Hoff, and then the two men and the dog disappear into the night.

"Any idea where we're at?" I ask Hoff.

"Not really," he says. He pulls a crumpled bag of sunflower seeds out of his pocket, shakes the last few into his hand, and tosses it out the door. "Kind of hard to navigate in the dark without a map or anything."

"You did good, big guy," Fletcher says from beneath the brim of his hat.

Hoff grunts in acknowledgement and shoves the seeds into his mouth.

"Will you quit shooting the shit and give me a hand, Hoff?" Lorento calls from behind him.

The big soldier rolls his eyes and moves down the narrow aisle and out the back of the truck. A few seconds later, I hear the front passenger door of the truck open and Lorento starts swearing and complaining and ordering Hoff around.

"Deep down, I'm sure she's a real good person," Fletcher jokes.

Blake and Quentin appear at the rear door of the truck a few seconds later.

"Looks clear," Blake says. "Let's get inside." He holds out a hand and Danielle hangs on to it as she steps down off the truck. Even though it is just a minor show of consideration, I can't help but notice it.

Steven gets to his feet and bends down to lift Stevie off my lap, but I stop him before he wrecks his damn shoulder again.

"Your shoulder," I remind him. I swat his hands away before he can scoop the kid up.

"Let me," Midhun says. He looks up at Steven. "If that is okay?"

"Sure," Steven says. "Thanks."

Midhun gently slides his hands beneath the sleeping child and cradles him in his arms. He stares down at the young face and even rocks him a bit like a baby as he hums softly and exits the truck.

I wait until everyone else is out of the truck to move. Steven waits for me at the door and eyes me for a long moment as I gather the motivation to get up and head inside.

"You coming?" he finally asks.

I roll my head to the side and stare at him through the narrow slits of my eyelids.

"Eventually," I smile.

"I'll wait for you," he says. He swivels his head to check the surrounding area, then he leans himself against the rear door of the truck. Really, I just wanted a minute to myself. A few moments to stop worrying and just listen to the crickets and feel normal again. I guess that is just too much to ask, even now. A pack of yipping dogs start howling at the moon. The sound is fierce and wild and haunting all at once. What were once our companions are now feral and vicious creatures that will not hesitate to murder you in order to survive another day. The sad truth is, we're not really all that different from them.

"Better get inside," Steven reminds me.

"All right," I agree. "I'm coming."

I shoulder the rifle and my pack and hop down off the back of the truck. The old wooden church creaks and groans. I look up and down the stretch of desolate country road, even though there isn't much I can make out in the darkness. It's more of a ritual now than anything; always looking over your shoulder so nothing sneaks up on you when you least expect it.

I turn toward the building when I hear Steven's boots scraping across the gravel lot loud enough to wake the dead. Usually, it's the kind of careless thing that would drive me crazy. Now, I just realize how tired he is, and I can't blame him for walking around like a zombie. So, I bite my tongue and follow him inside.

CHAPTER TWENTY-EIGHT

When I open my eyes in the morning, I stare at the gentle beams of sunlight angling across the rows of pews in the old church. For several minutes, I don't move but just enjoy the quiet and the stillness. The moment lasts until my stomach starts to complain to be fed. I can't even remember when the last time I ate was.

Once I manage to slip my arm out from beneath Stevie's head and tuck my jacket there instead, I tiptoe over the creaky floorboards and step outside. I stretch my arms and smell the earthy scent of the wet air that only comes after a storm. But I also notice another scent. I look around and spot Fletcher leaning against the front of the church.

"Is that pot I smell?" I ask.

He lifts a joint to his lips and takes a puff.

"You going to call the cops?" he jokes.

Fletcher holds the joint out for me to take, but I shake my head. I only tried it once before, when I was in high school, and I didn't much care for the stuff. It made me paranoid, which is my usual state now anyway.

"It keeps me sharp," Fletcher says.

"You don't have to justify yourself to me," I tell him.

"I wasn't," he says. Fletcher brings the joint to his lips again and sucks down some more smoke. He exhales another thick plume and watches it drift away into the sky.

"You and Lorento seem to get along really well," I say.

"Ha!" He laughs sarcastically at my sarcasm. "I guess you can say we got a history."

"A history?" I say. "Like you used to date?"

"Fuck no!" he winces. "Not like that."

"I'm just messing with you," I laugh.

His entire body shudders out of disgust. He shakes his head and resumes smoking the joint.

"But you did sleep with her, though. Right?" I ask.

"Don't make me shoot you," Fletcher grins. "There is no worse way to start the day than having to shoot an unarmed woman."

"Fine," I say, raising my hands in surrender. "Tell me about this history then."

"You ever met this scientist she's after?" he says.

I shake my head.

"Figures," he says. "If you did you wouldn't be in no rush to try and save him."

"Why not?" I ask.

"He ain't right in the head," Fletcher twirls his fingers holding the joint in small circles around his ear. "One look at the guy and it was pretty obvious he was not anyone who could stop this whole goddamn nightmare, so I refused to fly."

"So, are you going to bail on us now?" I ask.

He turns his eyes away and stares at the cornfield across the road and thinks for a few moments.

"I know you just met Danielle and Quentin, but they're good people," he says. "Nat is tough as nails, and College Boy isn't as stupid as he seems. Hell, even Blake is okay, I guess. Sometimes."

"So, you don't want to leave them," I say.

"That's part of it," he says. "I guess I still want a little payback, too. I owe it to the guys that were on that helicopter, even if they were too stupid to listen to me."

Fletcher drops the joint on the ground and smashes it with his boot. He kicks it around in the dirt for a few seconds then stops and stares up at the sky.

"You okay?" I say.

"Sure," he says. "I'm fucking stoned right now, of course I'm okay."

"You hungry?" I ask him.

"What do you think?" he laughs.

"I think I'll find us some food," I say.

"Got a few MRE's in my pack there," he gestures at the rucksack leaning near the front door. "If you feel like cooking, we can split one."

"How generous of you," I say and turn to walk over and retrieve the meal. I dig inside the sack and pull out one that says chili on the package.

"Not that one," Fletcher says.

I exchange it for a different box that says maple pork sausage patty. I hold it up so he can see.

"Jackpot," Fletcher gives me a wink.

I grab a water bottle from his pack and sit down on the front steps. My fingers pry open the package and I start sifting through the contents and place the heating pad in the bag of water.

"You're a doll," Fletcher smiles. He moves closer and leans back against the railing along the stairs. "I wasn't so sure about you at first, but you're growing on me already."

"I get the coffee," I tell him. "Deal with it."

"I spoke too soon," Fletcher says.

"Nuts or crackers?" I ask.

"I'll take the crackers," he says. "You can grab the nuts, doll."

I look up and can't help but roll my eyes at the stupid smirk on his face. Just when I started to like him, he had to go and make an immature remark like that. I toss him the bag of crackers a little harder than necessary and the package hits him in the chest and falls to the ground.

"So much for keeping you sharp," I say.

The look of surprise slips away from his face and he scowls at me before he bends down and picks the crackers up from the steps.

"You might think I was being rude," he says. "But I was just being considerate."

"Really?" I scoff before I put a handful of nuts and raisins in my mouth.

"Sure," he says. He holds up the crackers and points at them. "This is just empty calories. Those nuts got some protein and other healthy shit. I was actually doing you a favor."

"Whatever," I laugh. Even though he is completely full of shit, I can't help but find him kind of charming in a fucked up way. I always did end up falling for the worst kind of guys. The ones where you know it will just result in heartache and misery, but you find yourself agreeing to go along with them regardless.

Fletcher shoves a cracker into his mouth, and I watch him chew as the crumbs dribble down his chin like some kind of savage. We eat in silence for a few minutes and just stare at the quiet world around us. Out here, you can almost feel normal for a little while, if you can forget the fact that there are billions of dead people hunting you down every minute of the damn day.

"So, what's your deal?" Fletcher asks. He takes a sip from the water bottle and hands it to me.

"My deal?" I ask.

"You know, like, what your life was like before all of this." He waves a hand around to indicate everything surrounding us. "You married?"

"Come on." I say. "Let's not start that whole thing."

"What thing?" he says.

"The digging up the past thing," I say. "Nothing good ever comes from that."

"Suit yourself," Fletcher grunts.

"I was married, though," I say. "To answer your question. Had a couple kids, too."

"Seriously?" Fletcher cocks his head.

I nod.

"You look a little too young for that."

"We did get started pretty young," I admit. "I got pregnant in high school and had to grow up kind of fast."

"Damn," Fletcher says. "That's rough."

"I don't know why I'm telling you all this," I sigh.

"We're just talking, Scout," Fletcher soothes. "What kind of name is Scout for a girl anyway? Your parents were hoping for a boy or something?"

"It's just a nickname," I say. "When I was eight, I tried to join the boy scouts."

"Boy scouts?" Fletcher laughs. "Why not join the girl scouts?"

"Because I already knew how to bake cookies," I snap. "Besides, my friends were in the boy scouts."

"How'd you like being a boy scout?" Fletcher asks.

"Never got to find out," I say. "They kicked me out."

"For being a girl," he says.

"Yep," I nod. "So, my dad got me a uniform anyway and took me out on the weekends for the next couple of years. God, I can't believe you got me telling you this stuff."

"Seems like you've been dying to talk to somebody," he says.

It is the truth. I've spent so long surrounded by people that don't know me, that try to fit me into some kind of mold that I haven't really been myself with anyone for a long time. The realization is painful, and I clutch my hands together and hold them in front of my face to keep Fletcher from seeing how close I am to crying. I can't understand why, of all the people that have crossed my path, I decided to tell the most immature person of all.

"It's all right," Fletcher says as he takes a seat beside me on the step. "Sometimes it's easier to talk to somebody that doesn't think they know you because they aren't expecting you to be the person you try to be."

I let my hands fall away from my face and try to decipher what Fletcher is trying to say.

"Did that even make any sense?" he chuckles. "I think I smoked too much."

"I think I get it," I tell him as I tuck my overgrown bangs back behind my ear.

"Good," he smiles.

"You're not such a bad guy when you aren't acting like a complete asshole," I say.

His hand touches my shoulder, his arm wrapping around my back. I feel my body tense up as he caresses my arm. Before I can react, he leans in and tries to put his lips to mine.

"What the hell are you doing?" I say as I push his chest and squirm against the railing of the stairs.

Fletcher withdraws his hands and leans back, a look of confusion on his face.

"Shit," he sighs. "I thought you were like giving me a signal."

"What signal?" I say.

"You did that thing with your hair," he explains. "Like you were getting it out of the way so I could—"

"No!" I shake my head. "That wasn't anything like that at all."

"Oh hell," he sighs. "I'm sorry." Fletcher gets up again and moves to the other side of the steps and leans against the railing again.

"Maybe you did smoke too much," I tell him.

"I just felt like we had some kind of connection going there," he says.

"We did," I admit. "But I wasn't ready for that. Jesus, I don't even know the first thing about you."

"Okay. I can see your point there," he says.

"You were just moving in a little too fast there, don't you think?"

"Maybe," he shrugs. "But time isn't really a luxury we can really afford anymore."

"I'm sorry," I tell him. "I'm not ready for anything like that. I might never be."

The church door swings open and Lorento emerges from the dim light. I take a step back away from Fletcher and lean against the handrail. Lorento looks curiously at the two of us on the steps.

"Everything okay here?" she asks me.

"We're fine," Fletcher assures her.

Lorento ignores him and waits for me to respond so I smile and give her a nod.

"How's your leg doing?" I ask her.

"I'm dealing with it," she says. "Thanks for your concern."

"So, what's the plan this morning?" Fletcher asks her.

Lorento eyes him warily, as though she suspects his sudden cooperation must be some kind of ploy.

"Well?" Fletcher prods her.

"Sorry," Lorento says. "I'm kind of surprised at the moment. When I woke up and saw you were not inside, I thought I was going to have to spend the entire morning searching the countryside for you again."

"Not the first time you've been wrong," Fletcher smirks.

"Let's not start this again," Lorento huffs, and folds her arms across her chest.

"Relax. I'm not going anywhere," Fletcher relents. "Have a little faith."

"Right," Lorento says. "Since you've been so reliable in the past."

Fletcher shakes his head and laughs to himself. Even if they still don't really get along, Fletcher is hardly as combative as he was yesterday. It's probably just the effect of the drugs.

"We're going to need to find some more fuel for the truck," I say to redirect the conversation. "I can take a look around."

"Okay," Lorento agrees. "But don't go alone. Bishop is probably miles away by now, but just in case."

"Right," I say.

"I'll come along," Fletcher tells her.

Lorento nods and twists around and hobbles back inside the church. The fact that she is even walking today is incredible. She is a tough woman, but I am pretty sure the painkillers have something to do with it.

"I just want to bring Stevie some breakfast before we go," I tell Fletcher. "It'll just take a minute."

"I'll grab a gas can from the truck and meet you inside," Fletcher says.

I climb the steps and follow Lorento inside. Halfway down the aisle of the chapel she pauses to rest against a pew and glances back to the door to make sure Fletcher is out of earshot. She squints her eyes at me as I get close to her.

"What is it?" I ask.

"I don't know or care what you two talked about out there," Lorento whispers.

"We were just—" I begin, but Lorento cuts me off.

"I said I don't care," Lorento says. "Whatever you're doing, keep doing it."

CHAPTER
TWENTY-NINE

When Stevie opens his eyes, he sees the maple muffin top in my hands and gives me a smile. I sit beside him while he devours the thing, showering himself and the floor in crumbs.

"Slow down there, kiddo," I tell him. "Make it last so you feel more full."

He gives me an annoyed look, but he slows down and chews his food. I give him some water to drink, and he chugs the rest of the bottle. I kind of wish I had taken a sip before I handed it to him since I don't have anything else in my pack to drink. I might have to check the toilets and fill a bottle before we leave, even though just the thought of drinking toilet water again makes me nauseous.

"Listen," I tell Stevie. "I'm going to go away for a little while today to see if I can find us some more food and gas for the truck."

"I don't want you to leave me," Stevie whines. "Can't somebody else do it?"

"It will just be for a little while," I say. "And I'll see if I can't find a special treat for you. How does that sound?"

His face brightens and he nods his head in agreement. He holds up a fist and I make one with my hand and bump his gently. He makes an exploding sound as he spreads his fingers. I rub his filthy hair and give him a hug.

"I love you, Scout," he whispers. "Don't get hurt."

I hold him tight, clutching my fingers into the nylon fabric on the back of his jacket. The sound of a little boy saying that to me again stirs up a visceral emotion I find hard to contain. I feel like I should say the words back to him, but for some reason I still can't bring myself to say them.

"Ouch! Too tight," Steven complains.

My grip relaxes and I release Stevie. I hadn't realized how intensely I was squeezing him.

"You okay?" I ask.

"That was a big hug," he laughs.

"You're a good kid," I say. Then I get the strange feeling that comes whenever Steven is hovering behind me, and I whisper to Stevie. "Keep an eye on your dad. Make sure he stays out of trouble for me, okay?"

Stevie nods his head and gives me a smile.

I leave him to finish his breakfast and turn around to find Steven rubbing his sore shoulder. From the look on his face, I can tell he's been listening to the whole conversation.

"You need me to come along?" Steven asks.

"I think you should probably stay with Stevie," I tell him. "It might be too scary without one of us around. He hasn't known anyone else here more than a couple of days."

"I could go, and you can stay," he offers.

"It's all right," I say. "You should probably take a break while you can. Rest up that shoulder. I don't think lugging supplies around will do you much good."

He stops rubbing at the muscles and starts to speak, but I cut him off.

"Don't worry," I say. "We'll be fine."

"Who is going with?" he asks.

"I am," Fletcher interjects.

Steven turns to find him lacing up his boot on the closest pew.

"Nat and College Boy volunteered to come along, too. In case we find more than we can carry."

"They ready to go?" I ask.

"Already outside," Fletcher says.

"Just give me a minute," I say. "I'm going to have to check the bathrooms for water."

Fletcher makes a disgusted face.

"I think I have enough to share with you," Fletcher says. He stands up and lifts his pack off the floor.

"Thanks," I say. "I'll meet you outside."

Fletcher dips his head down in acknowledgement then heads for the front of the church. I grab my pack off the floor as Steven watches me and scratches at the stubble on his chin.

"You be careful out there," Steven says.

"I'm always careful," I remind him.

"I know," he says. "I just worry."

"I'll be back soon," I tell Steven. "Don't worry."

I head for the front door but before I can get there Lorento calls my name. I pause in the aisle and wait for her to speak.

"Keep a close eye on him," Lorento warns me. "I mean it. Don't let him out of your sight for a minute."

I nod and make my way outside where Fletcher waits with Nat and College Boy. We make our way across the parking lot and out to the road. The warmth of the sun is already drying the moisture from the storms that passed through yesterday. Billowy clouds sail like massive ships on the wind currents of the bright blue sky. The long desolate country road stretches for miles ahead of us through enormous fields of crops and grains. There isn't a sign of life or the dead. We don't have the slightest idea how many miles we might have to walk before we reach another town.

Even though it has been a long few days, getting a decent amount of sleep last night really helped. For the first mile or so, we walk alongside each other in silence, and it seems like the others are as content as me to enjoy the quiet and calm of the day. Out of the corner of my eye, I notice Fletcher turning his head to look at me a few times.

"I hope we're not walking all day," Nat says.

"You didn't have to come," Fletcher tells her.

"I thought I was going to be getting away from Kyle for a while," she says.

"Hey," says College Boy.

"Your name is Kyle?" I ask him.

"Yeah," he nods. "Only these jerks insist on calling me College Boy."

"It's because he thinks he's so smart," Nat says.

"Shut up, Natalie," he says.

"You know where we found him?" she continues.

"Come on," he protests. "Don't."

"He was hiding in a dumpster," she laughs.

"That's not true," Kyle says to me. "I was not actually in the dumpster."

"Yes, it is," insists Natalie. "He stank like old broccoli for days."

"Okay," Kyle admits. "That part is a little true."

"Sometimes, I swear, I can still smell it." She sniffs near him to make her point.

"Knock it off," Kyle says and pushes her away.

Listening to the two of them, I can't help but laugh.

"Cut it out," Fletcher scolds them. "Pay attention. I don't feel like dying today."

The two of them calm down and resume walking in silence.

"Are you guys the same age?" I ask them.

"Pretty much," says Kyle.

"I'm older," says Natalie. "He is still a teenager."

"Barely." Kyle rolls his eyes.

I can't help but think of Kyle as some older version of one of my boys. It is probably just because they share a name, but I can't help remembering my son every time I look at him.

"What about you?" Natalie asks.

"Me?" I say. "I'm twenty-eight."

"Really?" says Fletcher.

"Maybe I'm twenty-nine now. I don't really know what the date is."

"I thought you were older," says Kyle.

"You don't say that to a woman, you dummy," Nat whispers as she jabs him with an elbow.

"It's okay," I smile. "I guess, I've already lived a lot."

"Haven't we all," Fletcher chimes in.

"That must have been hard," Kyle says.

"What?" I ask.

"You must have been younger than me when you had your son," he finishes.

"What?" I say, confused. I hadn't mentioned anything about having kids.

"Stevie," he says. "That's his name, right?"

"No," I shake my head. "He isn't mine."

"Oh shit," Kyle says. "I just thought—"

"You're such an idiot," Nat says to him. "The kid doesn't look anything like her."

"I just thought he took after his dad," Kyle says to her.

"Well, he does," I say.

"Did you have kids?" he asks.

For a long moment, I let the question hang in the air.

"Yes," I finally say. "I had two boys. They were a little older than Stevie."

"Damn," Kyle mutters.

There isn't much else to say other than that.

"You're lucky," says Nat.

Her words catch me by surprise. I twist my head around to look at her walking alongside the road.

"I'll probably never get to have kids now," she says.

"That's not true," Kyle says. "We'll need more kids."

"No," Nat says. "I'd never bring a kid into this world. Not anymore."

"This conversation is fucking depressing," Fletcher interjects.

I want to say something, but the doubt in my mind does not allow it. Maybe Natalie has a point. With everything going on maybe we should all think like she does. If a child grows up in a place like this, could he still even be truly human? Who knows what kind of effects this world might have already had on Stevie. Only time will tell.

The four of us walk along the road quietly once again. The only sound is the breeze rustling the overgrown grass and the birds calling out into the morning air. Finally, I spot a committee of vultures roosting on the telephone poles in the distance.

"There's a town up ahead," I say.

"You sure?" Fletcher asks.

I nod. A few minutes later the top of a water tower appears above a copse of trees on the horizon.

"Finally," Natalie rejoices.

"Keep your eyes peeled," Fletcher reminds us.

"Maybe we'll get lucky, and it'll be pretty empty," Kyle says.

"I doubt it," I say. "How much ammo do we have?"

"Enough," Fletcher says. "Probably."

"I hope you're right," I say.

"It'll have to be enough," Fletcher says. "We don't exactly have a lot of other options. We need to get whatever we can here."

On the edge of town, we come upon a couple of vehicles on the side of the road. There is a black van with bullet holes in the windshield. A yellow sports car is parked on the adjacent shoulder. The windows are smashed in, and dried blood is smeared all down the door panel. We pause about twenty yards down the road and survey the scene.

Fletcher slips off his pack, unlatches the top, and begins digging around inside. He pulls out a long section of plastic hose and tosses it to Kyle.

"I'll check the cars," I say.

"I better," Fletcher says.

"It's okay," I tell him. "I can handle myself."

Fletcher raises his hands in surrender and watches as I head for the vehicles. I take the knife out of my jacket and grip it tightly in my fist. I can hear the damn vultures grunting in the distance. At least I hope it was the damn vultures.

As I come up on the rear of the yellow car, I walk in a careful arc toward the middle of the road to give myself a better angle to peer into the open front door while still keeping my distance. Once I can see inside the car, I spot a pair of boots and pants covered in blood underneath the steering wheel. After circling a few more steps, I see a body slumped across the front seats. I inch closer to the car, watching for any sign of movement, but the body remains still. When I get to the door of the vehicle, I cover my nose from the smell. The head of the man in the car is completely gone. Gore and tissue are splattered all over the inside of the vehicle.

I let out the breath I'd been holding and lower the knife. The relief doesn't last more than a moment before I hear a sound from inside the van behind me. I pivot around and raise the knife. The front seats of the van look empty, but I scurry across the road and peer inside the window. Nothing.

With my body close to the side of the van, I move toward the rear of the vehicle as quickly as I can without making any noise. I peer around the back corner of the vehicle and find the rear doors are closed. Something paws at the walls inside. I know I should just leave whatever is in there alone, but I reach for the handle of the door anyway, driven by some kind of irrational curiosity.

My fingers pry the handle on the rear door until it unlatches and springs open. A half-eaten face of a woman appears in the door and claws in my direction as the thing drags its body forward and flops onto the road. Below the waist, the entire body of the thing is gone. It drags a mess of mangled cartilage and bones that leaves a streak of black sludge along the pavement behind it. I jump back and get clear of the reach of the pitiful creature. I watch it for a moment in horror before I lift my boot up high and drive it down on the skull of the thing as hard as I can. It moans after its head strikes the pavement but continues to struggle up again. With a curse, I stomp on the thing as hard as I can again, feeling the skull give way and shatter beneath my heel. The sound wrenches my stomach. I gag and bring my forearm up to cover my mouth but regain control of myself a moment later.

Fletcher rushes around the back of the van and skids to a halt when he spots the half-eaten corpse with the skull splattered all over the ground.

"You hurt?" he asks.

I shake my head and lower my arm away from my mouth as I step away from the body. My boot leaves a bloody footprint on the ground.

"Should have let me check it out," Fletcher says.

"I told you I could handle it," I say.

Fletcher gazes back down at the mess in the road.

"Goddamn," he says. "I seen a lot of shit, but this one is right up there at the top of the shit list."

"The inside of the van is a mess, too," I say.

He glances inside the truck.

"Not much of anything inside there anyway," he says. He heads around to the front door of the van and climbs behind the wheel and searches inside the vehicle. "Found some keys," he informs me.

"Not sure I want to ride around inside there," I sigh.

"Any luck, Kyle?" Fletcher asks.

Kyle shakes his head and pulls the hose out of the gas tank and coils it around again. Natalie picks up the empty gas cans off the ground and follows Kyle over to the van.

"Jesus," Kyle gasps when he comes upon the remnants of the woman on the ground.

Natalie peers around the side of the van and curls her lip in disgust. Her gaze turns toward me as she studies my face and the gore on my boot.

I turn away and walk into the grass embankment beside the road and begin to wipe my boot off in the grass. Even though I twist my ankle and wipe it in every direction it seems impossible to get it all off. I give up when I hear the ignition on the van sputtering. It whirs several times then catches and turns over. A cloud of exhaust billows out from the tailpipe.

"Let's go," Fletcher calls.

"I'm not getting in that mess," Kyle says. "Let's put the gas in the car."

"Sorry pal," Fletcher says. "This puppy is diesel."

"Come on," Natalie says as she climbs into the back of the van. "Put on your big boy pants and get in here."

I move up the embankment and open the passenger door, but just before I climb into the seat, I hear Kyle puking his guts out on the side of the road. Fletcher laughs and drapes an arm over the top of the steering wheel. He jerks his head to encourage me to get in the van.

I leave the door and go to the back of the vehicle and place an arm on Kyle's shoulder as he hunches over and coughs. Spittle trickles from his lips and he swipes it away with his forearm.

"I'm fine," he says as he stands upright again.

"Why don't you ride up front?" I offer.

He gives me a quick nod and blinks away the moisture in his eyes. I watch him climb into the seat and then I get into the back of the van and crouch down in the blood-soaked upholstery.

"You got to man up, College Boy," Fletcher says as he shifts the van into drive.

"Whatever, man," Kyle shakes his head. "My breakfast just didn't agree with me."

"Sure," Fletchers laughs. "Whatever you say, kid." He wheels the vehicle around in a circle and we continue our search for supplies.

CHAPTER THIRTY

We park the van in front of a deserted gas station at the edge of town. The roads seem remarkably clear, which concerns me. The roads are never this clear anywhere. There are always a few bodies shambling around wherever we go.

"What do you think?" Fletcher asks.

"Looks like we lucked out," Kyle says.

"I don't know," I say. "Something doesn't seem right about this place."

We get out of the van, and I look up and down the empty roads. I scan the sky above. To the left, I spot a trio of birds circling in the sky.

"We'll check inside," Kyle says. He jerks his head and Natalie follows him toward the front door of the convenience store.

As I lower my eyes again, I happen to notice the sign of the gas station and the price of the gas. It says twenty bucks a gallon. Most areas I have seen never had time to raise prices before the power grid went down. This station must have had some means of pumping the gas. Maybe we can get the pumps to work again. In this tiny town people must have been spared for days, maybe even weeks after the dead began to rise.

"What is it?" Fletcher asks me.

"Shh," I hiss. "You hear that?"

I listen to the low, steady moans far off in the distance.

"We're good," Fletcher assures me. "They must be a mile away." He turns and heads for the door of the gas station.

"Fletcher," I say.

He pauses and turns and cocks his head.

"Did you notice the sign?" I ask him and point my finger at the prices for gasoline.

"Shit," Fletcher says a grin creeping on to his face. He walks over to check the pump, lifts the nozzle, and checks the display as he squeezes the handle. "It's off now. Maybe they have some kind of generator hooked up around here."

I follow him inside and am surprised to find the store is still somewhat stocked. Fletcher makes his way behind the counter and flips various switches that control the pumps. He steps back and rubs at the scruff on his chin as he tries to figure out how to get the gas flowing again.

"This place still has everything," Kyle says as he picks up a case of water.

"The prices are a bit high, though," Natalie says. She picks up a candy bar off the shelf and examines it. "Ten bucks for a chocolate bar."

There is a small selection of products on the shelves. I pick up a can of pasta and meatballs with a price tag of fifty dollars. I load the assorted cans of beans, vegetables, and fruit into my pack.

"Any luck?" I ask Fletcher.

He tilts his head to peer at me from beneath the brim of his cowboy hat.

"Must be a generator out back or something," he says. He glances over at a door on the back wall of the store. "I'll go see what I can find."

After he leaves, we continue to load up as much as we can. I grab some shopping bags from behind the register and load them with pretzels, chips, cookies, and trail mix. Not the best diet, but it beats starving to death. There's more than enough to last us a few days, long enough to get back to Missouri.

I notice road maps for Iowa and Missouri down an aisle alongside some air fresheners, oil, and wiper fluid. I shove as much as I can into the bags and leave them in a pile near the door. As I head behind the counter to get more bags, the lights turn on inside the store. The refrigerators kick on and an old boombox on the wall begins to play an old cassette tape of Johnny Cash.

"Holy shit," Natalie says.

Fletcher emerges from the backroom of the store with a smile. He glances at the radio and hums along with the music for a moment. He dips his knees and reaches a hand toward me with a stupid smirk on his face.

"Want to dance, Scout?" he asks.

"Let's just get some gas and get out of here," I suggest.

He grabs me around the waist and pulls me close to him. He laces his fingers through mine and tries to get me to dance.

"Jesus," I say and push him away. "Quit screwing around."

"Hell, I didn't even get to start screwing around," Fletcher whines.

On my way out the door I snatch up a few bags of supplies and hurry to the van. I unload the supplies in the front of the van and retrieve the gas cans from the rear. The digits on the pump screen appear when I remove the nozzle. I can't help but smile at the sight. After I remove the cap from the first gas can, I start pumping the gas. I wish it was always this easy to scavenge for food and fuel.

The blissful moment passes when I spot the vultures in the sky again. There must be a dozen of them now. I watch them swooping downward and disappearing behind the treetops before returning back up to the sky. They must be trying to feed on something but are encountering some kind of opposition that is chasing them away. I fill the last canister and hand it to Fletcher to load it into the truck.

"We must be near the highway," Fletcher says.

"What makes you think that?" I ask.

"A lot of states required gas stations located with a few miles of the highway to have backup power in the event of a catastrophe. I'm guessing the interstate must be on the other side of town. Maybe that's where all the fucking corpses are coming from."

"We should check it out," I say.

"First we'll head back and get the rest of them," Fletcher suggests. He lugs the gas cans toward the truck and sets them on the floor in the back. He slams the door and notices I am still standing beside the gas pump, holding the nozzle in my hand.

"Let's move, Scout," he says.

I glance up at the vultures in the sky, swooping down and then quickly back up again.

"We need to check it out first," I tell him.

"Quit acting weird," he says and stalks over to me.

"I'm not," I insist. "I think someone might be alive over there."

"You think?" he scoffs. "Come on. Just get in the truck, doll." His hand closes around my arm and he pulls me, but I yank my arm away.

"I'm serious," I say. "We need to have a look."

"Jesus," he sighs. "We can't go running around just because you got a hunch there might be someone alive over there."

"It isn't a hunch," I say. "Those things aren't all gathered on the other side of town for no reason. They're after someone."

"That's not our problem," Fletcher says. "We need to get this shit back to the church, now."

"Fine," I say. "I'll go on my own."

"No," Fletcher shakes his head.

I brush past him and cross the parking lot toward the road.

"Scout," he calls. "Get the fuck back here!"

"Take the stuff back and I'll get back on my own later." I glance back over my shoulder to see him staring angrily at me. Natalie and Kyle watch me from inside the truck.

"What's she doing?" Kyle asks Fletcher.

"Losing her damn mind," Fletcher says.

I give him a smirk, but it leaves my face quickly after a painful reminder from the stitches in my cheek.

"I'll be fine," I assure them. "Don't worry."

"Like hell," mutters Fletcher. He stalks over toward me as he curses and mutters under his breath. "You win. Just get in the truck and we'll go check it out."

The painful smile returns to my face. I follow him to the truck, climb inside the back, and squat against the wall across from Natalie. She gives me a hint of a smile, as if to show appreciation for my ability to manipulate Fletcher. The expression is a kind of wordless gesture of mutual female understanding in our struggle of dealing with the stubborn ignorance of men. It's something we've all had to deal with before. I smile back and shake my head as I roll my eyes back into my head.

The van pulls out of the gas station and wheels around toward the center of town.

"I can't believe I agreed to this," Fletcher complains as he hangs a right turn.

I crane my neck to see the road through the front windshield as he drives. Shops and boutiques line the road, their storefront windows still displaying mannequins wearing winter garments. There is a fire truck parked out front of the abandoned station. Cars are parked neatly alongside the road. There isn't a sign of the chaos we've come to expect as the standard. It makes me anxious when everything looks so much like the world used to look, but entirely empty. I manage to get a glimpse of the sky and notice the birds off to the left.

"Turn here," I tell Fletcher. "Left."

He turns down the next street and brings the van to a stop in the middle of the road. We sit there for a few moments in the idling vehicle just staring at the sight before us. A couple blocks down the road there is a massive crowd of the dead blocking the street. At first, I can't figure out why, then I notice they all seem to be gathered around one of the ranch homes along the street. I raise my rifle, peer through the scope, and spot a figure on the rooftop. It appears to be a man. He is shirtless, his khakis covered in dried blood. There is another body lying on the black shingles beside him in a pool of blood. At first, I think he must be one of the living dead, but then he notices the van in the road and waves his arms to flag us down.

Fletcher throws the van in reverse.

"Wait," I yell.

"Forget it," Fletcher says. "There's too many of those fucking things."

"There is someone on the roof," I tell him. "He's alive."

Fletcher squints his eyes at the person on the roof.

I look at the corpses again. The dead don't seem to have noticed our vehicle sitting in the road. They push against each other trying to get closer to the man on the roof.

"I can draw them away," I tell Fletcher. "Once it's clear pull up alongside the house so he can jump off onto the van."

"Whoa, whoa, hang on," Fletcher says. He shifts the car in park and stares at the crowd of corpses in the road. "I'll do it."

"Not a chance," I say. I open the back door of the van and sling my rifle over my shoulder. "We came all the way up here to get you because you can fly and no one else can. No way I'm going to risk you going out there."

"I'll come with you," Natalie offers.

"You sure?" I ask.

Natalie nods and gives me a little smile.

"I'll swing around and come up the other side of road," I tell Fletcher and Kyle. "Once you guys pick him up, we'll meet you back around by the gas station." I hop out onto the ground and wait for Natalie.

"Don't get any closer to those things than you have to," Fletcher says.

"We can handle it," I say. "Just be ready."

"I was born ready, doll," Fletcher grins. "Stay safe."

CHAPTER
THIRTY-ONE

Natalie leads me along the houses on the next block over. I do my best to keep up with her, but the younger girl runs much faster than me. Halfway down the first block she checks behind her and slows down to let me catch up.

I gasp for breath.

"Am I going too fast?" she asks.

"No," I shake my head. "I'm just getting old I guess."

She jogs alongside me through the yards in front of the small homes. As the sound of the dead grows louder, we slow our pace. At the edge of each house, we pause and check around the corner before dashing to the next house. Beyond the grassy lawns between each house, I see a crowd of them on the next block. I spot the man on the roof, but he still seems too focused on the truck to notice us. He calls out for help and keeps the attention of the dead on him. They moan and reach for the man, crawling over each other to get to the house.

We keep moving to the end of the block and then we turn left. At the next corner we pause behind the house and check our rifles.

"You ready?" I ask Natalie.

She nods her head, and then I step out and cross the lawn toward the street. I raise the rifle and fire from hip into the massive crowd. Natalie sidesteps beside me, firing as well. Several of the corpses along the edge of the group fall to the pavement. It doesn't take long to get their full attention. The crowd of the dead begins to surge toward us. The sight of hundreds of them headed our way with their eyes fixed on us is enough to instantly fill me with regret. I don't know what the hell I was thinking. Pull yourself together, Scout.

My magazine runs out and I reach into my jacket pocket to retrieve another as I move across the road. I reload and resume firing, pulling the rifle up to my shoulder to aim more accurately as the dead move in. It's hard to resist the urge to run, but the massive horde still surrounds the house. We backpedal around the corner of the intersection and move down the street. Every few steps we pause to fire a few rounds and take out any corpse that gets ahead of the pack.

"I think we got their attention," I yell to Natalie.

She nods and fires off a couple more shots before turning to run up the road. We race up the block to put some distance between ourselves and the dead. Natalie pauses at the next intersection and slips her pack off.

"Cover me," she says.

"What are you doing?" I ask as I bring the rifle up to my shoulder.

She ignores the question and thrusts a hand in her pack. I pull the trigger and manage to clip the head of a corpse in a softball jersey and watch the thing fall to the ground. Natalie grunts as she tosses a metal object in the road. Smoke begins to spew out of the canister and quickly fills the street. We resume firing a few rounds until the smoke makes it too difficult to locate targets, then we cut down a side street and make our way back to the main road.

After we round the corner, I collapse against the brick wall of the building and take a look back down the street. A moment later, the first of the dead shuffles out of the smoke and into the intersection a block away. I hold my breath and hope that they continue moving forward. The man in a business suit that is in front of the pack glances down the street causing me to pull my face further behind the wall. Then he looks straight ahead again and continues up the next block. The rest of the crowd follows mindlessly behind him, filling the air with their moans.

"We lose them?" Natalie asks.

"I think so," I huff as I push myself away from the wall.

Even though we slipped away from the horde, the move will likely only buy us a few more precious minutes to reach the van and get out of town. Now that they are on the move it is just a matter of time before the group begins to break up and wander off in different directions in search of a victim. I try to keep up with Natalie as she runs down the road, though I am still gasping for breath. After a couple blocks, I begin to fall further and further behind. Finally, she notices and slows to a jog to let me catch up.

The van is parked in the road near the gas station again. For some reason, Kyle and Fletcher are both outside of the vehicle. The man from the roof is hunched over on the ground. Maybe the man is hurt, I think. I squint my eyes to try and see what is going on, but the unsteady motion of running and the bright sunlight glinting off the windows of the van makes it difficult at first.

"What are they doing?" I ask Natalie.

"I can't tell," she says.

"Something must be wrong," I gasp as I pick up the pace and hustle down the street.

My heart begins to pound as we approach the scene. I am sure the running has something to do with it, but mostly it was a sudden sense of fear. From a couple blocks away, I can make out Fletcher standing behind the man from the roof. The man is hunched over on his knees staring at the street and rocking back and forth. His long, brown hair hangs down and conceals his face. Fletcher holds the rifle at his shoulder, the barrel pointing at the back of the man's head. I resist the urge to call out and tell him to stop. The sound of my voice would only attract the dead.

Kyle turns his head toward us and holds up a hand to block the sun. He spots us hauling ass down the road and says something to Fletcher as he gestures in our direction. I raise my arms and wave them wildly and shake my head. I hope the gesture will delay whatever was about to happen. Fletcher lifts his head and looks in our direction before returning his attention to the man on the ground. With every step, I anticipate Fletcher pulling the trigger, but he just holds his position.

Finally, we reach the intersection near the gas station, and I slow to a walk as I approach the van. Fletcher peers up at me again and notices the pained and confused expression on my face as I pant and wipe the sweat from my face with my sleeve. The fabric rubs against the stitches in my cheek and causes me to cringe from the sting.

"What the hell is going on?" I hiss.

"This guy is fucking nuts," Fletcher growls back.

The man continues to stare at the ground and rock back and forth. Then I notice something disturbing. He is laughing hysterically. The faint sound suddenly grows louder, and the man begins shake his head, spittle trickling from his lips.

"Put that thing down," I tell Fletcher.

"No fucking way," Fletcher shakes his head. "He's dangerous. Just look at him. He's out of his mind."

"So what?" I say as I step over and put myself between Fletcher and the man. "You're just going to shoot him."

"Move, Scout," Fletcher says as he shifts the rifle a few inches to the side. "Kyle, tell her what you saw."

"There was another body up there on the roof," Kyle says. "It was all torn apart. It looked like he'd been eating it."

The sound of crazed laughter from the man on the ground behind me sends a shiver through my spine. Fletcher cocks an eyebrow at me and jerks the gun to the side again a couple times to urge me to move.

"What did he say?" I ask Kyle and Fletcher. Neither of them answer. "Did you even ask him?"

"Nothing," Fletcher says. "Just a bunch of gibberish."

"We really don't have time for this," Natalie reminds us.

"He is too far gone," Fletcher whispers.

"So, we just shoot him?" I laugh at the craziness of the words coming out of my mouth. The sound gets caught in my throat.

"You know I'm right, Scout," Fletcher says. "It's the right thing to do here."

"No," I shake my head.

"Then we leave him here," Fletcher says.

"No," I repeat. "Not a chance."

I turn around and put a hand on the man's shoulder and he jumps at the touch. His hand whips up and snatches my wrist. His eyes lock on me, his teeth bared like a feral dog. He hesitates for a moment as he studies my face. He slowly loosens his grip on me.

"It's okay," I tell him.

"We need to move," Natalie urges. "They're coming."

"Help me get him in the van," I ask Kyle. The kid comes over to help grab the man by the arms and lift him to his feet.

"This is a big mistake," Fletcher warns me. "That son of a bitch is going to try to kill somebody. You'll see."

"I'll make sure that doesn't happen," I tell him.

"Sure," Fletcher laughs. He slings the rifle back over his shoulder casually and picks up his pack off the ground. "Whatever you say, Scout."

Kyle and I help the man into the truck. He can barely stand on his own and his legs buckle as he moves. The sudden strength that he showed when he grabbed my hand a moment before seems completely gone. He collapses against the wall in the back of the van, seemingly indifferent to the gore all around him on the floor of the rear compartment. Natalie scoots herself up toward the front seats and keeps her eyes fixed on him.

I wait until Fletcher starts the truck, then climb into the back and close the door as I spot the first of the dead coming up the road behind us. The truck begins to accelerate, and I stare out the back window at the dead receding into the distance as we make our way out of town.

CHAPTER THIRTY-TWO

"What's your name?" I ask the man.

I shift my gaze toward the rear-view mirror where I can see Fletcher's eyes fixed on me instead of looking through the windshield. Instead of making a smart-ass comment, I stare back until he returns his gaze to the road.

"Do you have a name?" I repeat my question to the man, but he just stares at his bloody hands for a long moment. After I let out a sigh, the man slowly lifts his gaze to meet my eyes.

"Thom," he says in a raspy voice.

"Tom?" I say. "That's your name?"

"No," he shakes his head. "With an H."

"Thom?" I ask.

The man nods.

I wonder what the hell difference it makes. Whatever.

"This guy is freaking me out," Natalie says.

I turn to look at Natalie and notice Fletcher watching me in the rear-view mirror again. He doesn't seem to notice that he is driving on the wrong side of the road. Not that it really matters anymore.

"Can you tell me what happened on the roof?" I ask Thom. "How long were you trapped up there?"

The man stares at the dried blood coating his hands as though he doesn't hear a word, I'm saying to him. Finally, he lifts his gaze and locks his eyes on me. Chills run down my spine when I see the empty expression on his face.

"I had to do it," he growls through clenched teeth.

"Do what?" I ask. I'm afraid I already know the answer, but I ask him anyway.

"I had to survive," he laments. His hands come up suddenly and I flinch and slide my hand down toward the trigger of my rifle. The man clenches a fistful of his hair with each hand and pulls it as he howls in agony.

The van begins to slow, and I look toward the mirror to see Fletcher watching me closely. Maybe Fletcher was right, and this man is completely out of his mind. He might even be as dangerous as Fletcher believes.

I can't even begin to imagine what kind of horrors this guy might have gone through, but we've all seen our fair share of carnage. Everyone one of us has a breaking point. I wonder if one day I'll snap and end up in the same state as Thom. After I brush away the thought, I reach out to place my hand on his shoulder. He flinches at my touch and his eyes dart around the van frantically like he has forgotten how he ended up here.

"It's okay," I whisper. "You're safe now."

He looks at my extended hand as though it was a snake about to bite him. I retreat to the other side of the van, and he begins to calm down. Instead of pressing him to talk any more, I decide to give him some more time. Maybe his nerves will settle, and he will be more coherent later on.

We ride in silence until we reach the church and pull to a stop near the delivery truck in the lot outside. Lorento leans against the doorframe and watches as me and Natalie begin hauling gas cans out of the van.

"Get everyone ready to go," Fletcher directs Kyle as he makes his way toward the rear of the truck to help us with the gas.

The kid jogs across the lot and up the stairs toward the entrance. Lorento blocks his way, so he has to pause and talk with her on the way inside.

"Lorento's going to have a fit when she sees him," Fletcher mutters as he twists a nozzle cap onto the gas can.

"That's her problem," I say.

"I'm not taking the heat," Fletcher informs me. He twists off the fuel cap and begins to pour gas into the truck.

"Don't worry," I say. "I'll deal with her."

When I look back to the door, she is already hobbling toward us. She shakes her head as she mutters something to herself.

"What the hell is wrong with you?" she asks me. She brushes past me to walk to the back door of the van and has a look at the man inside. Her expression sours at the sight. She keeps her eyes on the man as she takes a couple of unsteady steps backwards.

"He was going to die if we didn't help him," I tell her.

"Are you out of your mind?" she seethes.

"That's what I said," Fletcher agrees. "She wouldn't listen to me."

I shoot him an accusing look. Thanks for having my back. Asshole.

"Look, Scout," Lorento sighs. "We don't need to be looking after some lunatic when we have plenty to worry about already."

"You don't know he's a lunatic," I say. "You didn't even try to talk with him."

"I don't have to talk to him," Lorento says. "It's a bloodbath in there."

"That's not from him," I say. "Well, not all of it."

Lorento waves a hand to silence me.

"Forget it," she says. She reaches her hand to her waist and grabs the handle of her gun. "I'll get rid of him."

"No," I growl. I raise the rifle and point it at her.

"Whoa," Fletcher says. "Easy everybody."

"She's not going to shoot me," Lorento smirks.

"I wouldn't bet on that," I tell her.

Lorento studies my face for a long moment, then slowly puts the gun back in the holster.

"Fine," she says. "You want to look after him, then that's on you. But if he gets out of hand, I won't hesitate to put a bullet in him."

I keep the gun steady and follow her as she limps past me and heads for the front of the delivery truck. Once she climbs in the passenger door, I lower the barrel and slide the strap over my shoulder again.

"You're lucky she didn't shoot you," Fletcher says. He removes the gas can from the tank and twists the nozzle off.

"She won't shoot me," I tell him. "She still needs me."

"Guess that's something else we have in common," Fletcher smirks. He tightens the nozzle on a full gas can and hoists it up to fill the tank some more. "Once that changes you might want to watch your back."

I shrug indifferently. Lorento talks a lot, but after a while it's hard to believe she's as tough as she thinks. Especially when she can barely walk. I'm not worried about her.

"I mean it," Fletcher warns. "Don't trust her."

The rest of the group begins to file out of the church. As soon as Stevie spots me he sprints for the truck with a big smile on his face. The dog runs along beside him, tongue dangling out of the side of its mouth. I bend down to scoop Stevie up as he jumps into my arms.

"Were you good while I was gone?" I ask him.

"I played ball with Stitch," he says.

"That sounds like fun," I say. It makes me so happy to see him finally smile again. Something about getting a dog seems to have made coping with this dismal world a lot easier for the kid.

The dog circles around my legs and pants. He pauses and cocks his head as he sniffs the air. Stitch lets out a whimper then follows the scent to the rear door of the van. Something causes him to emit a low growl, though I can't tell if it's the smell from the corpse that was inside, or the sight of the savage man sitting on the floor.

"It's okay, Stitch," I tell him.

The dog looks at me and back at the van, then retreats from the door with his tail tucked between his legs. Blake calls him over and the dog follows him into the back of the delivery truck. I notice the dog seems to be trembling and continues to eye the van from the inside of the truck. Something definitely has him spooked.

"Let's get moving," Hoff says. "We only got a few hours of daylight left."

I set Stevie back down on the ground and notice the shadow on the ground of his father hovering behind me as usual.

"Who's in there?" Steven asks.

"Some guy. He says his name is Thom," I tell him. "Found him surrounded on a roof. God knows how long he was stuck up there."

"He's a real headcase," Fletcher chimes in. He swaps the nozzle to a full can of gas and resumes filling the tank. "Had some half-eaten body up on the roof."

Steven cranes his neck around to look back at the van.

"That doesn't mean he did it," I say. "It was probably those things."

"Is that what he said?" Steven asks me.

"Not exactly," I say. "He's a little too rattled to talk at the moment."

Fletcher empties the last of the gasoline into the truck and bangs on the chassis to get Hoff's attention. The loud engine turns over and rumbles against the backdrop of the quiet afternoon.

"Let's go, Scout," Stevie says as he hops inside the back of the truck. As much as I want to keep him company, I know I should ride in the van and try to connect a little more with our new friend. At least, I hope he is a friend.

"Wish I could," I tell Stevie. "But I'm going to have to ride in the other truck."

The smile fades from his face and he turns away from the door.

"Don't worry," I call to him. "As soon as we stop for the night, I got that special treat for you."

"Okay," he sulks. He lets out a sigh as he sits down in the truck. Stitch presses up beside him and tries to lick his face. Stevie smiles and fends off the dog before he rests a hand on the dog's head and scratches the scruffy hair.

"Want me to ride with you?" Steven asks me. "In case he gives you any trouble."

"You should be with Stevie," I urge him. "Fletcher will be with me."

"Me too," Midhun adds. "Maybe I can try to talk with him."

I'm not really sure if more people will just make the man feel more anxious. It might not matter either way. On the other hand, Midhun might have the best chance at making some kind of connection with the man. He always seems to know what to say to help me feel better when this painful world becomes too much.

"That would be great," I tell Midhun.

We help Fletcher load the rest of the gas cans, and then we all squeeze into the reeking van again. I lose what little appetite I had as I squat down and rest my back against the wall. Thom has hardly moved and appears to have drifted off to sleep while sitting upright. The sound of the engine starting causes his eyelids to snap open and he scans the interior of the van with a look of panic on his face. Finally, his eyes settle on me, and after a long moment, he rests his head against the side of the van and closes his eyes again. As we turn onto the highway, he begins to mumble softly in his sleep. I try to listen, but I can't make out any words. It's hard to hear him over the sounds of the vehicle.

"Can you tell what he is saying?" I ask Midhun.

Midhun turns his head to the side and shifts his weight to lean closer to the man. Creases appear on his brow and his mouth goes slack.

"What?" I repeat.

"This man," Midhun shakes his head. "He is a very sick man."

"What did he say?" I ask.

"He says he ate someone… a woman," Midhun whispers. He shifts uncomfortably beside me while he keeps his eye on the man across from us.

The man ceases mumbling and snores lightly now. My hand rests on the rifle with my finger on the trigger. It would be easy to kill him now. Maybe it's even the right thing to do. But I can't bring myself to do it.

CHAPTER
THIRTY-THREE

After a couple of hours of driving, we come upon a gun store on the outskirts of a small town. We park a few hundred yards down the road and Hoff and Fletcher get out of the vehicles to recon the area. Through the windshield, I scan the surroundings. There is a vulture pecking at the bones of a corpse up the road. Several more of the dead wander around outside the storefront. Beyond the store, the road curves sharply to the left toward the center of the town. From this vantage point, it's hard to see just how many of those things could be further down the road.

"You think you can keep an eye on him?" I ask Midhun. "I'll see if those tough guys need any help."

Midhun nods and returns his attention to the sleeping man across from him. I pop open the back door of the van and jump down onto the street. I decide to leave it open so Midhun can see down the road and keep an eye out for any signs of trouble. Or just in case Thom gives him any issues and he needs to get out fast. I push those thoughts away and join Fletcher and

Hoff in the road beside the delivery truck. As I approach, Hoff hears my boots on the pavement and lowers the binoculars.

"Count half a dozen," he says.

"Nothing we can't handle," Fletcher says.

"Might be more around the corner," Hoff says.

"That's a big ass gun store for such a tiny town," Fletcher notes.

Hoff grunts in agreement.

"Looks like it's pretty much untouched, too," Fletcher adds. "Probably a lot of shit we can use in there. We should bring the truck."

"Too risky," Hoff says. "The noise could draw out more of them from town."

"Are we going or what?" I ask them.

The men both turn their heads and look at me. They lock eyes again and Fletcher smirks and shakes his head as he chuckles to himself.

"We'll come too."

I turn around to find Blake standing behind me with Quentin, Danielle, and Natalie. The thought occurs to me that maybe we should leave more people to protect the trucks. Maybe I should let the rest of them go without me. I glance back down the road toward town and watch as another vulture flaps into the sky from behind the store. As much as I would rather stay behind and make sure Stevie is safe, I get the feeling that they might need my help. I look back at the van and notice Midhun watching us through the windshield. He gives me a thumbs up and I wave my hand. Even though I still feel some apprehension about it, I turn and follow the rest of the group down the road.

We move slowly along the pavement, keeping our eyes on the grassy fields on each side of the road. As we near the half-eaten corpse in the road, the vulture lifts its bloody head from the carcass and hisses at us before it vomits on the ground.

"It's sick or something," Danielle says.

"No," I say. "It's fine. Just a defense mechanism."

"That shit is disgusting as hell," Quentin cringes. "Nasty ass bird."

The vulture spreads its wings, and it flaps angrily away, leaving the rotting body in the road. I try not to look when we walk by, but I just can't help it. The eyes have been eaten out of the skull. Scraps of flesh have been torn away from the torso, and the contents, organs, and muscle, have been dragged out onto the pavement beside the corpse. As disgusting as it is, the thing that really bothers me is the moving mouth that opens and closes. Hoff grimaces as he raises his rifle and brings the back of it down with a grunt on the skull of the corpse. The cranium gives way with a crack and chunks of brain and congealed blood squirt onto the highway. Hoff shakes off some gore clinging to the rifle resumes walking down the road.

"Shame College Boy wasn't here for that," Natalie says. "He'd be throwing up all over the place."

The guys all share a moment of quiet laughter. Danielle just rolls her eyes.

A few weeks ago, that would have probably caused me to puke my guts out on the side of the road, too. It is scary how most of us have become used to something like that now. It kind of makes me ashamed that it doesn't affect me more. Maybe being like Kyle isn't so awful. The truth is there might be something wrong with the rest of us for not having the same kind of reaction anymore.

The dead take notice of us as we approach the gun store. The first corpse, a huge guy in a pair of jeans and a red shirt leads several others in our direction. Quentin raises his rifle and takes the big guy out with a single shot. The clunk of the suppressed rifle shots spurs on the others in the crowd. With any luck, the noise won't attract any more of them from town. Quentin pauses and fires off another round. The head of a girl in a blood-soaked tank top snaps back and she collapses to the ground. From this range, I doubt I could do the same. At least, not on the first try.

"Lucky shot," Fletcher taunts him.

Quentin ignores the comment and stops walking again as he lines another one of the dead up in his sight. He pulls the trigger again and a guy wearing only swim trunks or boxer shorts plummets to the pavement.

"Damn," Hoff grins. "That's impressive."

"He's a regular killing machine," Blake adds.

"Fuck you, boss," Quentin says. He pauses again and fires off one shot, then shifts targets, fires again, and repeats once more.

When I look back down the road, none of the corpses are standing anymore. One of them lays face down on the road and feebly gropes at the ground.

"Ha!" Fletcher laughs. "Missed one."

"Damn it," Quentin snaps. "I didn't miss."

"It's still moving," Blake joins in.

"Whatever man," Quentin waves a dismissive hand. "I still hit the motherfucker."

"Take it easy boys," Danielle says. "Play nice." She turns her head to gaze in my direction and rolls her eyes.

I smile back and then I bring the barrel of my rifle up to my waist and keep it ready but pointed at the ground like I have learned to do from being around the soldiers. The building has surprisingly little damage considering the value of the weapons inside the store. There are a few cracks in one of the windows, but the iron bars seem to have deterred any looters.

We reach the front door and Fletcher tries to open it, but it is still locked. He lunges at it with his shoulder but only ends up hurting himself. Hoff moves him aside and lifts one of his big boots up and kicks out at the door. The wood splinters around the handle. He kicks a second time and the door swings open.

"I got it loose for him," Fletcher informs us.

Flies buzz around the interior of the store. The stench of rot hangs in the air. I follow Hoff inside, gripping the rifle tightly in my hands. Hoff takes a few cautious steps, then relaxes and scans the inventory of the store.

"We're good," he says. Hoff steps to the side and in the dim light I see a body in a chair at the back of the store. A shotgun sits on the floor beside it. The body has no head at all anymore. There is just a massive splatter of tissue and dried blood plastered to the wall behind it and a puddle of gore on the floor.

"Looks like somebody decided to check out," Fletcher says casually.

"Can't blame him," Quentin says.

"Gross," says Natalie. "He could of at least had the decency to go outside and do that." She swats her hand at a fly buzzing around her face.

"Enough sightseeing," Hoff says. "Let's hurry it up. We don't have much daylight left."

I force myself to look away from the gruesome scene and search the gun shop. As much as I have gotten the hang of shooting guns, I still don't know much about them at all. I don't know what kind of ammo goes with what guns. Not sure what to grab, I ask Hoff.

"You can check out the back room," Hoff says as he crouches down and retrieves several boxes of ammo from beneath the display counter. He sets the boxes down on the glass display case and points to the numbers on the box. "See if they have any five point five-six-millimeter rounds. Grab any forty-five- or nine-millimeter ammo you see, too."

"Got it," I say. "I think."

"Holler if you need me," he says.

I move past the remains in the chair, cringe as my boots stick in the mess on the floor, and brush aside a curtain that leads to a storage room. Dim light filters through a couple of small nicotine-stained windows high up on the wall. There's a mini fridge, and a desk with invoices heaped beside an ancient computer monitor, and a back door that hangs open a few inches. The afternoon sunlight blankets the exterior of the door and spills inside across the floor.

There are piles of boxes along the wall and on rickety metal shelves. I start to scan the labels on the boxes to find the right kind of ammunition. I find a case of 5.56-millimeter rounds with an eagle on the cardboard box, and I lug the heavy thing back up front and set it on the counter.

"Nice," Hoff grins. "Find any more?"

"Yeah," I say. "Just can't carry the rest."

"Hang on," he says as he stuffs a few more boxes into his pack. "I'll give you a hand."

Hoff leaves his pack and his rifle on the counter and snags a couple of duffel bags off a shelf near the door. I follow him back to the storage room again. He spots the boxes of ammo on the shelf and begins to load them into the first bag.

"We should be in pretty good shape again now," Hoff says as he zips up the first bag. He slides it to the side and begins filling up the next bag with more ammunition. He starts talking again, but I stop listening when I notice a slight change in the light near the door out of the corner of my eye.

When I turn my head, I spot the shape of a head silhouetted on the bottom of the door. At first it just seems strange to see something down there. But the shadow slowly rises up the door until I can make out the shapes of shoulders and arms. Then other shadows appear and blot out the sun on the door as the first one of the corpses crashes inside.

I bring up the rifle and start firing without even taking the time to aim. Bullets punch the wall and I hit the thing several times and it tumbles to the ground. I release the trigger and take a moment to aim then fire off a round that punches through the side of his skull. The second corpse stumbles inside and I reach into my pocket for a fresh mag and jerk my head to tell Hoff to get moving. For a moment he looks uncertain about leaving me, but without a rifle he isn't doing me any good anyway.

"Go on," I say as I slap a fresh mag in the rifle.

Hoff scoops up the heavy bags and bursts through the curtain as I open fire again. I hear some yelling from the front of the store, but I can't make out the words over the ringing in my ears from the rifle report. The dead continue to push through the door. Three, four, five, six of them, before I stop counting. My heart is racing in terror, but I try to measure my shots and aim each one carefully because I can't afford to change magazines again. When the rifle finally does click empty, I pivot and race through the curtain. There is no sign of anyone else in the front of the store, so I sprint for the entrance.

As I step outside, I see Hoff waving to me from the road while the others run ahead. Corpses come staggering around the side of the building. The first few spot me near the door and moan wildly as they stumble after me. The only thing I can do is run for it. I glance back over my shoulder as I reach the street and see dozens of them trudging along the road behind me. Thank God we didn't drive the trucks down here.

Since everyone else is hauling weapons and ammo from the store, it doesn't take me too long to catch up to them. Even though it was close, I can't help but smile that we all made it out alive, and maybe that wouldn't be the case if I hadn't come along. The moment doesn't last long, though. The smile fades from my face as we get close to the vehicles and spot a pair of lifeless bodies in the road.

CHAPTER THIRTY-FOUR

Kyle is face down in a pool of blood beside the delivery truck. Spurts of red fluid still dribble out the side of his neck. Further down the road, Midhun slumps against the rear tire of the van. His lifeless eyes are open and stare vacantly in my direction. Blood soaks the front of his shirt. As I approach the scene, there is no sign of anyone else. My heart races.

Danielle rushes over to Kyle and clamps her hand over the wound in his neck. She rolls him over and he coughs. Blood and spit gurgle out of his mouth.

"Hang on," Danielle urges him.

I move past them and spot Lorento and Steven on the easement behind the van. They have their guns drawn and pointed at someone beyond my line of sight. I move between the two vehicles to the other side of the road and see Thom holding Stevie with a knife to his throat. My knife. It must have fallen out of my pocket in the truck. Stevie whimpers softly. A trickle of blood trails down his slender neck.

"Stevie!" I yell.

Screaming probably isn't the smartest thing to do, but it is a pure visceral reaction to the sight. As soon as I open my mouth, Thom jerks his head in my direction.

Lorento capitalizes on the distraction and fires off two rounds that hit Thom in the face. His hand releases the knife, and he staggers back several feet and falls to the ground. Stevie charges toward me and sobs into my chest as I wrap my arms around him.

"You're okay," I assure him. I remember the mob of the dead pursuing us down the road. I pick the kid up and carry him over to the delivery truck and set him down. His fingers cling to my shirt when I let go of him. "I need you to get in the truck now, Stevie."

Gunfire erupts as Stevie scurries inside the truck. I hold my position by the door, unsure whether to get in the truck or go help the others hold off the dead.

"Stay here," I tell Stevie.

Steven helps Lorento as she hobbles up to the shoulder of the road toward the truck. He hands me back the knife I dropped. The one that cost two people their lives. I don't want to take it back from him, but I do.

"What's going on?" Steven asks me.

"They're coming," I say. "Hurry."

I step around the back of the truck and nearly bump into Blake as he rushes toward the vehicle. He pulls Danielle along with him. Her arms are covered in blood up to her elbows, and her knees as well.

"We can't do anything for him," Blake urges her as he drags her into the truck.

Danielle curses in rage but stumbles into the van.

"Give me a hand," Blake orders me as he runs back toward the street. I run along and scoop up the ammunition and weapons left in the road. I haul the supplies back and toss everything into the back of the truck. We run back out to the road to get the last of it. After I grab a few stray shotgun shells off the street and shove them in my pocket, I can't help but notice Midhun slumped against the van. The pistol feels heavy as I slide it out of the holster and walk toward the body. I raise the gun but hesitate to pull the trigger.

"What the hell are you doing?" Fletcher yells as he opens the front door of the van.

I reach a hand into Midhun's jacket and pull out the book tucked away inside. Then I take a step back and point the pistol at his head and fire.

The rest of the group begins to fall back to the vehicle as the dead close in. I climb into the truck and wrap my arms around Stevie as he sobs on the floor. Hoff starts the engine and the tires squeal as he wheels the truck around. The dead bang their fists on the side of the vehicle as we roll past them. One of them lunges for the open back door as we drive away and manages to grab on to the frame of the door. Blake grabs onto a shelf and lifts a boot up and kicks the thing in the face as it bites the air. Finally, it releases hold of the truck and skids to a stop on the asphalt.

Behind us, Fletcher speeds backwards down the road in the van. Once he puts more distance between the vehicle and the dead, he swerves sideways and spins the vehicle around. He shifts the van into drive and peels out leaving trails of rubber on the road.

I let out my breath and try to soothe Stevie some more.

"It's okay now," I tell him. "You're safe now."

Lorento pokes her head into the passageway from the front of the delivery truck. I try to avoid her gaze, but she just continues scowling until she knows I am aware that she is pissed.

I already know this whole mess is my fault. If we never helped that lunatic, then none of this would have ever happened. Now, because of me, two innocent people got killed. Stevie was nearly killed, too. I hear Danielle let out a sob as she wipes the blood off her hands. Blake wraps an arm around her and kisses her head.

"It's not your fault," he tells her. "Nothing you could have done about it."

I want to tell her it wasn't her fault as well. It was all my fault. Me and my stupid instinct to try and save everyone, even people that aren't worth saving.

"Fuck!" Quentin curses as he slams a hand against the wall of the truck. The loud noise reverberates through the metal and Stevie jumps in my arms.

I feel like I should say something. Maybe I should apologize to everyone and own up to the fact that two people are dead because of me.

"This is all my fault," I admit. "I should have never brought that guy back with us. I'm sorry."

"You couldn't have known that was going to happen," Blake says.

"Sure she did," Lorento scoffs. "I told her it was just a matter of time before something like this happened."

"Maybe," says Blake. "But we can't just turn our back on people either. She wasn't wrong to try to help him."

"Two people are dead," Lorento says. As if I needed a reminder. "We are lucky that asshole didn't manage to hurt anyone else."

"She's right," I say. "I fucked up."

"No," Blake shakes his head.

"It's true," I insist. "I should have known better than to put everyone in jeopardy. I won't let it happen again."

Lorento retreats to the front of the truck as we continue down the highway. The tires rolling over the pavement is the only sound for a long time. I hang on to Stevie, as much to console myself as anything else.

I can't believe I was so stupid.

I squeeze the little boy in my arms and realize how terrified I am that some harm will come to him. I know I need to be the kind of person that is strong enough to protect him; to kill for him, if necessary. Even when that guy was holding a knife to his throat, I hesitated. I could have shot the man myself. Should have. That isn't who I am, but that might be the kind of person I need to become.

"I won't ever let anyone do that again," I whisper to Stevie. "I promise."

The words are directed at myself more than the scared little boy that is crying too hard to listen. I got so distracted trying to help everyone that I nearly lost what matters most to me.

The truck rolls along as the sky turns a golden orange. The sun sinks into the horizon and night draws closer. We eventually reach a bridge and Hoff slows the truck down.

"There's a town up ahead," he says. "Jefferson City."

"Can't we go around?" Blake asks.

"Only so many places to cross the river," Hoff says.

"Let's get across," Lorento says. "Then find a place to stop for the night."

Hoff shifts the truck again and accelerates over the bridge. Once we reach the other side, Hoff takes a left down the first side street. It's really not ideal staying this close to a town, but we don't have a lot of other options.

Eventually Hoff pulls to a stop, and we get out of the truck in front of an old sandy brick colonial with two large white pillars on each side of the door and white railings all around porch. A hanging sign that reads

'Burkhead & Associates, LLC' squeaks over the door. Crickets chirp in the overgrown grass and a pack of wild dogs howl and yap somewhere nearby. In the air hangs the foul scent of the dead. I glance up and down the road but only spot a couple of them shuffling after us down the street. There must be more nearby.

I scoop Stevie up and follow Steven up the stairs to the front door. He checks the handle then pushes the door open and scans the inside of the offices. Steven cocks his head to the side and listens for any signs of the dead inside. I check back on the rest of the group as they make their way across the lawn. Quentin raises the rifle and fires a couple of suppressed rounds into the approaching corpses, and then the lifeless bodies collapse in the street.

"Let's go," Steven says and ushers me inside the dark building. The wooden floors creak under our boots as everyone files inside. Steven lingers on the porch a moment longer and checks the street once more before he closes and bolts the door.

CHAPTER THIRTY-FIVE

Inside the creaky old house that served as an office for accountants, we wait for the dead to come. Even though we slipped inside without drawing too much attention to ourselves, all it takes is one or two riled up stiffs to draw a whole crowd. Quentin watches the street from behind the blinds on the front window while the rest of us pick through the food we scavenged from the gas station. The only sound is the occasional crinkle of a wrapper or Steven chewing with his mouth open like an animal. For several minutes, no one talks. The world outside is so quiet, that even a casual conversation might be enough to draw attention to ourselves. Hoff helps Lorento over to a couch in the waiting area and sets her down. She grunts and curses from the pain and then settles with a long sigh of exasperation.

"I need to get cleaned up," Danielle finally says. Her hands and clothes are still covered in dried blood. She shrugs off her gear and then Blake escorts her down the hallway toward the rear of the house.

After everything that happened today, I don't have much of an appetite. I grab a can of alphabet pasta and meatballs for Stevie and watch him slowly spoon letters into his mouth. Stitch plops down beside the kid and licks his chops, watching each spoonful in case a noodle happens to fall.

Stevie is a resilient kid, but I can tell that today has not been easy on him either. Hell, he almost died. That can rattle anyone. It must be ten times more traumatic for a kid. I can only imagine what is going through his head right now. When Stevie gets down to the meatballs, he licks the spoon and stares sorrowfully into the can.

"You should try and finish it," I whisper.

"They taste bad," he says.

Even though he needs some protein, and the mom in me wants him fed, I let it go tonight. I don't have it in me right now. And the last thing we need is for him to start whining while we're trying to stay quiet. I take the can and force myself to finish the meatballs, so they don't go to waste. After I taste one, I can hardly blame the kid for eating around them. They're like dog food, which I can say because I have already had the lovely experience of eating dog food since the dead started walking.

I almost finish the can, but then I notice Stitch staring at me and I toss him the last meatball. The dog flinches when the food hits him in the face and falls to the floor. Stevie covers his mouth to stifle his laughter. Stitch sniffs the meat on the floor, then delicately picks it up in his mouth and eats it. He swallows the meatball, and his little tail starts to wag as he stares at me.

I grab a bottle of water from my bag and wash the taste out of my mouth before handing it to Stevie. He takes a sip, and then he tries to give it back to me.

"Finish it," I tell him. I might have been a pushover about dinner, but I know he needs to drink enough to avoid dehydration.

"What about my treat?" Stevie remembers.

I reach into the plastic bag beside me and pull out a bag of chocolate covered raisins. A smile appears on his face as I pry open the bag and hand it to him.

"I found some coffee in the kitchen," Blake announces from the doorway. "It's Starbucks."

"That's the best news I've heard all day," Fletcher grins as he rubs his hands together.

"What's with you white people and motherfucking Starbucks?" Quentin asks.

"Don't knock it until you try it," Blake says.

Quentin shakes his head. He turns around and peeks through the blinds to scan the dark street.

"Still pretty clear out there," Quentin reports. He removes his finger from between the blinds. "There's a few out on the street, but they don't seem to have any idea we're in here."

"We should keep someone watching the street anyway," Hoff says. He spits a sunflower seed shell between his lips. "Just in case. If more of those things start to show up during the night, I want us to have as much time to get out of here as possible."

"I got it," Fletcher says. He gathers his pack and rifle off the table and gives me a wink when he notices me watching him. "I'll check out the second floor. Might get a better vantage point up there."

I don't know if he expects me to follow him or what, but I just roll my eyes as he heads up the stairs.

"What's that all about?" Steven asks me. He cocks an eyebrow and curls his lower lip, clearly disgusted.

"Nothing," I shake my head. The grime on Stevie's face suddenly becomes too much to look at and I reach into my pack and look for a towel and a bottle of water.

"That wasn't nothing," Steven says.

I ignore him and continue to dig in my pack.

"You got a thing going with him or something?" Steven asks.

I toss the rag on the floor with a little more force than necessary.

"So, what if I did?" I say. "What does it matter?"

"It doesn't," Steven stammers. My standoffish demeanor seems to have softened his tone. "Just want to look out for you, that's all."

"I can look after myself," I remind him. The irritation causes my voice to rise and Lorento promptly shushes me from across the room. My emotions got the better of me for a moment. Steven has some nerve. Hell, I'm the one

taking care of his kid. Asshole. I pick up the rag again and pour a trickle of

water to soak it and begin to wipe the grime off Stevie's face. The stubborn

dirt seems to cling to his skin, so I rub harder until he winces.

"Sorry, kiddo," I whisper to him.

"Are you mad at me?" Stevie asks. His tired eyes stare back at me.

"Of course not," I assure him. I wrap my arms around his head in a hug

him and kiss the greasy hair on his head. "It's just been a bad day, that's all."

"You can say that again," Steven sighs.

"Why don't you get some sleep now?" I encourage Stevie.

"Can you do a story first?" Stevie asks.

"Not tonight, kiddo," I say.

"Please?" he pleads.

"Bed," I tell him. I tilt my head and press my lips together to let him know

I mean it this time.

His shoulders droop and he lets out a frustrated sigh. I know I should

make him sleep now. There's no telling how long we'll be able to stay in

this building. When I see the disappointment on his face I cave.

"Fine," I whisper. "Just a quick one, and then you go right to sleep."

He grins and nods his head. He takes another sip of water and relin-

quishes his hold on the bottle to let me screw the cap back on. I set the

bottle beside him as he rests his head on his backpack full of clothes. I shrug

off my jacket and cover him with it.

I begin to recite the story about the Sneetches. It's one of the stories I had read my kids over and over so I will never forget it. Before I get to the part where the Sneetches realize they are all the same, Stevie closes his eyes. I abandon the story and watch him drifting off to sleep for several minutes.

When I look over at his father, his head is tilted back against the wall and his mouth hangs open. He snores slightly. The unease I still feel over the losses we suffered makes me feel that sleep isn't likely to happen just yet. I gather up my stuff and stand up to leave the room. The noises I make wake Steven again and he opens his eyes.

"Where are you going?" Steven mumbles.

"Upstairs," I tell him. The wounded look on his face begs me not to go. "I'm just not tired."

"Look, Scout," he whispers. He takes his baseball cap off and pretends to inspect it. "I'm not trying to tell you what to do."

"Then stop it," I cut him off. "Jesus Christ, Steven. Just go back to sleep."

"Whatever," he grumbles. He puts the hat back over his face and rests his head against the wall again.

I know he just cares about me, but I can't stand him trying to control my every move. It's the same damn thing that made me feel like I'd stopped loving my husband. I got so tired of feeling like something that only existed to satisfy the expectations of a man who never bothered to care about what I wanted or how I felt. So even though I know that nothing is going to happen upstairs, and I didn't really have any desire to be near Fletcher at that particular moment, I am damn sure going up there anyway.

"Well, well, well," Fletcher grins when he spots me at the top of the stairs. I follow the sound of his voice to a darkened office along the front side of the building. He sits in a leather chair with his feet propped up on a metal file cabinet beside the window.

"No coffee?" he asks as he watches me step through the doorway.

"I'm not your secretary," I remind him.

"Something about a feisty gal that always gets me going," he says.

"Calm down," I tell him. "I'm not here for that."

The smile fades from his face and he shifts his gaze back to the corpses in the street.

"You just want to talk or something?" he asks. He cups a hand over his mouth and lets out a long yawn.

It suddenly feels like coming up here at all was a mistake.

"Just thought you might want some company," I smile.

"Company?" he smirks and cocks an eyebrow.

"God, not like that," I roll my eyes.

"Can't blame a guy for trying," he mutters as he turns back toward the window.

I take out the book of quotations from my pocket and stare at the dried blood on the cover. I flip it open and start to scan the pages for the quote that Midhun said. Something about how tyrants always fall. I see a different quote that makes me stop turning the pages.

"Where there is love, there is life."

"What?" Fletcher mumbles. I look up and realize I must have read it aloud. Fletcher rubs his eyes and then looks outside again.

"Shit," Fletcher gasps.

He jerks upright in the chair and cranes his neck to see out the window. I lean over to get a better angle and see the crowd of dead at the end of the block. There is at least a couple dozen of them so far, but it's impossible to tell how many more might be trailing along further down the street that we can't see through the treetops.

"We need to get out of here," I panic.

"Wait," Fletcher grabs my arm. "They don't know we're in here. If we just keep cool, they should pass right on by us."

"I need to warn the rest of them downstairs," I say.

"No need for that," Fletcher says. "Listen. They'll hear them soon enough."

The moaning of the dead grows louder and louder as they filter down the street. The sparse group out front is followed by a much larger horde of hundreds and hundreds of corpses shambling down the road. Their bodies fill the street and spill out onto the front lawns along both sides of the roads.

I step back from the window even though I doubt any of them would notice me from the street. The sight of so many of them is still terrifying. Suddenly, I can't help but feel trapped inside this building. My elbow bumps into a lamp on the desk as I move away from the window, and it topples over and crashes on the floor. Fletcher whirls around and stares at me then returns his focus on the street.

"Did they hear?" I ask.

"We're still okay," Fletcher whispers. "Just stay calm."

I settle myself into an armchair on the opposite side of the desk and try not to hear the dead outside. I slump in the chair and rest my head on the thin cushion. As Fletcher stares down at the street and eyes the crowd below, I stare up at the ceiling. The noise goes on and on for what seems like hours until it seems like it will never end. I will just have to get used to it.

Get comfortable being uncomfortable, I remind myself.

Eventually, my eyelids get heavy, and I finally drift off to sleep.

CHAPTER THIRTY-SIX

Before the sun rises, we make our way back out to the vehicles and silently pile inside. It's been a couple of hours since the horde of the dead passed through, but more likely than not, they are still in the area. A few of the things still linger along the street and stare vacantly at the empty houses.

We drive for a couple of sleepy hours along country roads as the dawn breaks, and then Hoff turns down the long driveway to the farmhouse where we left Fawn with the soldiers a few days earlier. My heart sinks when the vehicles pull to a stop. I step out of the truck next to the spot where we buried James, but now there is just a hole in the ground. A pack of feral dogs fight over pieces of the remains a few yards away. The sight of us getting out of the vehicles scares most of them off into the woods, but a German Shepherd with half an arm in its mouth lingers and watches us.

"Sons a bitches," I growl. I raise the rifle and fire off a round at the dog that misses. The noise sends the dog dashing for the bushes. Firing the rifle was probably a mistake. If there are any corpses in the area it won't be long before they descend on our location.

Stitch growls and bolts out of the truck. He takes off after the German Shepherd, even though the other dog must be twice his size.

"Stitch!" Danielle calls after him. "No, Stitch!"

The dog ignores the shouted commands and continues his pursuit of the pack.

"Stupid dog," Blake complains as he grabs his rifle. Danielle and Natalie follow him out as he chases after the dog.

I turn around and discover the farmhouse is gone. A pile of ashes, blackened boards, and the remnants of the stone fireplace are all that is left. Beside the house, a body hangs from the tall oak tree. The arms and legs flail aimlessly, the random and pointless movements of the dead. While I knew it was unlikely that we would arrive and find the others were alive and well, and Piper was on the mend, I never imagined we'd come back to find something this awful.

"Fucking hell," Hoff says as he gets out of the truck.

"What the hell happened here?" Quentin asks. His eyes scan the farmhouse and then fix on the figure dangling from the tree branch.

"Somebody had a fucking barbeque," Fletcher says.

"Bishop," I say. "It had to be."

"This is a waste of time," Lorento decides. "Let's keep moving." She climbs back into the front of the truck and slams the door.

"Some of them might still be alive," Steven says. "Maybe they took off into the woods or something."

I notice Stevie poking his head out of the truck and looking around.

"Get back in the truck, Stevie," I tell him.

"Where is Stitch?" Stevie asks. His eyes search the area, and then pause on the figure below the tree branches.

"They'll find him," Steven says. He herds the boy back inside the truck and climbs in behind him.

"I hate to admit it, but Lorento is right this time," Fletcher says. "We should go. That gunshot is going to bring every walking stiff in the area."

"I just need a couple minutes," Hoff says. "Keep the trucks running just in case."

We leave Fletcher and Quentin guarding the trucks and I follow Hoff as he walks across the lawn and approaches the tree beside the house. He pauses when we get close enough to see the camouflaged clothing.

"It's Morris," Hoff whispers. "Fuck."

Even though the soldier is dead, it isn't difficult to see that he had been severely beaten before he was killed. Most of his teeth have been knocked out. His nose is fractured with bone fragments poking through the skin. It looks like they even sliced off one of his ears.

Hoff removes the pistol from his holster and fires a round into the forehead of the corpse and then the limbs of the soldier go limp. He adjusts his aim and fires again at the rope and then the body crashes to the ground.

Hoff stares at the dead soldier for a moment before he turns and begins to walk through the rubble of the house, scanning the ground for something. More bodies, I guess.

"I'm sorry," I say to Hoff. I don't know what else to say to him. Words don't seem to matter.

The soldier grunts and stares at the ground.

"Lot of guys in the military liked to talk about the shit hitting the fan," Hoff says. "They figured they were the best soldiers, so they'd survive the longest. You know, last man standing. All that tough guy bullshit."

Hoff laughs to himself as he steps through the ashes.

"The truth is, the best soldiers are the ones that die first," Hoff explains. "They make that sacrifice, so that the rest of us can live." The soldier stops walking and squints down at something on the ground.

A bony hand jerks up out of the ashes and seizes hold of Hoff's boot. The corpse in the rubble tries to sit up and dislodge itself as it reaches for Hoff. The entire body of the thing is burned to a crisp, but it still struggles to take a bite out of the big soldier. Hoff jerks his boot free and staggers backward. He stumbles over a loose board and falls hard on the ground with a grunt.

I bring the rifle up and nearly fire off a shot, but I worry that I might miss and hit Hoff. The corpse hauls itself out of the rubble and lunges at Hoff again as he scoots away from it on his back. I stomp a boot down on the back of the corpse to pin it to the ground. The butt of my rifle slams down on the back of the thing's skull with a sharp crack as it hisses. The force is enough to crack the back of the cranium open and the writhing body immediately goes limp.

Hoff gets to his feet, his camo fatigues coated in soot. He swipes away the dirt and coughs out the residue in his mouth. His eyes fix on the body on the ground. The remains are unrecognizable now. There is no way we can tell who it was. It could have been one of Bishop's guys, or it could be one of our friends.

I scan around the rest of the rubble for a moment and realize how futile it is to continue searching. There is no way anyone could have survived the fire and the collapse of the building. The only thing we might find is more indistinguishable bodies.

"This is pointless," Hoff coughs. He tries to find a clean bit of fabric on his sleeve to wipe the chalky dust off his face but eventually gives up.

I slip my arm out of a strap of my pack and slide the bag around my other shoulder. After undoing the zipper, I retrieve the old towel and a water bottle and soak the rag for Hoff and hand it to him. I gaze off at the tree line in the distance while he cleans himself off. Something still seems strange about the whole situation.

"Why would Bishop burn down the farmhouse?" I ask Hoff. "Seems kind of pointless."

"Probably just for the hell of it," Hoff shrugs.

"Maybe," I agree. "I don't know."

"What are you thinking?" he asks.

"What if they did it to hide something?" I speculate.

"Like to dispose of all the bodies?" Hoff says. "What would be the point of that?"

"No," I shake my head. "Maybe to conceal the fact that they didn't kill everyone."

"I know you want to believe the rest of them are okay," Hoff shakes his head. "But that sounds like wishful thinking to me."

Stitch begins to bark behind us, and I turn to see him racing back for truck followed by Blake, Danielle, and Natalie. The way they are sprinting through the long grass tells me something must be wrong. I look to the sky and see dozens of vultures circling. It looks to be the largest kettle of vultures I've seen since all this started.

"Come on," I say to Hoff. "Let's get out of here."

"What is it?" Hoff asks.

"I don't think we want to sit around and find out," I say.

We stumble through the rubble and hurry to meet the others in the vehicles. As I glance over to the tree line on my left where Blake and the others had emerged from the woods, the first of the dead reach the clearing. I climb into the parcel area of the truck and look back to find the crowd has doubled in size. More and more of the things keep pouring out of the woods. The line of them extends from the north edge of the field to the south end, and probably well beyond that. There are tens of thousands of them surging forward like a wave of death.

"Get us out of here, Hoff!" Lorento yells as Hoff climbs in behind the wheel.

I watch as Fletcher and Quentin reverse the black van down the driveway behind us. As Hoff wheels the big delivery truck around, I hear the collective moaning from the dead over the loud roar of the engine. The scene is the most horrifying thing I've witnessed since this all started. The delivery truck kicks up a cloud of dust as Hoff accelerates down the driveway and we leave the massive horde behind us.

"What the hell was that?" I ask. It's more of a general question of astonishment. I don't really expect anyone to give me an answer.

"I haven't seen anything like that since we left Chicago," Danielle says.

"What are they all doing out here, though?" Quentin wonders. "A crowd that size couldn't have come from any of these little towns."

"Maybe they're moving this way for the same reasons we are," Blake speculates. "The devastation could be driving them this way in search for prey."

"Those things don't think like that," Steven shakes his head.

"It's just a theory," Blake says. "I don't have any other way to explain that."

"If what you're saying is right," I say. "That could just be the beginning. There could be more of those things coming this way. A lot more."

The possibility makes our whole situation even more urgent. We need to get this scientist and fly to somewhere safe before the dead completely overrun the area. There is also the chance that we could use this to our advantage. No matter how well-prepared Bishop may be, I don't think there is any way that he could defend his compound against such a massive swarm of the dead. It might be the thing we need to tip the odds in our favor if we can survive long enough. I contemplate these thoughts as we speed down the country roads, feeling as uncertain about the chance that I will wake up tomorrow as I have felt since the beginning. I wrap my arm around Stevie and try not to appear as terrified as I am inside.

"Is everything going to be okay?" he asks me as he strokes the dog that pants and laps a tongue at his fingers.

"Of course, kiddo," I smile. "There's nothing to be worried about."

I know it isn't true. There's a lot to worry about, but I can't bring myself to tell him that. Even now, I find it in me to lie and try to preserve the false sense of security that children used to have; the feeling that the family around you could protect you from anything bad that might happen.

Our convoy heads west, toward Bishop and away from the dead. Once we clear the area, Lorento pokes her head into the back of the truck and addresses all of us.

"We're heading to Fort Leonard Wood," she announces. "I want to secure that V-22 before we move on Bishop."

She pauses to look around for any indications of resistance among us.

"I'll be honest," she begins. "It is possible that we will encounter some hostiles when we reach the base, so I want you all to be ready."

Lorento glances around once again to gauge our reactions. Natalie stiffens her features and gives her a mocking salute. Lorento scowls at her before retreating to the front of the truck.

"I wouldn't piss her off if I were you," I warn Natalie. "She doesn't have a sense of humor."

"Yeah, I noticed that, too," Natalie rolls her eyes. "She can bite me."

"If this doesn't end well for us, she just might," Fletcher says.

We all crack a smile over his sarcasm, then we shift our focus to getting the weapons and ammo prepped for our arrival at the military base.

CHAPTER
THIRTY-SEVEN

"We're almost there," Hoff says as he takes his foot off the gas pedal. I move toward the front of the truck to look through the windshield at the military installation. It's the first time I've ever seen a base in my life, and I'm kind of surprised to find it looks just like any number of other towns that we have seen along our journey.

"This is it?" I ask Hoff.

He nods and steers toward a ramp beneath a large green sign riddled with bullet holes that says Fort Leonard Wood.

"Not what you were expecting?" Lorento asks.

"It looks just like the suburbs," I say.

Hoff laughs to himself.

"I thought there'd be like walls or something like that," I admit. "I didn't expect there would be a Holiday Inn."

"It's more of a training facility than what you think of as an actual fortification," Hoff explains. He steers the truck around an empty security building and passes a stone sign for the base carved in the shape of Missouri with the waving American flag engraved across half the stone.

"I can see that now," I say.

"There's a Dunkin' Donuts," Hoff jokes as we cruise down the main road.

"No wonder nobody survived this shit," I grumble.

"Knock it off," Lorento says. "Keep your eyes out for anything suspicious."

"This whole town looks suspicious," I say. "It's so empty. I haven't even seen a single corpse on the streets."

"Bishop," Lorento says. "When we first arrived, he had hundreds of soldiers occupying the installation while they cleaned out all the supplies and the dead."

"There used to be maybe fifteen thousand people on base," Hoff adds. "Most of them are probably dead now. The rest must have either fled town or joined up with Bishop."

The fact that Bishop managed to clear out and secure a small town speaks to how large and well-stocked his forces are. Some of them were even military. It makes me realize just how much the deck is stacked against us.

As we approach the heart of the base, the signs of the battles fought here become more apparent. The barracks along the left side of the street are mostly reduced to heaps of rubble. Burned remains of cars are scattered up and down the roads. Smashed windows, bullet pock marks, and splatters of blood are evident on nearly every building that remains standing. Rotting bodies are strewn about the lawns. The smell of rancid meat still hangs in the air. It is the closest thing to a war zone that I have ever seen.

We take a left turn at the airfield and drive along a chain link fence. The vehicles roll slowly down the road as Hoff swivels his head to scan for threats.

"There it is," he says and juts his chin toward the right side of the road.

The V-22 Osprey parked beside the hangar is unquestionably the strangest looking aircraft I've ever seen. It's like someone couldn't decide whether they wanted to build an airplane, or a helicopter so combined them into a single awkward mechanical nightmare. I have a hard time believing the thing could actually fly at all.

"I can't believe Bishop left that thing here," I say.

"He probably didn't have a pilot who could fly it," Hoff says. He steers the delivery truck through an open gate and drives across the runway. We pull to a stop beside the Osprey and exit the vehicle as we check the surroundings. The emptiness of the military installation seems to make everyone a little cautious and edgy. Even if we aren't walking into a trap, it still feels like we are. As soon as I am satisfied that we aren't about to be ambushed, I walk over to where Fletcher is examining the aircraft.

"This is the strangest helicopter ever," I say.

"Watch it, babe," Fletcher says. "This is a seventy-five-million-dollar state-of-the-art badass piece of modern warfare right here."

Stitch brushes against my leg and sniffs near the landing gear beneath the cockpit. He lifts his leg and sprays a stream of urine on the tire.

"Get out of here," Fletcher complains and chases the scruffy mutt away. "Stupid dog."

"Are you sure you can get it to fly?" I ask.

"No faith," Fletcher shakes his head. He caresses the side of the Osprey. "She might just be a little jealous, honey. Don't listen to her," he whispers to the thing.

"Fletcher," Lorento barks. "Quit hitting on the helicopter and make sure it is still operational. We need it ready to go by dark."

"Yeah, yeah," Fletcher waves a dismissive hand. "I got it."

"Everyone else gather over here so I can go over the plan."

"There's a plan now?" Fletcher asks.

"Of course, there is a plan," Lorento says. She limps over to the black van and spreads open a map on the hood. "There was always a plan."

Lorento proceeds to explain her plan to raid the compound where Bishop is holding the scientist. She wants me to lead her to the access point along with Quentin. Blake, Danielle, and Natalie will take up a position near the main entrance in case they try to escape with the scientist before we can locate him. Fletcher is going to fly the Osprey with Steven and his son aboard, and Hoff will man the fifty-cal to provide air support. Lorento finally points to a large clearing in a forest preserve about a mile from the facility.

"This is the rally point," Lorento says. "Anybody that doesn't make it back there by the time we return with Dr. Schoenheim gets left behind."

"What happens if you don't make it out of there?" Natalie asks.

"As long as you all do your jobs right that won't happen," Lorento snaps. She holds her gaze on Natalie for a few awkward moments until the younger girl looks away. "Any other questions?" Lorento asks.

When no one speaks up she snatches up the map off the hood and folds it back up. She slips the map back in her satchel and pulls back the hem of her sleeve to check the watch on her wrist.

"Hoff," she says. "You got the phone?"

The big soldier reaches into his pack and retrieves a black handset with a thick antenna. It looks like a cell phone from twenty years ago.

"You guys had a phone this whole time?" I ask.

"Actually, we had two," Lorento says. "Unfortunately, Bishop has one of them now."

"Would have been nice to know that before," I say.

Lorento notices the anger on my face and glances at Hoff.

"I'm not sure what you're upset about, Scout," Lorento smiles. "It's not like I was hiding it from you. Did you have someone you wanted to call?" She holds out the satellite phone to invite me to take it from her.

I realize her point. A satellite phone wouldn't be particularly useful to me.

"Couldn't you have called for help before now?" I ask.

"Who exactly do you think is in any position to help us?" Lorento turns the question back on me. "We're mostly on our own."

"So, who are you calling?" I ask.

"You're not ever going to trust me, are you, Scout?" Lorento says. "That's a shame."

She turns and hobbles toward the back of the delivery truck and it takes a moment before I stop feeling like a jerk and realize she managed to get out of giving me any information. That sneaky bitch.

"Who is she calling?" I ask Hoff.

"You think I know?" he laughs. "That's above my pay grade."

I squint my eyes at him to get him to fess up if he is lying to me, too.

"What?" Hoff says. "I'm serious. I don't know shit."

"You better be telling the truth," I warn Hoff.

Hoff holds his hands up in mock surrender, and then he steps away to help Fletcher prep the Osprey. I debate trying to go eavesdrop on Lorento by sneaking toward the back of the truck, but then I hear Stevie calling my name behind me.

"Hey kiddo," I smile. I crouch down so that our faces are just a few inches apart. "What's up?"

"Are you going to fly in the helicopter with me?" he asks.

"Not just yet," I tell him. "First you and your dad are going for a ride, but later you will come get me and then we can go for another ride together."

Stevie frowns and lowers his eyes to stare at his sneakers. I glance up at his father beside him. It isn't hard to see he wants to say something to me as well.

"I really wish you wouldn't go in there," Steven says.

"I'd rather not go down there either," I admit. "But I'm the only one that has been around that area before. I have to go."

"I got a bad feeling about it," Steven says.

"You always—" I begin.

"I know," Steven says. "I always say that. But this time it's different."

Even though I don't want to admit it, I know that he is right. This time it is a lot different. We aren't just dealing with some mindless zombies. These are real people and that makes them much more dangerous.

"You're right," I agree. "I'm scared, too. But as long as I know Stevie is out of danger and he will still have you there to protect him, I know I can deal with whatever might happen."

The sound of laughter makes us turn our heads and we watch as the dog chases after the little boy with the ball. The two of them being oblivious to the mood of everyone around them reminds me why I need to fight to protect that innocence, even if it means risking my life.

"He needs you," Steven says. He lowers his gaze and shoves a rock around the tarmac with the toe of his boot. "More than me. More than anything."

"No," I shake my head. "He needs a world where hope still exists. Where he can have a chance at a normal life someday. That's what he needs most. That's what I'm fighting for."

Steven stares at the pebble for a long moment. I anticipate him coming up with some other excuse to try and change my mind, but when he lifts his head, he just stares into my eyes and nods. I stretch my arms out and wrap them around his shoulders and give him a hug. At first, the gesture seems to have taken him by surprise, but a moment later I feel his hands on my back.

"I don't even care what happens to Bishop," Steven whispers. "Just come back in one piece, Scout."

"Don't worry," I assure him. "I'll be fine. And we're going to kick his ass."

I release my hold on Steven and try to smile to keep him from seeing how close to crying I am. Before he notices I turn and scoop up my pack and head toward the back of the truck to get myself ready to leave. I can only hope this won't be the last time I get to see him and Stevie.

CHAPTER THIRTY-EIGHT

Even though the inside of the black van is still drenched in blood, the six of us cram inside the vehicle, along with the smelly dog, because it makes less noise and will be less noticeable in the darkness. We head out in the late afternoon, which will allow us a little time in case we run into trouble. Nothing is guaranteed anymore.

Quentin steers the van down the rural highway cautiously to avoid the debris in the road and keep an eye out for any threats. As we get closer and closer to the compound, the likelihood increases that we will run into one of their patrols. If that happens, it won't just be the patrol we have to deal with. If they happen to tip off Bishop, we will lose the element of surprise and the whole operation could be in jeopardy.

"Can I ask you something, Lorento?" Blake says as he strokes the scruffy hair on the skull of the dog.

Lorento waits for a long moment before she answers.

"Sure," she says.

"How long did you know that massive horde was headed this way?" Blake asks.

"What makes you think I knew anything about that?"

"You didn't seem at all surprised," he says. "You also weren't the least bit shocked when I told you how bad things had gotten on the other side of the Mississippi. So, you must have known about all of it."

From behind her sunglasses, Lorento stares through the windshield at the road.

"You're a smart guy, Blake," Lorento compliments him. She pauses to consider her words before speaking again. "I still get intel on a daily basis, and those briefings often include what has been observed from satellite surveillance."

"How many of those things are we talking about?" Blake asks.

"It's a sizable crowd," Lorento says and brushes back a loose strand of blonde hair behind her ear. "At least two hundred thousand. Maybe two or three times that many. The number grew substantially when the pack moved through the St. Louis area."

"Why didn't you say anything?" I interrupt. "You knew this whole time and you didn't warn me about it. After everything I did for you?"

"Would it have made any difference?" Lorento asks.

"Maybe," I snarl. I'm not sure how to answer her.

"Would you have decided to skip town instead of helping me, Scout?" Lorento asks.

"That's not the point," I say. "You lied to me. People died because I thought I should trust you."

"God damn," Quentin gripes. "Calm down."

"You might not agree with the way I do things, Scout," Lorento says. "But I never lied to you. I might not have told you everything, but I never lied. I don't care what your opinion of me is. At the end of the day, I did what I had to do to try and save my country. I can live with that."

Her speech makes me realize just how expendable we all really are in her eyes. At the same time, I can't help but respect her sense of duty. In her mind, she has always done what she felt was best for everyone, even when it cost those around her their lives. I wish I could believe in what we are doing that much, but I am not sure I ever will. To me, this whole thing is personal. It always has been.

"Take this exit," I tell Quentin.

"You sure?" Lorento asks.

"Yeah," I say. "Bishop probably has eyes along the highway heading into Springfield. We can take the back roads."

Quentin steers the van onto the exit ramp, and we turn onto a small country road that runs for miles beneath the shade of towering trees. When we reach highway 65, I tell Quentin to take a left.

"This will take us straight into Springfield," I say. "The entrance to the compound is just off this road at the edge of town."

The mood in the truck is tense with each passing mile. Natalie pulls a piece of gum out of her pocket and pops it in her mouth. Danielle chews on her bottom lip anxiously. I watch as Blake notices her tension and reaches out to grab her hand.

"We're going to be okay," he whispers to her.

He catches me staring at the two of them and he gives me an awkward smile and releases her hand. I almost want to apologize for staring. If anything, I wish he would have kept holding on to her hand. For some reason, just watching them was making me feel better, too. When I look through the windshield, I can see we are approaching the expressway along the north side of town.

"Pull over here," I tell Quentin and direct him to a cemetery on the left.

"The cemetery?" Quentin asks. "For real?"

"We can't drive any farther on this road," I say.

"At least we know we won't run into Dom in the cemetery," Danielle says. I don't understand why, but Blake and Quentin seem to find her comment pretty damn funny.

Quentin steers the van through the gates and drives through the rows of graves toward the back of the cemetery. We are greeted by the sound of crickets and buzzing cicadas as we get out of the truck. Night is not far off. There isn't a lot of time left before we have to make our move.

"So how long did you know about that massive crowd heading this way?" Blake asks Lorento once again.

"About a week," Lorento admits. "But I was never sure they would make it across the rough terrain out here. It seemed like hitting the Mississippi could potentially stop them altogether. But that only thinned their numbers slightly."

"Guess we're lucky some of them made it," Blake says.

"Only if this operation works," I say. "Otherwise, we'll be dead along with everyone inside the compound."

"It will work," Lorento winces. She retrieves the bottle of painkillers from her satchel and dumps a few in her hand. She quickly tosses them in her mouth and swallows them with a gulp of water.

"Easy," Danielle snaps. "Christ, how many pills did you just take?"

"Don't worry about me," Lorento says. "I can take care of myself."

"Oh my god," Danielle rolls her eyes. "It's not you I'm worried about. If you can't think straight down there—"

"I appreciate your concern," Lorento interrupts her. "But we don't have time for this. Let's move out."

We grab our weapons and ammunition out of the truck and follow Lorento as she walks toward the road. Her shape is just a silhouette against the giant orange setting sun on the horizon. Even with a bullet wound in her leg, she moves along quickly, driven by a compelling urge to finish her mission.

"Anyone else a little worried about her?" Danielle asks.

"I still like our chances better with her here," Blake says.

"Is she always so pleasant?" Natalie asks.

"You should see her when she isn't on painkillers," I say. "It's not pretty."

We move toward town through the woods alongside the road. Stitch leads the way, weaving between the trees and pausing now and then to lift his nose toward the sky and sniff the air. The pain medication seems to kick in and Lorento starts to move more fluidly as we tackle the tricky terrain. It makes me feel a little better about the amount of pills she took. Maybe she knew she couldn't physically handle this otherwise.

We come to the highway overpass along the edge of town. A pair of parked Humvees sit sideways in the road. We pause before we reach the edge of the tree line and wait for darkness to fall. As the sun dips below the horizon, the clouds turn orange, then blood red and finally cool to a soothing violet. A lone bullfrog that lurks nearby begins to croak.

Along the highway a corpse in a filthy denim shirt and ripped khakis shuffles past our position. The thing spots the soldiers on the overpass through the stringy strands of dark hair dangling over his face. It slowly wanders up the exit ramp toward the roadblock. One of the sentries eventually spots it and takes it out with a shot from a sniper rifle. The corpse falls to the ground immediately, but the sound of the gunshot lingers for a few moments in the air.

There isn't another corpse to be found anywhere. The fact that Bishop was able to clear out this entire town is pretty remarkable. There must have been over a hundred thousand people living in this city before the outbreak. Somehow Bishop and his group not only survived here, but they've also actually started to rebuild.

"What happens if the dead go by north or south of here?" Blake asks. "They could miss this town completely."

"They won't," Lorento assures him.

As though to explain her certainty, bright lights power on along the roadways that lead toward the underground office facility. The sounds of generators humming fills the dusky air. It looks like they have construction light stands along all the roads for several blocks around the entrance to the underground facility. The sight is pretty amazing after weeks of spending nights in total darkness.

"Pretty ballsy," Quentin says. "Every corpse for miles is going to see and hear that."

"Seems like they've done okay so far," Danielle says. "It's kind of amazing."

"They haven't dealt with anything like what is coming this way tonight," I say.

The sound of twigs snapping draws my attention to the woods behind me. Stitch lets out a little whimper and sniffs the air. I listen closely for more sounds from the forest. It doesn't seem like that horde could have gotten here so quickly.

"Is that them?" Danielle asks.

No one needs to ask what she is referring to. We all listen quietly for a moment.

"No," Blake says. "We'd hear a lot more noise from a group that size."

"It won't be long before they do get here, though," Lorento whispers. "Let's get moving."

CHAPTER
THIRTY-NINE

We slide down the grassy slope toward the highway in the darkness. I keep my eyes on the overpass and the men that linger near the Humvees and exhale smoke from their cigarettes into the night air. The bright light from the portable construction lamps might make it easier to monitor the overpass, but it also makes it less likely that they will be able to see us moving through the darkness beyond.

After we scurry across the highway, we come upon a chain link fence surrounding a factory. Quentin reaches into his pack and pulls out a pair of heavy-duty clippers and begins snipping the metal to create an opening. The sound of the metal snapping seems so loud in the surrounding quiet. I keep my eyes trained on the sentries, listening to their voices as they talk casually. If I can hear them, it seems like they will certainly hear the noise we are making if they stop talking long enough to notice it. One of the men must have cracked a joke, because I can hear several people laughing in the distance.

"Got it," Quentin whispers.

He pries the fence open to create a space for us to move through and holds it for us as we pass through into the empty lot. Even though we're a block from the main road where all the lights and blockades are positioned, we could still run into trouble on our way to the compound. This is no time to get careless. If something happens to tip Bishop off, we might not have a chance in hell of walking out of there alive.

I follow Lorento along the side of the old brick factory and step through the glass of the broken windows as quietly as possible. We reach the front of the building and wait while Lorento scans the road. Once she is sure it's clear, she scurries toward the street. I crouch down and hustle along behind her, keeping my eyes glued to the intersection to my right. There is another blockade, but I don't see any signs of activity as I hurry to get to cover again. Once we all reach relative safety once again, we continue our advance along the corrugated steel building until we come to an open field.

We make our way through the tall grass cautiously. The rocky ground is tricky and full of ruts. I catch the scent of pond water in the air and hear more frogs croaking in the darkness. It's just a little further now. We eventually reach the end of the field and find ourselves in a lot with about a dozen trailers parked side by side. Crouched down between the large tires, we look beyond the trailers at a junkyard filled with the remains of damaged and cannibalized vehicles.

"How much further?" Blake asks.

"The back entrance is just on the other side of the road," I say. "The sinkhole is just a couple hundred yards beyond those train tracks."

"Quiet," Danielle whispers. "Do you hear that?"

We all listen in silence. The faint sound of distant moaning can be heard coming from the direction of the highway behind us. It's a sound that you might not notice if you weren't listening for it, but the second I hear it a chill runs down my spine. The dead are returning to take back this town.

"We need to hurry," Lorento says.

She advances toward the front of the junkyard, crouching as she creeps alongside the rusty cars and trucks. We follow along behind her in a column until we reach a garage beside the road. From the back corner of the building, we can see the rear entrance to the underground facility. The back loading bay doors are barricaded by eighteen-wheelers, but only a handful of men stand guard.

We move to the front of the building and duck across the road, using the tall weeds for cover. Beside the driveway of the back entrance there is a steep drop-off to a small pool of water. We make our way around the pond, keeping low and moving fast. My hands start to get slick with sweat and I can feel my heart racing in my chest. As we slip past the rear entrance, I begin to hear the massive crowd of the dead approaching. The radio held by a guard outside the building comes alive with chatter. Any minute now all hell is going to break loose when they figure out what is headed this way. As much as I want Bishop to get what is coming to him, some feelings of guilt creep up inside me when I think of the innocent people that have no idea what is coming. Maybe they aren't any more innocent than us. I push the thought away. There's no time for that now. Focus. People are still counting on me.

I scan the surroundings, spot the fence across the clearing, and point it out to the others. We hurry across the rocky dirt and gaze through the barrier into the dark hole that leads to the underground facility. Quentin goes to work with the clippers as the rest of us keep our eyes peeled for any signs of trouble. Alarmed voices from below can be heard from the opening and the sound of the approaching dead grows louder. As Quentin finishes opening the fence, an alarm goes off inside the facility.

"Where is the rope?" Blake asks.

"I got it," Natalie unslings her pack and fishes out a spool of rope from inside and hands it to Blake. Blake begins to tie off the rope to one of the fence posts. As soon as he is finished, Lorento grabs up the rope and wraps it around her waist. She glances over her shoulder into the hole and then leans back and lowers herself into the darkness.

"You next," Blake says to Quentin.

Quentin grabs the rope and peeks down the hole as he readies himself.

"Don't do anything stupid down there," Blake tells him with a smirk.

"Can't make any promises, boss," Quentin grins as he lowers himself into the darkness.

"Ready?" Blake asks me.

I nod and take the rope from him with my trembling hands.

"Good luck, Scout," he says.

I wait until Quentin reaches the bottom to wrap the rope around my waist. Then I lower myself into the darkness. Within a few moments my fingers burn from the friction with the rope. I can't help imagining losing my grip and falling to the rocky pool of water at the bottom. Boots stomp along the rock floor below as the men inside begin to organize to fight the dead. From above comes the sound of gunfire in the distance as the big machine guns on the Humvees at the bridge begin to battle against the horde of the dead.

I reach the bottom and feel my feet touch the pool of cool water on the floor of the sinkhole. Inside the compound, the alarm continues to blare. The voices are tense and panicked. A voice repeats an announcement over an intercom system.

"All available personnel to the north entrance. This is an emergency."

We stay around the edge of the rock wall and keep out of sight while we wait in the darkness for a break in the sounds of people passing by in the tunnel. It seems like there might be more people inside than we had guessed. The thought fills me with even more dread.

This is insane. We're going to die in here.

"Relax," Quentin whispers.

I look at him and he gives me an easy-going smile.

"Just stay cool," he advises. "We got this."

I let out a breath and give him a nod. It helps to know the other two people around me aren't losing it.

"Okay," Lorento says. "We can't wait any longer. Let's move."

We follow her out through the opening and into the lighted tunnel. The place is like a giant system of caves with structures built right into the rock. There is a bright blue four story office building in a giant cavern directly across from the sinkhole. I can't help but pause and stare at it in wonder for a moment until Quentin nudges me with his elbow.

"Maybe act a little more natural," he whispers.

I turn my head to look at him and notice the enormous shadows cast on the tunnel wall of several figures approaching our position.

"Let's move," Lorento urges.

We follow her toward the approaching group. She moves along the corridor quickly, without seeming to show much interest in her surroundings. It even makes me forget for a moment that we have no idea where we are going. I notice Quentin doing the same. There is a map along the wall of the facility with a directory of the various offices. I try to glance at it as we walk by but only catch a glimpse. We pass by the group of soldiers, and I take my eyes off the map and make the mistake of making eye contact with one of them. I quickly avert my gaze. Maybe I tried a little too hard not to look at him. We don't get more than a few feet away from the group before I hear a voice call out behind us.

"Hold up," one of the men orders the others.

"What is it?" another man asks.

"Don't stop," Lorento hisses between her teeth. "Keep walking."

I hold my breath and keep marching forward behind Lorento. Any second I expect to hear the soldier order us to stop, or to hear a rifle opening fire from behind us. My stomach twists in anxious anticipation. The sweaty palms of my hands grip the rifle with my finger poised beside the trigger.

A crackle of gunfire erupts over the radio carried by one of the soldiers. The sound makes my head twist around and I nearly start shooting, but realize the soldiers are no longer paying attention to us.

"There's a whole fucking army of those things," a voice screams on the radio. "We need more people out here. They're going to overrun us!"

There's a pause and then more sounds of gunfire, maybe even artillery.

"Is that a helicopter?" another voice asks on the radio. "Who the fuck is flying a helicopter up there?"

"Is that ours?" another soldier asks.

The realization that Fletcher is flying above the compound almost makes me smile until I hear the radio one last time.

"Shoot that goddamn helicopter out of the sky," Bishop growls into the radio. "This is an attack you stupid assholes. Lock everything down."

The sound trails off as we move farther along the corridor away from the soldiers. We can hear the footsteps of more people heading toward us.

"We can't keep wandering around like this," Quentin says. "It's just a matter of time before they figure out we're here."

"Calm down," says Lorento. "There was only one science research facility listed on that sign. That's where we will find the asset."

CHAPTER FORTY

It isn't long before we start to hear gunshots echo inside the facility. The dead must have broken through the barricades on the street and are attempting to breach the north loading bay doors. We are running out of time, but the facility is a couple miles of winding tunnels.

Finally, we reach a building marked with a large number 4 and follow Lorento toward the entrance. The outside appears completely unguarded. Perhaps this is the wrong building. We push through the front doors and step into an empty reception room.

"There's nobody here," Quentin says.

"He has to be here," Lorento says. She moves down a corridor toward the rear of the building.

There are a series of office doors before we reach a staircase. We climb a flight of stairs to the second level and see a red "ACCESS RESTRICTED" sign on the door. Lorento twists the handle cautiously and eases the door open to peer inside. In a swift motion she pushes her way into the hallway and begins firing her pistol. Quentin plunges through the doorway behind her with his rifle raised and checks the hallway, then he lowers the rifle and holds the door open for me. I step into the hallway and spot two bodies at the far end of the hall.

"Someone had to hear the shots," Lorento says. "Let's keep moving."

There is a light coming through the window of a room at the end of the hall. The radio on the belt of the closest guard crackles to life in the quiet hallway.

"Hold up," Quentin says. He pauses to crouch beside the guard and slips the radio free. The corpse behind his back opens it's eyes and sits up. Before Quentin realizes what is happening, I fire a round into the head of the corpse splattering the wall with gore as it slumps to the ground again.

I shift the rifle to fire another bullet into the head of the other guard but see that it is already moving and it lunges at Quentin snapping his jaws around the hand that holds radio. Quentin curses and shoves the thing away as he falls backwards. Before I can pull the trigger again, Lorento fires a round from the other end of the hallway. I watch the corpse as it collapses back onto the floor. Quentin clutches his palm as blood soaks between his fingers and dribbles down to the floor.

"Goddamn," Quentin growls. He takes his eyes off his hands and finds Lorento pointing her pistol at his face.

"Just say the word," Lorento says. "I'll make it quick."

Quentin thinks about it for a second then he shakes his head. The bite itself isn't necessarily a death sentence. The bites always carry some kind of nasty infection, but I've heard that it's possible to recover. Everyone has heard a story about someone that got bit and survived. Maybe they severed a limb off, or just beat the infection. I never actually met anyone that has yet though. Everyone I've seen with a bite died a slow and painful death within a few days. I lower the rifle and reach into my pack to find something for Quentin to use to wrap the wound on his hand that is covered in blood.

"I'm good," Quentin assures her. He takes the dirty towel from me and frowns at it but wraps it around his hand. He cringes from the pain. "You guys might still need my ass to get through this."

"You sure you can keep going?" Lorento asks. It's almost like she'd rather shoot him than worry about him slowing her down.

"I'll be fine," he says. "Fuck it."

Quentin gets back to his feet, and we advance toward the lighted window at the end of the hall. I keep the rifle ready to fire. It only took a moment of carelessness for something bad to happen. We can't afford to rush, even if we don't have a lot of time. Lorento pauses at the doorway and listens. As I approach, I notice the opaque glass conceals the room within. Lorento curls her fingers around the steel handle and raises the pistol as she prepares to breach the room. She pushes open the door and we rush in.

"Hold it right there," someone says before I even make it through the door. The thick accent tells me immediately who I will find inside. Arkady has a gun pointed at the head of an old guy in a lab coat that I presume to be Dr. Schoenheim. "Lower your weapons," he says.

"Who the fuck is this guy?" Quentin wonders.

"Arkady," I whisper to Quentin. "He's an asshole."

We lower our weapons, and for a long moment, Arkady sits there and smirks as though he is enjoying the hell out of this moment. The scientist continues to stare through a microscope, seemingly oblivious to anything else going on the room.

"Miss Lorento," Arkady says finally. "It is quite a pleasure to see you again."

"Go fuck yourself," Lorento spits.

"I had a feeling that this was your work," he gestures vaguely with the gun. "Very impressive, I admit."

Lorento just continues to scowl at him.

"Aww," Arkady tilts his head and pouts in mock pity before a smirk returns to his face. "Still angry, are we? It was just business my dear."

"Cut the bullshit," Lorento says.

"Put your guns down," Arkady says.

"Fuck that," Quentin says. "I'm gonna shoot your ass."

Quentin begins to raise his rifle slightly. Arkady gives Quentin a hard look and then cocks the hammer of his revolver beside the cranium of the scientist.

"Don't do anything stupid," Arkady warns him.

"You won't shoot Doctor Schoenheim," Lorento says. "You need him alive."

The doctor lifts his eyes from the microscope from the first time and looks around the room. He pushes the wire glasses up the bridge of his nose and then his gaze settles on Lorento.

"Hello, Judith," Doctor Schoenheim smiles at Lorento. "When did you get here?"

"How do you think this ends, Arkady?" Lorento asks. "You'll never make it out of here with him alive."

"Perhaps," Arkady muses. "Maybe the three of you will help me."

"Not a chance," I sneer.

"Then we all die in here together," Arkady growls. "And everyone else in the world. Is that what you really want, Scout?"

He pauses to give me time to answer, or maybe just to emphasize his point.

"That was your helicopter I heard outside, no?" Arkady asks.

"What helicopter?" Quentin asks. He knows damn well what helicopter, but I can't blame him for trying to play stupid.

"Don't speak again, big man," Arkady growls at Quentin. He shifts his gaze to Lorento. "You will bring me to that helicopter and we all get out of this together. Or we all die. It is up to you."

"What about Bishop?" Lorento asks. "You think he won't try to stop you?"

"Fuck him," Arkady cackles. "Polezni durak."

"What the hell does that mean?" Quentin wonders.

"Useful idiot," Lorento mumbles.

A machine gun rattles out in the caverns nearby. The battle is definitely getting closer to this end of the facility. We really don't have time to keep trying to rationalize with this freaking lunatic. I feel my shaky finger hovering near the trigger guard as I wait for the man to get a little too careless, to shift his head just far enough to give me a clean shot without injuring the scientist. I have to wonder how the hell this doctor is supposed to be worth all this. He seems completely out of his mind. If I had any idea we were rescuing some kind of mental patient, I would have never agreed.

"Is someone having a party outside?" Doctor Schoenheim asks. "It's very hard to focus with all that racket going on out there."

"Shut up," Arkady snaps at the scientist. He grabs a fistful of the white lab coat and hauls Doctor Schoenheim out of the stool that he is sitting in. "Come on, everybody. Let's all go for a nice little walk now, okay?"

"I need my pants," the old scientist pleads. "I took them off. I always think better—"

"Move it," Arkady demands.

"Judith this man is very rude," the doctor tells Lorento as Arkady shoves him toward the door.

"Ladies first," Arkady says, and then he waits for us to move out into the hallway.

Quentin and I walk shoulder-to-shoulder a step behind Lorento. Behind us, Arkady watches us all with the handgun pressed to the back of the skull of Doctor Schoenheim.

"What do we do now?" Quentin mumbles under his breath.

"We get outside," Lorento whispers. "Then make our move."

"Quiet!" Arkady shouts. "Get down the fucking stairs."

We move down the staircase, out the entrance of the office building, and into the cavern. The lights along the walls have begun to flicker on and off. The gunfire is constant and close although it is hard to tell how close since the shots seem to be amplified by the tunnel walls. In between rifle reports, the growing moans of the dead begin to fill the air. There is no question they are inside the compound. So, if we don't get moving, we may never get out.

CHAPTER FORTY-ONE

The lights continue to pulse and dim as we walk through the compound. People are running past us in both directions now. Some are heading to the north end of the facility to try to hold off the dead, but most of them are just trying to get to the main entrance and escape.

At this end of the compound, the people seem more like terrified refugees than soldiers. They grab as much as they can off the rows of shelves in a storage area. No one seems concerned with our presence. Not one of them even seems to notice the doctor walking around with no pants, or the man holding a gun to his back. Everyone is just trying to get what they can and get out alive.

A young girl walks along beside me calling for her mommy every few seconds. Since I can't stop and help her like I want to, I scan the faces around me, as if I might be able to guess which person is her parent.

I glance over my shoulder to see how closely Arkady is watching me. Maybe I can catch him off guard. It wasn't the best move to let us keep our guns, but he probably realized he might need us to help defend him, too.

"Keep moving," he urges me and emphasizes his point by shifting the barrel of the gun in my direction.

It isn't the right time. Wait for the asshole to make a mistake. Get him where you want him, and then make your move. It all seems plausible until Dom appears further up the tunnel. I notice her eyes squint when she spots Quentin beside me, and a look of confusion settles on her face as she marches toward us.

"Wait," Arkady barks, but it's too late. Dom pauses and she lifts a radio to her lips.

"Bishop," her voice crackles through the radios that Quentin and Arkady are holding. "I've got eyes on Arkady," she says. I hear her saying something else, but a burst of gunfire down the corridor drowns out the words.

"Fucking traitor," Bishop barks into the radio. "I'm on my way. Hold him there."

The lights flick off again and when they come back on Arkady had already shoved the doctor down on the ground. He points the pistol at Dom and fires off a round from the revolver. The bullet hits a man in the chest as he steps into the line of fire. Dom raises a rifle and aims it at us across the crowded corridor.

I realize all hell is about to break loose, so I lunge at the girl that had been calling for her mother and shield her with my body as the gunfire erupts. People scream as the first shots are fired. Bullets zip past my body as the lights flicker off and on again. I look over and see a trio of bullets rip through Lorento's chest. As her body topples over beside him, Quentin trades shots with Dom. Arkady is still firing with the revolver, so I lift my rifle up and pull the trigger. Half a dozen bullets tear open his midsection and knock him backwards. The whole exchange takes place in a few seconds, but it feels like an eternity.

In the aftermath of the firefight, I sit up to allow the little girl to scurry out from beneath me. Her hands still tremble with fear. I'm still not sure if I actually saved her, or if trying to protect her was what happened to save me.

"It's okay," I tell her.

She ignores my words and turns to run away in terror. A pair of hands reach out from the shadows and grab her, and she lets out a terrified scream. The lights flicker off again and I lose sight of her in the darkness. When the lights come back on, I find Fawn crouched beside the girl. She points the girl in the direction of the front entrance, then turns her head to find me lying on the ground.

"Scout?" she asks as if she doesn't believe her eyes.

"Hey," I manage to say. Seeing her alive again has me in shock as well.

"You're alive!" Fawn exclaims. She reaches out her hand and pulls me to my feet and wraps me in one of her bear hugs. "I never thought I'd see you again."

There are bodies all over the ground from the stray bullets that were flying around the crowded tunnel. Anyone that is still alive is rushing away from the scene. I watch as they recede into the darkness of the caves.

Lorento groans on the ground and the sound causes Fawn to look in her direction. Quentin winces in pain as he kneels beside Lorento. I notice there is a dark red stain just below his knee. Fawn hurries over to Lorento and applies pressure to the wound in her chest.

"Where is Schoenheim?" Lorento coughs.

I look back to see him feeling around for his glasses on the floor.

"He's fine," I assure Lorento.

"Get him out of here," she chokes.

I start to give her some kind of assurance that we will get the scientist to safety, but she cuts me off by lifting the gun with her quivering hand and pointing it at my face.

"Just go," she gags. Her head collapses back on the ground. Her pupils gaze up at the ceiling, then her head lolls slightly to the side and I realize she is gone. Fawn lowers her head and lifts her bloody hands off Lorento's body. I spot the satchel on the ground beside her, and I remember the satellite phone. I grab the leather bag and slip my head and shoulder through the strap.

"Come on," Quentin urges the doctor as he pulls him up by the arm.

"Let me look at your leg," Fawn says as she gets to her feet.

Quentin just waves her away and cringes as he drags the stumbling doctor to his feet alongside him.

I grab Fawn by the shoulder and hold her until I have her attention.

"Listen to me," I tell her. "You have to run. Take the doctor and go. There is a helicopter waiting a mile southeast of here."

"I'd rather stay together," Fawn says. "Let me help you."

"You can't," I remind her. I glance over at Quentin as he hobbles toward us. "We'll just slow you down anyway."

The sound of gunfire echoes down the hall. I look back and can see the muzzle flashes around the corner on the dark stone walls. Fawn pinches her lips together and gives me a sharp nod. Then she takes the scientist by the arm and leads him through the dark tunnel.

Quentin leans his forearm on my shoulder and rests for a moment. I wrap my arm around his waist and help him as he limps along beside me. Quentin pauses as we approach Dom lying on the ground. She has taken a round to the kneecap and another to the shoulder.

"Quentin," Dom gasps. She reaches out a hand, but Quentin just stares at it. "Help me."

Quentin scowls down at her pleading face.

"We have to keep moving," I urge Quentin.

"Help me up," Dom demands. "You know me."

"I know you all right," Quentin growls.

"You can't leave me like this," Dom pleads. "Please. I'll do anything. You know I will."

Quentin takes his hand off my shoulder and kneels and reaches out a hand toward Dom. It seems like he is considering helping her, but then he grabs the collar of her shirt into a fist.

"Fuck you, Dom." Quentin snaps as he shoves her back down toward the ground. "It's my turn to leave your ass to die."

He gets back to his feet and jerks his head to let me know he's ready to move. Dom twists around on her belly and claws at the ground to grab at our boots as we walk away.

"Quentin," she screams. "Come back here."

"Let's go," Quentin urges me. He places a hand on my shoulder as he limps down the corridor beside me.

"You fucking monkey piece of shit!" Dom screams behind us.

I hear the victims from firefight returning from the dead. Even as the dead descend on Dom and she howls in pain, Quentin just lowers his eyes and hobbles forward. The dead moan and she screams louder until they tear into her throat and she gurgles and finally goes quiet, and then the only noise in between the approaching rifle reports is the sound of the dead devouring her flesh.

"She had it coming," Quentin mumbles to himself.

Another sound causes me to turn around. I hear voices coming toward us. Bishop barks orders at some of his men. I try to urge Quentin to hurry but he stumbles and there is a cracking sound from his leg as he collapses to the ground. He grimaces to keep from bawling in agony. For a moment, I watch in frozen silence as Bishop and about a dozen of his men round the corner about a hundred yards away and approach our position.

There is a stack of crates along the wall, and I bend down and grab Quentin by the shoulders and drag him along the floor. He scoots himself along to help me until his back rests against the crate.

"How many?" Quentin asks me.

"At least ten," I whisper.

"Shit," Quentin mutters.

I peer around the crates to see Bishop's men and notice that Lorento's corpse is getting up. The sight fills me with remorse. I should have never left her like that. She was a heartless bitch, but she doesn't deserve to be like this. Bishop pauses in his tracks when he spots her.

"Good God almighty," Bishop exclaims. "Will you look at that?" He indicates the corpse to the other men nearby.

"Just go, Scout," Quentin says. "I can hold them off long enough for you to get out of here."

"I'm not leaving you," I tell him.

"Look at me," Quentin holds up his bloody hand. "I'm not getting out of this shit."

"You're not quite as pretty as I remember," Bishop laughs. I glance over to see him lift a boot and kick Lorento's corpse in the face. It topples her, but she immediately pushes up from the ground again.

"Go, Scout," Quentin says. "Now."

"We can take them out," I insist.

"No," Quentin shakes his head. He reaches up his bloody hand and clenches my shoulder. "Please go now. Don't make me die down here for nothing."

"Give me that ax," Bishop says.

I nod to Quentin and squeeze his hand before I let him go. The sound of glass breaking draws my attention back down the corridor. As I rise, one of the men tosses Bishop a fire ax. He catches it with one hand and turns around to face Lorento again.

"I have to admit," he says. "I've been looking forward to this for a while."

He brings the ax down on her neck as I turn to run. I don't dare look back. The only thing I want to do now is get the doctor to the helicopter and get the hell out of here. The firefight ignites a few moments later.

"Come get some, motherfuckers," Quentin yells.

But the shooting doesn't last very long. There's a howl of pain a few moments later. Then nothing except the approaching moans of the dead.

CHAPTER FORTY-TWO

I step outside through the bay doors of the main entrance and raise my rifle as I scan the shapes in the dim light in the hopes of spotting the white lab coat. The corpses are scattered up and down the road, feasting on bodies scattered on the ground. Sporadic bursts of machine gun fire rattle nearby. Out here without any weapons, or hell even any pants, I don't give the mad scientist much of a chance.

"Schoenheim!" I call out. "Fawn!" Maybe that was stupid, but I felt like I had to do it even if it draws attention to me. Not like I'll be sticking around here long anyway.

A corpse staggers toward me from the field on my left. I fire several rounds at the thing but miss the mark in the darkness. The mag clicks empty, so I pull the rifle back and smash the thing in the face with the back end of it. It crumples to the ground for a moment before it struggles back up again.

Several more shambling figures emerge behind the corpse I just took down. The sound of an assault rifle inside the compound reminds me that Bishop is not that far behind. There is no time to wait around. I have to start moving in the direction of the helicopter and hope that Fawn was able to get the scientist out of here.

I hustle up the drive, weaving between the corpses as I load a fresh magazine. I spot a worn dirt trail through the grass on the left and I head for it. Before I get there, I hear more shots fired behind me. The bullets zip past me as I stumble to the ground. Over my shoulder, I spot a trio of figures emerging from the compound. It's Bishop, flanked by two of his scumbags. I can tell it is him because he still carries the blood-soaked ax. A corpse lunges toward him and he raises the ax and slams the blade into the face of the thing. He removes the ax from the skull and wipes the blood off his face.

As I get back to my feet, I realize Bishop and his men haven't actually spotted me yet. The bullets that nearly tore me apart were only strays that missed the corpses. I know I should turn and run away as fast as I can before they get any closer. But this might be my only chance to kill Bishop and get revenge for everyone he has harmed.

I lift the rifle to my eye and begin firing. My first burst manages to hit the soldier to the left of Bishop in the leg. The man yowls as he buckles over on the pavement. Bishop and the other soldier crouch and scurry in different directions for cover as I open fire again. I keep spraying bullets until the mag is spent and Bishop lunges behind a Humvee.

Instead of waiting around to find out if I hit the bastard, I turn to sprint up the trail and immediately collide with a towering corpse. A yelp of terror escapes my mouth as I use the rifle to fend the thing away. It takes every ounce of strength to keep the giant dead man from sinking his teeth into my face. It clutches the rifle with both hands as it lunges forward. As much as I try, I can't twist the weapon free from the dead hands. Bullets tear into the dirt beside me as Bishop and his man fire in my direction. I finally just sidestep and release the rifle sending the corpse sprawling on the ground. There isn't much I can do now except to leave the rifle behind and make a run for it. I don't like it, but at least I still have the handgun and my knife if I need them.

As another volley of bullets pursues me, I scramble over the path toward the hillside. Before I can reach the top, I feel a cramping ache in my behind. I stumble forward a few more steps then collapse on the ground and grab my leg. My fingers come away wet after touching the hole in my jeans. It only takes me a second to realize I must have been shot, in the ass no less.

"Fuck," I growl as I struggle to get back on my feet again. Instead of running, the best I can manage is an urgent limp. Out of pain and anger I grip the pistol, raise it up and fire several wild rounds behind me as I retreat into a shroud of darkness beneath the canopy of trees. The moans of the dead seem to be coming from everywhere in the woods around me. Behind me I hear Bishop tell the other guy to "man the fuck up."

"I ain't fucking going in there," the man insists.

"You afraid, Charlie?" Bishop growls. "Afraid of one little girl in the woods? You goddamn pussy, get the hell in there."

"Come on, Bishop," Charlie pleads. "Those things are everywhere, man. Let's get the fuck out of here. What the—"

A burst of automatic rifle fire ends the discussion.

I slip the knife from my jacket pocket as I retreat deeper into the woods. Even as my eyes adjust to the darkness, I struggle to make out the shapes, but I can tell from the moans and the sounds of snapping twigs that the dead have me surrounded. As I drag my ass from the trunk of one tree to the next, I try to avoid thinking how screwed I really am right now. I'm not even completely sure I am still headed toward the helicopter.

I pause to scan the dark shapes in the woods again and to slow my breathing. It seems like my heart is beating so hard that anything close by could hear it. When I glance back in the direction I came from, I spot a tall shape moving toward me quietly over the branches. A corpse comes snarling at the figure from the side and then there is a grunt and the sound of bone cracking, and the corpse falls to the ground and goes silent.

Any hopes I had that Bishop might give up disappear from my mind. I turn around and limp to the next tree, making too much noise as I drag my gimpy leg over the leaves and twigs. A corpse with long hair and a bikini comes toward me from left, crashing through the foliage as it hisses. I can't even outrun the thing anymore, so I lean against the tree and wait. As it reaches me, I jab the knife upwards into the neck of the thing. The blade goes halfway in and skewers the corpse as it snaps at me. I grab the thing by the hair and drive the knife up with all the strength I can manage until it is buried to the hilt. The chick in the swimsuit finally goes limp and collapses to the ground.

After I remove the knife again, I look around for Bishop but there is no sign of him. My blood runs cold as my head swivels from side to side to scan the woods. I know I need to keep moving, but the fear of making the wrong move has me bound to the trunk of the tree.

"Where are you, princess?" Bishop beckons.

A corpse growls at the sound and shuffles through the trees. I hear a grunt as Bishop brings down the fire ax and silences the thing for good.

It sounds like he is just a few yards behind the tree I am using for cover. My fingers tighten around the grip of the handgun as I lean to the left to peer around the tree trunk. In the sparse moonlight, I can barely make out his frame in the darkness. Bishop grunts as he pries the fire ax free from the skull of a corpse on the ground and looks up to scan the woods again.

I duck back behind the tree as he begins to laugh softly to himself. If I stay hidden, maybe he will abandon the search or move on to another area of the woods. The other option is I can take my chances and take a shot at him.

"Come on out, Scout," Bishop says. "I know you're out here."

Another corpse staggers toward the sound of his voice on my right. The sound of it hissing and crashing through the brush cuts off after the sound of an axe cracking bones. The cramping pain in my ass begins to throb. I need to take the shot. Running isn't an option. If I stay put it's just a matter of time before Bishop finds me or a corpse stumbles upon me in the darkness.

I pivot around the tree, raise the handgun, and fire the rest of the rounds at the figure in the darkness. Several shots tear through his chest and abdomen and the last bullet punctures his skull and drops him to the ground. The body remains motionless on the ground, so I lower the gun and step out from behind the trunk of the tree.

The sound of the gunshots seems to echo endlessly through the air. Even after I know the noise is gone, I still hear it in my mind. As I move toward the lifeless body on the ground, I feel a tightening in my chest. I killed another human being. Even if he deserved it, I still killed him in cold blood. I thought that I would get some satisfaction or resolution from doing it, but I feel nothing at all.

When I look down at the face of the man I shot, I realize it isn't Bishop at all. It was a corpse.

I look up and start to search the forest, but when I turn my head, I see the butt of a rifle heading toward my face.

Not again.

There is a sharp crack as the stock strikes my nose and it sends me sprawling back on the ground. My vision blurs as I reach a hand up to my face. Somehow, I managed not to lose consciousness this time, but my balance is totally gone, and I can't seem to form any words. In a daze, I raise the gun and try to fire but nothing happens. Bishop laughs as he shoulders his rifle. He reaches down and rips the gun from my hands and tosses it into the woods. Bishop pauses his pursuit to swing his axe at a corpse that crashes through the branches. While he is distracted, I turn to try and get to my feet. I stumble and crash to the ground. My balance is still gone from the blow to the head. So, I crawl away on my hands and knees.

"Where do you think you're going, Scout?" Bishop sneers.

A boot crashes into my midsection and knocks the wind out of me and flips me on my back. I try to swallow oxygen, but my diaphragm is paralyzed. I drag myself over the ground a few inches on my back until Bishop bends down and grabs a fistful of my shirt and pulls me close to his face.

"You got a lot of nerve," he growls. "I offered to take you in and take care of you and your asshole friends."

A fist appears out of the darkness and bashes the left side of my face. Bishop gets on his knees and straddles my body on the ground. He leans close until I feel his breath on my face.

"And this is the thanks I get?"

Another blow falls on the right side of my jaw. It sounds like something cracks inside my face. My body goes limp as Bishop pulls me up by the shirt again.

"You have any idea who you are messing with?" Bishop sneers. "Nobody does this to me. Nobody."

His fist crashes into my bloody nose again and everything dims for a moment. The moans of the dead fill the night air. It also sounds like a dog keeps barking nearby, but I can't be sure of what is going on anymore. Through the blurry slits of my eyes, I see Bishop standing above me.

I wait for the next punch to land without even trying to fight him off anymore. His fist crashes into my eye socket and snaps my head back against the ground. With my blurred vision of the spinning world, I see Bishop cringe and shake the hand he hit me with. At least I hurt the bastard. I cough out a laugh but must stop to swallow the blood in my mouth.

"What's so goddamn funny?" Bishop says. He rubs at his knuckles. "You lost. You're about to die out here. Laugh it up, princess."

He pulls back his other fist and punches me again. I let out a groan as the world goes dark again. This is it. I wish he'd just get it over with.

"You might kill me," I say. "But you didn't win."

"Wrong," Bishop bares his teeth.

"You've got nothing now," I tell him. "Nothing."

"Shut your damn mouth, woman," Bishop growls.

I watch as his fist goes up in the air, then close my eyes and wait for it to be over. My rattled brain suddenly reminds me of the knife still clutched in my hand. Moving my limbs seems impossible at the moment. Even though the voice in my head keeps telling me to stab him, I just can't seem to find the strength to save myself.

The sound of rifles nearby causes me to open my eyes to see Bishop scanning the trees nearby. A bright white beam of light washes over us and he reaches up a hand to shield his eyes. It's the helicopter. They must have taken off without me.

Bishop reaches for the rifle on the ground beside him and raises it up to take aim at the Osprey. For a second I can picture Stevie strapped into a seat on the helicopter as Bishop begins to fire. The vision gives me a surge of strength and I reach up and grab Bishop by the shoulder and lunge at him with the blade off knife. Even though I can barely see through the slits of my rapidly swelling eyes, I feel the blade dig into the skin and slide deep into the tissue. The man releases a harsh hissing sound as he topples backwards, and beneath the bright beam of the search light he grabs at the crimson blood that pours out of his neck.

"You bitch," he spits blood from his lips.

From the darkness the dead begin to emerge behind Bishop. Their morbid bodies step into the light and descend on the helpless man. Dozens of hands seize his body before he realizes what is happening. For a moment, he looks up at their faces as though asking for help, until he realizes it is only the dead that have come for him. A corpse grabs his face, leans in, and tears a chunk of his cheek away between his teeth. Bishop begins to wail. I know I need to run, but I am stuck watching the horror as the dead claw his stomach open and unspool his innards. The last thing I see before I turn and try to get to my feet is Bishop staring at me, his eyes already vacant and unblinking.

I get my legs working again but stumble to my knees after walking just a few yards through the trees. I dig my fingernails into the bark of a tree and pull myself up again and stagger ahead. My balance is totally gone. I veer to the left, and then back to the right, before I lose my footing and crash to the ground again. It's just a matter of time before the dead catch up to me, and I have nothing left to use to defend myself. Still, I crawl through the dirt. I have been through too much to give up now.

As my eyes swell shut, the world seems to fill with sound. I hear the blades of the helicopter overhead and the moans of the dead in the woods behind me. Their noises get louder and louder until it seems like they are right at my back.

I scream when the first pair of hands seize me and pull me back. With my last bit of strength, I break free and crash to the ground again. The force of the fall seems to ignite a fresh sensation of pain all over my body. I know I am hitting the wall and my body has just given up. I feel the cool mud between my fingers, smell the earthy bark of oaks. Something wet caresses my cheek. Then I feel the sensation again. I hear a soft whimper in my ear.

"Get her up," someone whispers.

I feel my body being lifted off the ground and carried away before everything goes black. The last thought I can remember is wishing this would just be over but knowing somehow that it will never really end.

EPILOGUE

There are loud thumping sounds all around me.

"Easy," I hear a woman yell over the noise. "Careful with her."

I feel my body being lowered until I'm resting on a hard metal surface.

"Get us the fuck out of here, Chuck," says a man with a gruff voice.

The thumping picks up speed and then the air gets still all around my body. The deafening noise fades to a roaring patter.

"Damn it," says the woman. "She's not breathing."

I feel rough fingertips on my neck. Warm lips press against mine. I hear air moving inside my body as a force pulls my body upward again.

"Jesus," I hear Steven say. "He beat the hell out of her."

A pulsing pressure pushes down on my chest.

"Come on, Scout," says the gruff voice. "Hang in there."

My mouth is opened again, and air fills my lungs once more. Hands press down on my chest again and again.

"Wake up mommy!" I hear the voice of a young boy and my eyes snap open as I suck in a painful breath of air. Danielle and Fawn are leaning over me. They turn me onto my side as I cough out a few breaths.

"Holy shit," Blake gasps.

I try to move, but Fawn keeps me still with her firm grip.

"Just take it easy," she urges me.

"Thought she was a goner for sure," Natalie says as she lowers the handgun she had pointed at my face. She tucks the firearm back into the holster and gives me a smile.

Stevie pushes by Danielle and wraps his arm around me and squeezes my aching body. The pain is excruciating, but the sight of the kid makes the pain seem irrelevant for the moment.

"She needs to rest awhile, Stevie," Danielle tries to pull him away.

"I want mommy," Stevie cries as he pulls away from her grip.

"It's okay," I say, and hold up a hand to stop her from pulling Stevie away.

"I thought you were gone," Stevie sniffles.

"I'd never leave you, kiddo," I assure him. He presses his face into my neck and even though my arms don't have their usual strength, I close my swollen eyes and hold him tightly until he stops being afraid. I grimace in pain from the effort and allow Danielle to pull Stevie away from me again.

"You should probably stay in your seat while we're flying," Danielle says to the kid.

Stevie looks back at me but goes back to the seat between his father and Dr. Schoenheim when I nod in agreement. I feel a prick in the back of my leg, and it makes me wince.

"Sorry," Danielle says. "It's just a little morphine for the pain."

I nod in appreciation. The aches in my bones and the throbbing in my head are unbearable. The drugs can't kick in fast enough for me right now.

"Did Quentin get out?" I crane my neck around to see Blake crouched down at my back.

"Sorry," I tell him. I cringe when my weight shifts on to the bullet wound in my ass.

Blake looks at Danielle, and then he lowers his eyes to the floor. His hands knot into fists and he turns and slams one against the seat behind him. He turns back around and lets out a deep breath.

"What happened?" Blake asks. The words slip through his clenched teeth.

"Not now, Blake," Danielle says. "Let me look at that wound. Were you shot?"

"Yeah," I groan as I roll on to my stomach.

"You got shot in the ass?" Steven asks.

"It's fine," I assure him. "Don't worry. You're still the biggest pain in the ass ever."

The doctor cackles loudly in the seat beside Steven.

"At least your sarcasm still works," Steven smirks.

"This still works, too," I say and give him the finger.

Steven smiles and shakes his head.

"Really it doesn't hurt that bad," I tell Danielle.

"That's because I didn't start taking the bullet out yet," she says. "We need to get your pants off."

"I'm fine," I insist. The drugs work fast. I already start to feel a little numb all over.

Danielle ignores me as Fawn hands her a pair of scissors from the medical bag beside her. Danielle slices open my jeans from the bottom. Seems like a waste of a good pair of pants, but suddenly the only thing that is bothering me is how tired I am now.

"I just need to sleep it off," I mumble as I let my eyes close.

"If you're lucky, you'll pass out," Danielle says.

My lower body feels cool as my pants are removed. I feel a vague sense of embarrassment and open my eyes again but can't keep them open for very long.

"Don't let Steven look at my ass," I complain, but the words are so slurred that it probably sounds like nonsense to everyone else. I feel a brief stab of pain in my ass, and then everything goes dark again.

I awake to a sound like an alarm clock going off, but when I open my eyes again, I'm staring at a long line of cables along the ceiling. Steven and Hoff lift me off the floor and strap me into a seat beside Stevie. Some kind of emergency alert is going off in the cockpit.

"Are we going crash?" I ask Hoff.

"Just a precaution," Hoff says as he fits a helmet on top of my head. "Don't worry. Fletcher has it under control."

I give him a nod as he returns to his own seat and blink my eyes a couple times to fight off the grogginess from the medication. Through the small window, the pink light of daybreak fills the cabin. The Osprey dips for a moment and my stomach twists. Across from me, Blake looks pale. He turns and vomits on the floor.

"Nasty," Natalie cringes.

Hoff was mistaken. Fletcher doesn't have anything under control. No one does. There is no such thing as control anymore. There is just living again, which only feels like a curse if you let it.

"No one is fucking answering the radio," Fletcher complains over the intercom. The concern in his voice is apparent over the headset.

"How far out are we?" Hoff asks.

"Bout ten miles," Fletcher says.

I feel Stevie's fingers wrapping around my hand.

"We'll be fine," I assure the boy.

"How do you know?" he says.

"Where there is love, there is life," I tell him. "And I am always going to love you, Stevie."

The Osprey rumbles over some rough air again, so I let go of his hand and try to tighten up the straps of his seat a little more. Like the rest of this world, the seat isn't meant for a child.

"I see it," Fletcher says over the radio. "Goddamn things are everywhere down there."

"Fucking hell," Hoff curses.

"I knew this whole thing was a bad idea," Fletcher says. "We're almost out of fuel."

"Get us the hell out of here," Hoff barks.

"No can do, big fella," Fletcher says. "This is the end of the line. We're going down."

But somewhere inside I know that this isn't the end of the line. This is just the moment I start fighting again.

ABOUT THE AUTHOR

Jeremy Dyson is a fiction author who loves all things related to post-apocalyptic horror. He graduated from the University of Iowa where he studied English and dreamed of writing books one day. When he isn't writing he spends his time drinking beer, listening to metal, and gaming. He currently lives in Crystal Lake, Illinois with the love of his life, their two amazing daughters, and black goldendoodle named Duke. He is currently at work on another post-apocalyptic series.

amazon.com/Jeremy-Dyson/e/B01CZ41PIE/

facebook.com/jeremydysonauthor

instagram.com/jeremydyson

twitter.com/writerofthedead

♪

tiktok.com/jeremydysonauthor

For more information visit: **http://www.jeremydyson.com**

If you have enjoyed this book, please take a moment to **leave a review** to show your support for the author.

Also By Jeremy Dyson

ROTD Series

RISE OF THE DEAD

RETURN OF THE DEAD

RAGE OF THE DEAD

REFUGE OF THE DEAD

REMNANTS OF THE DEAD

Printed in Great Britain
by Amazon

23346860R00220